Miracle

At

Indian Key

J. Thomas Stovall

A Novel

Keys Publishing

Franklin, NC

Library of Congress Cataloging-in-Publications Data
ISBN: 978-0-692-31826-3

Acknowledgments

The original draft of the first chapter of this book was written over fifteen years ago. Massacre at Indian Key was the original title due to the history of the island. As with time, things change, and in this case for the better.

No one person can put together a novel. It takes a concerted effort from many people. Below are several whom I would like to recognize and offer my sincere thanks.

This book would not have been possible without the many hours that Diane Strickland sacrificed in editing this book. She has continually provided support, encouragement, and advice. Thank you so much!

I also want to thank my sister, Bonnie Mills, for her undying support and spiritual uplifting.

A special thanks to Neil TS Flanders for his artistic design of the cover for *Miracle at Indian Key* and *The Cuban Sanction*. You're the best!

If you can read, you can do anything.

J. Thomas Stovall

Miracle at Indian Key

Chapter 1

Three hundred feet over U.S.1, in the middle of Big Spanish Channel in the Florida Keys, the pelican rode the gentle thermals up and down over the bridge without flapping his wings. It was so quiet he could hear the fishermen on the bridge speaking with each other. Some spoke in English, most spoke in Spanish, but he couldn't understand what they were saying.

This view is spectacular, he thought, as he gazed into the pristine water below. He could see the bottom of the channel, which was at least thirty feet deep, if not more. Out in the distance, the water danced in assorted colors of emerald-green and turquoise, and finally out in deeper water, purple. To the north, he saw thousands of mangrove trees sprinkled about, which formed what is known as Florida Bay, his home where his friends call him Flapper.

Flapper made a steep right turn, then headed north by northeast along the Seven Mile Bridge. His keen eye spotted a school of mullet circling in a clockwise motion. Tighter and tighter, the school of mullet closed. This was his chance for a quick and easy dinner. He quickly slowed, reduced his altitude to about eighty feet above the fish, and began a slow circle, waiting for the right moment. *Now!* He decided. He lowered his head, folded back his wings, and made a high-speed plunge dive into the water. He caught two mullets in his pouch and headed for the surface. After bobbing up and down, he swallowed his dinner and gracefully took to the air.

His belly full and content, he continued his course along the bridge, flying about ten inches above the clear water.

Skye Somers and CJ Jansen were fishing along the catwalk on the Seven Mile Bridge. They would rather have been out on CJ's fourteen-foot McKee Craft, but today the wind was blowing out of the south at about sixteen miles an hour, making the waves too high for CJ's little boat to handle. Reluctantly, they had to settle for fishing on the bridge.

Fifteen-year-old Skye was short and petite. Every year for the past five years, she left her home and parents in Connecticut to spend the summer months with her grandfather, George Hudson, whom she lovingly called Poppy.

She loved the summer vacations at his island home on the water next to Florida Bay on Islamorada. It had a long wide dock. At the end was a twenty-two-foot Seacraft boat hanging from its davits. Her grandfather occasionally allowed her and CJ to take it into deeper water to dive into the reefs.

CJ, on the other hand, lived the year round on Islamorada. He was a sixteen-year-old junior at Coral Shore High School, where he was first in his class. He was tall and gangly, with long skinny arms and legs. Most of his friends told him he should be playing basketball because he was about eight inches taller than most of them. CJ was not an athlete and had no interest in team sports. Sports didn't interest him unless they were on the water.

Skye stood next to her sixteen-year-old companion. She considered CJ her best friend, even though they only saw each other in the summer. Since Skye was so short, the difference in their height was a minor irritant to her, along with the fact that she had to take two steps to his one. Other than those two slight annoyances, she was happy to spend her days enjoying his company. They were a lot alike and enjoyed doing the same things, especially when it involved being on Florida Bay or the Atlantic.

Skye looked down and noticed the pelican. *How does he do that?* she wondered. Her small hands clutched her heavy rod as she leaned out over the bridge railing to get a better look at the bird. It amazed

2

her how he could skim just inches above the water without crashing into a wave. She was very envious of this prehistoric yet graceful creature.

Relaxed, satisfied, and enjoying the warm breeze, Flapper had not noticed the fishermen along the bridge railing casting their rods.

One fisherman drew back his rod and heaved with all his might. The heavily weighted hook flew through the air in a high graceful arc. The next moment, searing pain ripped through Flapper's body as the hook took purchase in his right wing.

Almost simultaneously, Skye felt an electric shock shoot up from the back of her neck and into her head. She felt like she was on the brink of passing out but somehow managed to stay on her feet. Something strange was happening to her, and it was frightening. Skye felt she could mentally hear the bird screaming in pain for some unknown reason. Terrified, she wondered, *What is happening to me? Am I dying?*

The fisherman was startled when he realized that he had hooked the bird, which was struggling to stay in the air. He had never caught a bird before. His first instinct was to pull on the line. He quickly realized his mistake and released the tension on the line so that the pelican could have some kind of flight control.

The heavy weight was just too much for Flapper to handle. He heard, and at the same time felt his right-wing snap. He knew it was broken. The only thing he could do was fall into the water. A fast-moving, incoming tide instantly grabbed him and began pushing him toward Florida Bay.

The fisherman panicked and pulled back the stop on his reel, causing the line to go tight. Flapper began painfully skipping like a pebble across the water as the line held him in the grips of the current.

Help me, please! Somebody, please help me!

Skye's ears were ringing with Flapper's words. *How can I hear the pelican?* she thought. *Am I going crazy?* "He's going to drown," she whispered aloud. She knew she had to do something.

The man holding his rod with the bird attached was less than ten

3

feet to the left of Skye. Instantly she threw her rod on the catwalk and grabbed fishing pliers from the old bait and tackle box her grandfather had given her. Almost simultaneously, she sprang like a tiger toward the fisherman. In less than two seconds, she was next to the man, yanking the rod from his hands and cutting the line with her pliers, freeing the injured bird.

The man just stood there, paralyzed and in shock. *How dare this girl grab my fishing rod*! he thought. Not knowing why Skye had done it, he was enraged.

Skye could only stand there trembling, with adrenaline flowing through her body, staring at the fool who had nearly killed the poor pelican.

Deep in thought, CJ drew his eyes away from the slight tugging of his fishing line and saw Skye cutting the fisherman's line. *What in the world is she doing*? He hadn't noticed that the line was attached to the pelican floundering in the water. He dropped his rod and ran to her side.

"What's going on? What happened?" he questioned, looking into Skye's eyes. Suddenly, her eyes rolled back, and her knees buckled. CJ barely caught her before she hit the catwalk, and then he gently laid her down.

Just before Skye passed out, the last image she had of the pelican was of him being carried by the fast-moving current into the vastness of Florida Bay. He was flapping his good wing, trying to take to the air, but weakened and in terrible pain, his strength was waning. He was out of sight of the bridge within minutes.

Chapter 2

A short distance away, CJ quietly watched Skye rocking back and forth on Poppy's dock, staring into the water. He sensed that she was deep in thought as he walked to the end of the dock to join her.

"Are you okay?" he asked quietly, sitting beside her.

Skye squinted in the early morning sun and looked over at him. The glare hurt her eyes as it reflected off the water behind him. Seeing CJ always made her happy.

They had met five years ago. Her thoughts briefly returned to the first time she had seen him. Shy, tall, and lanky, he seemed to be a misfit. She supposed that was what attracted her to him. She wasn't exactly Chelsea Cheerleader herself. Poppy had always told her that she danced to the beat of her own drum.

Turning her attention back to CJ, she answered, "Yeah, I guess so." She stared down at the dock. "What's up with you?"

"Thought I'd stop by and see how you're doing," he said, leaning back and stretching his arms behind him. "I've been worried about you."

With a slightly embarrassed smile, Skye said, "After what happened yesterday, you probably think I'm nuts, don't you?"

"No. You know I would never think that about you. It was just so freaky, that's all. What happened out there, Skye? How could you hear what a pelican is saying?"

"I've been trying to figure it out myself," she said, looking a little self-conscious. "When the pelican got hooked, something happened. I can't explain it, CJ, but it was like an electric shock going into my head. It hit me like a bolt of lightning, and then I heard him screaming for help. It was so real, but I just couldn't believe it. I've been sitting here all morning thinking about the pelican and wondering what happened to the poor thing. Do you think he's dead?"

Before CJ could respond, Skye suddenly knew what she had to do. Excitedly, she said, "CJ, we've got to go find it." Her big, beautiful blue eyes begged him to agree.

"What do you mean find it? I wouldn't know where to start. Heck, it could be a hundred miles from here, or a shark could have eaten it for all I know."

"Please CJ, we've got to try. I won't be able to live with myself if we don't at least try. Please," she pleaded.

CJ paused as he looked into her persuasive eyes. Since they met, he had never been able to refuse her. She always got her way.

"Okay, you win," he said. "I'll have to go fuel my boat and get some charts. When I come back, we'll try to figure it out."

Skye jumped up from the dock. Grinning, she gave him a big hug as he stood up. "Oh, thank you, CJ! I owe you big time."

"Give me half an hour, and I'll meet you back at the dock. In the meantime, why don't you pack us one of your world-famous lunches?"

"It's a deal!" Sky shouted as she ran for the house. She was so excited. *We're going to find the pelican! I just know we will*! she thought.

About thirty-five minutes later, Skye stood at the end of the dock holding a small cooler as she waited for CJ to return. Inside the cooler were several gourmet sandwiches of turkey and ham. She had added cheese, pickles, lettuce, tomato, and mayonnaise to them. She had also included a couple bags of chips to their lunch. For dessert, she had thrown in some Oreos. They both loved Oreos. She had included two bottles of water and some Gatorade because the temperature would be in the low 90s. The summer weather in the Keys was always hot. *This should hold us for a while,* she thought with a smile, her enthusiasm growing.

She heard the sound of an approaching boat, and a moment later CJ's fourteen-foot McKee Craft sped around the mangroves at thirty miles an hour. He leveled the boat, lowered the speed on the twenty-five horsepower Mercury motor, and then headed straight for the dock. Skye watched as he expertly reversed the engine and slowly and gently glided the boat within inches of where she stood.

Skye reached over and handed her cooler to CJ. After putting the cooler down on the deck, he reached up and took Skye's hand. She stepped down into the boat next to him.

"Are we good to go?" he asked, smiling down at her. She smelled of coconut suntan oil. He noticed that she had changed into her boat shoes and had put on a pair of white shorts and a red sleeveless blouse tied in a knot at her waist. He also saw that she had used lip gloss to protect her lips from the hot sun. Petite and tanned, she looked beautiful, even though they were just going on a pelican rescue mission. For the first time, CJ felt a strange little tugging at his heart. *What is that?* he thought, his forehead wrinkling a little.

With excitement on her face, Skye looked up at CJ and replied, "I'm ready. Let's go save a pelican."

CJ broke out one of the charts he had brought along. He unfolded it and laid it on top of the center console. "Here's the bridge," he said and pointed so Skye could get a reference point on the chart. "This isn't going to be easy," he said as he looked over the chart. "There have been two tide changes since yesterday; one incoming, the other outgoing, and now it's about ebb tide. We can figure two hours into yesterday's tide before the incident. If the currents were flowing about five miles an hour, within the following four hours the bird could have traveled as much as twenty miles. Assuming the outgoing tide did the reverse, it could be back where it started."

Underway and without thinking, Skye held onto CJ's arm for balance as the small boat rocked back and forth. She hadn't realized how much pressure she was applying to his arm until CJ broke her grip. "Hey girl, not so tight," he said. He knew the pressure on his arm had come from her enthusiasm.

"Sorry, I didn't realize I was hurting you. I'm just so excited about finding the bird. If we find him, maybe I'll be able to understand what happened to me yesterday."

"Okay, let's go to the bridge and start there. It'll probably take us about an hour to get there, so hang tight."

CJ pushed the throttle forward, and the little McKee Craft jumped out of the water and settled to thirty knots within a matter of seconds.

Off balance, Skye stumbled backward a half step before seating herself.

CJ glanced down at her and saw the anticipation in her eyes. A slight smile tugged at the corners of his mouth. He had never met anyone like her. They had had some wild times together in the past five years. Every summer she took him from one adventure to another, which sometimes resulted in several days of restriction for both of them. He couldn't understand why he kept agreeing to her wild schemes. But thinking about it, he knew he wouldn't change a thing, even if it did mean trouble for him.

Chapter 3

The ten o'clock sun shone warmly on their backs. The June north wind blew steadily at eight knots. The light breeze allowed the little McKee Craft to skim effortlessly over the water. Small islands and mangroves flew by as CJ and Skye headed for Big Spanish Channel. CJ chose to follow U.S. 1 on the ocean side, which was called the lee side. It protected them from the wind and offered smoother water.

With one hand, Skye gripped the metal bar that framed the windshield, her knees slightly bent. It helped to absorb the shock of the leaping boat. She loved to feel the wind blowing through her hair, and she always felt closer to nature on the water. Poppy had taught her to snorkel and scuba dive, and since first being introduced to the water, she felt lost when she was not near it. She especially missed it during the long months she was at home in Connecticut.

Because of her love of the water, Skye had fleeting thoughts of becoming a marine biologist, but she wasn't sure she could handle several additional years of schooling after she graduated from high school. She was a "hands-on" girl and didn't know if she had the patience to sit in a college classroom for an additional four years. She knew what she wanted, but she wasn't sure how to go about getting it. *Who knows?* she mused. *I'm only in the tenth grade, and I've still got a couple years to think about it. Hmmm. Maybe the only way to reach my goal is to go to college. I'll have to think about that another day.*

CJ's long arm pushed the throttle forward to its last stop. He was not satisfied with their progress. The little boat leapt five knots faster, which pleased him. Of course, he preferred Poppy's larger Seacraft. Faster and more comfortable, it also cost twice as much to operate, and his meager budget wouldn't allow such luxury. An occasional gig working as a deckhand on local charter boats did not exactly make him a man of means. Then again, his McGee Craft could navigate the much shallower water of Florida Bay. With the engine tilted in the up position, the boat could move in as little as fourteen inches of water. "Another five minutes and we'll be at the bridge," CJ shouted over the roar of the engine. "Keep an eye out for the pelican."

Skye nodded her head to confirm that she had heard CJ. "Maybe we should slow down a little," she shouted.

CJ eased back on the throttle, and the boat came to rest under the Seven Mile Bridge. He reached for the chart. "I need to check the chart again. There are lots of tributaries that run along the channel."

"Don't you think the bird could have been pulled along the main channel?" Skye asked.

"It's possible, but there's no way to know for sure. It may have gone down any of them. Why don't we follow the main channel for a while, and if we don't find it we'll double back and start checking the tributaries, okay? You check the left side, and I'll watch the right."

CJ eased the throttle forward until the little boat rose to the surface and settled into an easy fifteen knots.

The sweltering sun was directly overhead, and CJ finally decided they had gone far enough. "Let's turn back and try the first tributary. Maybe we'll have better luck there." Skye nodded in agreement as CJ turned the boat around.

On their way back to the bridge, both remained silent, each consumed in thought. Skye hoped they could find the poor injured bird. *What will we do if we do locate it?* Skye said a silent prayer that they would find it alive. *Please, please, God, let it be alive.*

They rounded the last curve before the bridge.

"There's the first tributary!" Skye shouted as she pointed to her left.

CJ followed her instructions as they headed toward the narrow channel. They moved slowly through the mangroves. Occasionally, they would have to duck the overhanging branches. Mosquitoes buzzed around them. Within seconds, Skye was covered. She reached into the center console and retrieved a can of insect repellant. CJ was slapping himself all over, trying to get rid of the pesky little bloodsuckers.

Skye sprayed her entire body with the strong-smelling repellent.

"Want some bug spray?" she said.

"Yes! Hurry, they're eating me alive!" CJ shouted. He was frantically hopping around, beating at the insects.

Skye had to laugh at his gyrations. "Close your eyes and hold your breath," she said as she sprayed him from the top of his head to his feet.

CJ coughed several times. The strong odor was overpowering. Remarkably, the repellent took effect immediately. Mosquitoes were still buzzing all around, but none was landing for a human happy meal.

"Let's get out of here," CJ groaned, scratching his bites as he moved the boat forward.

Suddenly, Skye shouted at the top of her lungs, "Stop, CJ! Stop the boat! My ears are ringing. I hear something." She closed her eyes and tried to focus on the pelican.

CJ immediately pulled back on the throttle.

"Shut the engine off!" Skye ordered. "I can't hear it very well."

CJ reached for the ignition key and quickly turned it off.

"It's the pelican!" Skye said excitedly. "It has to be close, but it's too far out of range for me to pick up what it's saying."

"Okay," CJ said quietly, "I'll move the boat up a bit, and you tell me if it gets louder."

CJ started the engine and put it in gear. They began to move up the channel at a snail's pace.

Skye placed a finger in each ear and concentrated on the bird. The sounds got stronger and stronger as they moved forward.

"We're getting closer. I can hear a little better now. Just keep going."

The pelican called out again hoping that someone would understand his cries for help. "I'm over here. I'm in front of you. Please help me!' Skye looked up at the far end of the channel and saw the pelican about a hundred fifty feet from the boat. She bumped CJ's arm and pointed toward the pelican.

"I see, I see," CJ whispered. He didn't want to scare the poor thing.

Skye was almost ready to jump out of the boat. She couldn't believe they had found him.

As the boat moved closer, they could see that the bird was entangled in some fishing line. It was apparent that he had struggled to free himself and had only made matters worse.

"We're coming," Skye said aloud, hoping that he understood her. He began to struggle.

He heard me, she thought, and then said, "No, don't struggle!" she cautioned. "It'll make things worse. You'll just hurt yourself more."

The bird understood what Skye said to him. He quietly floated on the water and waited to be rescued.

CJ eased the boat next to the mangroves and reached over to grab a limb to steady the craft, and Skye reached into her old tackle box and pulled out her fishing pliers. Balancing herself fearlessly, she leaned over the side and began cutting the bird free.

The pelican flinched as Skye worked her way up the line to his broken wing. He moved his large beak back and forth picking at the line. *My wing sure hurts. I hope this girl can help me,* he thought.

"Easy big guy," Skye said. " I'm trying not to hurt you."

The injured bird responded. "My wing is broken. It hurts a lot."

"Sure, looks like it," Skye responded to the bird. *Am I actually having a conversation with a pelican?* she wondered.

"Be careful of that thing with my wing," the bird groaned in

12

obvious pain.

Skye finally got the line clear and cut it at the back of the hook.

"Free at last," she said with a sigh of relief.

"CJ, I need some help here!" she shouted, trying to move the bird. "He's a lot heavier than I thought he'd be."

CJ let go of the branch, reached down with both hands, and then lifted the injured pelican into the boat. "Easy," Skye said as CJ gently settled him down in the boat.

"Thank you so much," the pelican responded to Skye.

"You're quite welcome," Skye responded back to the bird. "Just try to relax. We'll take you ashore and get you all fixed up."

Relieved, he looked at the boy and girl who had rescued him. The pelican knew he was so lucky that they had found him. *They must have been searching for me for quite a while,* he thought. Realizing that he and the girl had communicated, he wondered in amazement how it had been possible.

Chapter 4

CJ had the boat cruising at about fifty percent power, and the ride was comfortable. It was Flapper's first boat ride, and CJ didn't want to scare him to death. The bird seemed to be adjusting reasonably well to the slight up-and-down movement.

Assured that the pelican was comfortable and secure, Skye pulled her iPhone out of her duffle bag and pressed Poppy's speed dial number.

Poppy answered on the first ring. "Hello," he said.

"Poppy! Thank God you're home!" she yelled over the engine noise.

"What's wrong, little bit"? her grandfather asked anxiously. "Are you okay?"

"Yes, we're okay. CJ and I just rescued a pelican with a broken wing, and we're bringing it in to take care of its injuries. Would you mind calling the bird sanctuary and see if they'll meet us at your dock?"

"Of course, honey. I'll get right on it." Hesitating, he said, "Skye, are you sure you're okay?"

"We're fine Poppy. Don't worry. We should be there in about an hour."

"Okay. Please be careful."

Skye eased herself down next to the live well. She gently stroked the injured bird's head. The pelican looked into her eyes. "Thank you so much for your help. I didn't know what was going to happen to me."

Skye still could not believe or understand how she had been able to communicate with the bird. *How is it possible?* she wondered. *I hear his thoughts as if he is actually speaking to me, and he understands me.* She kept trying to think of a rational explanation but knew there was none. She finally decided that for some unknown reason, there was a special connection between her and the pelican. *I'll just accept it as a special gift. I sure hope it lasts. It's kind of cool,* she thought.

Skye and the pelican began a longer conversation with each other. CJ couldn't understand it, but he knew it was happening as he listened to Skye. She spoke, nodded her head to the bird, smiled briefly, and her forehead wrinkled a little as though she was listening to what the bird was saying to her.

Skye looked at the bird and said,. "I'm glad we found you. Are you doing all right? Do you have a name? How old are you?" Skye knew that most pelicans live between ten and twenty-five years. Questions to the pelican overflowed from her mind. Since Skye had discovered the connection between her and the bird, she wanted to find out all she could in case this was a one-time fluke, and she lost the ability to communicate with him.

"I'm glad you found me, too. My wing hurts, but I'm okay," the bird responded. My friends call me Flapper. I don't understand your question about how old I am. Why would I care how old I am? I guess age matters to humans, huh? What is your name and how old are you and the boy driving the boat?'

"My name is Skye, and I'm fifteen years old. My home is in Connecticut, but I visit my grandfather in Islamorada every summer. CJ is driving the boat, and he's sixteen. He's my best friend, and he lives in Islamorada year-round."

Skye couldn't believe she was carrying on a thought conversation with a pelican. *Wow! I'm beginning to understand that there is*

15

another world around me that I never realized before. Surely, if I can communicate with Flapper, there have to be others who can do the same. She briefly wondered if she would ever meet any of them.

"Where do you live?" Skye asked Flapper.

"In a tree in the mangroves," Flapper answered. "That's where most of us live, and we like living there. There is one place, though, where none of us will go."

"Where's that?" Skye asked.

"Indian Key," Flapper replied. "It's a bad place."

"What do you mean by bad place?" Skye pressed. She knew it was a tiny island close by, but she had never heard anything about it, nor had she ever been there.

"It's haunted, and bad things happen there."

"What kinds of bad things?" Skye continuing questioning Flapper.

"All my friends have heard noises, and now we're afraid to go over there."

"What else can you tell me about it?" Skye questioned. Indian Key sounded like a place she would like to investigate.

"If you fly over it at night, there are strange lights, but nobody lives there. The strangest thing is none of us has ever seen lights over there until recently," Flapper answered, sounding scared. He and his friends thought it was a spooky place, and they all stayed away.

———————

About an hour later, CJ, Skye, and Flapper pulled up to Poppy's dock. A white van was parked in the driveway, and two men in white jackets were waiting with Skye's grandfather.

Seeing CJ and Skye arrive at the dock, Poppy and the two men headed to the boat.

Suddenly, Flapper became frightened and started flapping his good wing. *Who are those men?* he thought. *Are they coming to take me away? Will they hurt me?*

Noticing Flapper's distress, Skye responded in thought, *It's okay, Flapper. The white-haired man is my grandfather, Poppy, and the two other men are from the bird sanctuary. They are going to put you in the white van and take you to have your wing fixed. They won't hurt you. They're only here to help you. After they get your wing fixed up, CJ and I will come to the sanctuary to visit you. You'll be fine, I promise.*

Even after such a short acquaintance, Flapper felt strongly that Skye would not put him in danger. He finally settled down and waited to be taken by the two men.

Chapter 5

The building was dark except for a small light shining in the reception area. Moonlight shone through the tree branches, casting ghostly shadows across the sign that said Visitor Welcome Station. It was a nondescript structure typical of most welcome stations throughout the state parks in Florida.

Though no one could tell from outward appearance, this building was vastly different. Visitors walking into the building would never know that in the four rooms in the back were some of the most sophisticated electronic equipment in the world. All of it was connected to a worldwide network of seismic monitoring stations. near Orlando in the Disney Wilderness Preserve,

The seismic center was located on twelve thousand acres of the most pristine property in the United States. The University of Florida, along with the U.S. Geological Survey, used the facility to train future seismologists from fifty-seven nations.

Central air conditioning hummed a steady quiet noise that kept the equipment and its occupants cool.

Of the four rooms, one was a meeting room with a twelve-foot oak conference table. Ten plush reclining chairs surrounded the table. Framed photographs hung on the walls around the room. Each of them depicted scenes of devastation and human suffering. All were scenes of earthquakes, man's oldest killer. Today, countries around the world hunt them and spend billions of dollars scouring the earth for them. Unfortunately, no one had any idea what to do with them, or how to stop them.

The other rooms in the building consisted of a small kitchen, a bathroom, and a twelve-by-twenty command center. The seismic monitoring room was painted a nauseating shade of green, typical of most government offices.

Twenty-one-year-old University of Florida archaeology student, Nathaniel Brown, sat in the command center at his computer. Half asleep, he kept nodding in and out of slumber. In the past three days, sleep for Nathan, as he liked to be called, had been elusive. Final exams at UF would be in one more day. Several nights out partying with friends and working an eight-hour part-time job at the seismic center didn't exactly give him much time to study.

Tall and skinny, Nathan had shaggy brown hair and a slightly blemished face, making him look as though he had not completely made it through puberty. His thick, black-rimmed glasses gave him an owlish appearance. He was not the kind of guy to whom pretty girls usually were drawn, but he did have one redeeming quality. His parents were very wealthy, so he never lacked for friends. That made him part of the "in" crowd.

Exhausted, Nathan yawned deeply and rested his elbow on his desk, his chin in his hand. Nodding off, his head weaved back and forth as if swaying like the sawgrass blowing across Payne's Prairie about ninety miles north of the seismic center near Gainesville.

A slight digital sound from his seismometer broke his sleep. He opened his eyes, stretched his long arms back over his shoulders, yawned again, and then slowly swiveled his chair around to look at the graph on the circular chart. For a moment, he couldn't see anything until his eyes adjusted to the ambient light around him.

Leaning forward for a closer look, he saw a faint jagged line on the paper disk. *That's strange. I've never seen anything like it before.* He reached over and changed the screen that was connected to the computer to "Analyze." The wave appeared as a small but distinct line. Nathan enhanced the image until it became too pixelated to interpret. He made a few minor adjustments which cleared out all the extraneous noise.

I wonder where it's coming from. Surely, it's not an earthquake, particularly not in Florida, but it sure looks like one. Staring at the monitor, Nathan was mesmerized by what he saw.

Pondering his next move, he wondered if he should call his boss. *No, it's too late to disturb the director. He really gets ticked off when he's called in the middle of the night. In fact, he turns into a real bear if he's called for anything other than an emergency.* Making a quick decision, he picked up the phone and dialed Brewton, Alabama.

Brewton was one of three seismic centers connected to Disney Wilderness. Turks and Caicos, and Yucatan, Mexico, were the other two affiliates.

His friend Mac answered the phone on the first ring. "Hello."

"Hey, Mac, it's Nathan." Nathan liked him a lot because he was always so helpful when Nathan called him. Nathan was also a little envious because Mac was already working on his Ph.D. in seismology.

"What's going on Nate? Long time no hear. How's sunny Florida?"

"It's okay. I've been busting my butt with finals."

Mac heard the fatigue in Nathan's voice. "What can I help you with, buddy?"

Nathan paused for a moment, not knowing what to say. *This is probably going to be a ridiculous question,* he thought.

"Mac, would you mind checking your computer at about 0207 your time for any anomalies?"

"Okay, give me one sec," Mac replied. "My computer is slow tonight."

Moments later, Mac was back on the line. "I see a faint registry on the template. Let me check the audio."

Mac switched to the audio spectrum. "I'm looking at the audio. Based on the frequency and wave spacing, I would guess it's an explosion. Let me check my data bank. It will only take a minute."

Brewton was the official Operations Center for the Southern

United States, the Caribbean, and the Central American Region. All seismic data since the early 1960's was stored there. Information from airplane crashes, coal mine drilling, and subway noises were also registered there. There was almost nothing that could not be identified.

"What kind of range and bearing do you get?" Nathan questioned.

"Hang loose for a minute buddy, and I'll let you know."

Moments later, Mac was back on the line. "I've confirmed that its most likely dynamite, bro. It's about five hundred miles south of here. I'm reading latitude 24' 88" 81 sec N and longitude 80' 69" 44 sec W. You'll have to check with Turks and Caicos or the Yucatan for a more precise triangulation."

"I appreciate your help, Mac. Thanks." He replaced the handset in its cradle.

Nathan leaned back in his chair and studied the monitor. He was still puzzled. Using Mac's calculations, Nate wondered who would be using dynamite at this hour of the morning, especially around the Florida Keys.

As Nathan leaned back in his comfortable chair, he tried to relax. Memories of his reasons for coming to work at the seismic center flooded his mind.

As a kid growing up in Central Florida, he and his buddies loved to swim in the shallow lakes around Ocala and Silver Springs. When he was thirteen, he had his first encounter with his current passion for archaeology.

On a hot sunny day, Nathan and some friends had been swimming in a small lake outside Ocala. It was the site of their favorite camping spot. On this particular morning, they were wading and snorkeling in about five feet of water on the opposite side of the lake from the campsite. As he was waded into deeper water, Nathan's foot struck a sharp object lodged in the packed sand. His curiosity forced him to investigate. With limited visibility, he saw what appeared to be a piece of charred pottery.

Leaning down and picking it up, he shouted, "Hey guys, look

21

what I've found!" In his hand, he held a piece of broken, curved, Indian pottery. He could see by the color, which was dark brownish black, that it was old. He wondered how long it had rested in the lake covered in water.

That afternoon, he and his friends brought up about one hundred fifty pieces of broken pottery. Some had distinguishable marks, and others were bare. All were crudely made, and none was fired. What remained of the pieces was very primitive, brittle dry clay.

Nathan's mind raced with questions. *Which Indians made it? Where did they get the clay? Why was it all broken? Was the lake formed from an ancient sinkhole after the Indians had abandoned the site?* Those questions were puzzling to Nate.

The incident was a turning point in his life. He had to have answers to those questions, which brought him full circle to the study of archaeology.

Snapping back to the problem at hand, Nathan reached for the phone for the second time and dialed Turks and Caicos. Third-world countries had antiquated phone systems, so he figured it would take some time to get through. He briefly wondered if there was anything there, or if he was just bored.

He tried to clear his mind. *Coffee, that's what I need.* He pocketed the remote phone and headed for the kitchen. As he walked into the kitchen, the phone rang. *Crap, Third-World countries suck. Why can't they fix their communications systems?*

As he reached for the coffee pot, a voice spoke from his back pocket. "Yo, Mon. Whatcha doin?"

Surprised by the accent, Nate took the phone from his pocket. "Hey, this is Nate at Disney Wilderness. What are you guys doing down there? Outsourcing?"

"No, Mon. I am a student from Jamaica. My name is Joel. How can I help ya?"

"I need some help to triangulate a source."

"Okay, Mon, give me the coordinates."

Nathan gave the student the latitude, longitude, and time, and then the line went silent.

22

Four minutes and thirty-one seconds later, which seemed a lifetime to Nathan, Joel was back on the line. At that same instant, the coffeemaker beeped.

"Hey, Mon, you still there?"

When Nathan responded with a "Yes," Joel said, "I barely got a signal, ya know, but I'd say it's 'round Islamorada, Florida."

What the heck? Responding to Joel, he said, "Thanks, man. Check you later." Nathan pressed the off button. *That's strange. I wonder what's going on down there.*

―――――――――――

Alexei Kovalchik squeezed his two hundred fifty pounds out of the tight hole. Sweat poured from his round face as his body strained for release from its dirt prison. Free at last from the grasp of the small opening, he lay on the sand trying to catch his breath. Exhausted and ready for a break, he mumbled, "I should be used to this by now."

He and his partner, Anatoli Krasnoff, had been secretly blasting and digging out the tunnel for months. They had always done it on moonless nights because the local fishermen were unable to spot their boat moving up and down Indian Key Channel.

They had chosen Indian Key for their base of operations because of the solid limestone. The island had been abandoned for over a hundred fifty years, since just after the Seminole Indian War. Only raccoons, mosquitoes, and giant aloe plants remained. The soft limestone was waterproof and perfect for tunneling. Alexei's electricians in Miami had come down to the island and had secretly connected an underwater electric cable to a power pole on the shore. Without electricity, none of this would have been possible.

Anatoli's head, and then his shoulders, carefully rose out of the hole. Unlike Alexei, Anatoli was trim and fit. He bounced out of the hole in one easy movement. He sat next to Alexei and cupped his hands to shield his lighter from prying eyes and lit a cigarette. Taking a deep drag, he exhaled a long breath of smoke as if it would be his last. He had been working non-stop in the tunnel for hours and was dying for a cigarette.

Alexei rolled over and looked up at Anatoli. In his usual deep voice, he said, "I think we're ready to begin our operations, don't you? Tomorrow we'll finish the tunnel door and put up a camouflaged door at the base of the cistern."

"What the heck are you talking about, bird brain? I told you that the last blast would be too big. Now it'll take us two more days to clear out all that crap," scolded Anatoli. "Anyway, our comrades in Miami will be pleased at our progress. On the next moonless night, we'll have the supply boat come in." Sometimes Anatoli was a little gruff with Alexei and could be a jerk, but he was smart and made a good partner.

Anatoli looked at his luminous watch. "It'll be light in about an hour. You cover the entrance, and I'll get the boat ready."

Though he didn't want to get up, Alexei finally raised himself, and groaning with exhaustion, he stood. He didn't like the manual labor they had to do, but the thoughts of all the money they would make gave him renewed energy.

Chapter 6

Poppy sat on a stool on one side of the kitchen island in his spacious home in Islamorada. He raised his head and looked at Skye and CJ, who were sitting at the opposite end. They each nursed a Cherry Coke that Poppy had made for them from his specially installed soda fountain. He leaned over to look at a nautical chart of the lower Keys. His right index finger rested on a small island named Indian Key. Skye had just told him about Flapper and had confided in him what Flapper had mentioned to her about Indian Key.

As Poppy sat in silence listening to Skye's incredible story about her ability to communicate with Flapper, he was having difficulty understanding this new gift. He knew Skye was telling him the truth. She had always been honest with him, but in all his seventy years he had never heard of such a thing. He knew she wasn't making up the amazing story, but with his limited knowledge of her mental telepathy ability, or whatever it was, it failed to penetrate his rationale. *Is it a gift or a curse? How is it possible? What will her friends and the rest of her family think? Will she be labeled as a freak? My God, what is in store for my sweet little granddaughter? Will she ever be able to lead a normal life again?*

Getting up from the table, confused and bewildered, he walked over to the coffeemaker to start a fresh pot of espresso. With Skye's revelation, he needed something stronger than regular coffee. While he was making the strong brew, he was assessing what Skye had been saying. *I'll have to give her the benefit of the doubt. What else can I do? She is an emotionally stable, realistic, and honest young girl, and I will support her in what is happening to her, even if I don't understand it.* While the espresso brewed, he walked back to the table, sat down, and changed the subject to Indian Key.

"I've been doing a little research on the island," he said as he looked up from the map.

Skye fidgeted on her stool, anxious to hear what Poppy had to say.

"In the early 1800's, wreckers inhabited the island. They cleared away most of the scrub and underbrush, built a few small cabins, and even had a couple of streets intersecting in the center of the island. Lack of water was their main concern, so they built a large cistern to catch rainwater."

Continuing with the history of the island, Poppy got up from his stool and walked over to stand by Skye, who seemed mesmerized.

"There was a rickety boathouse extending out over the water with a small dock attached. Below the dock was a wire cage in the water where they kept sea turtles. Turtle soup was a delicacy back then."

"Poppy," CJ interrupted, "why in the world would people want to live on such a primitive island? I mean, there's nothing there."

Poppy told CJ and Skye what he had learned about the wreckers. "Wreckers were people who made their living standing on the edge of the island at night with lights in their hands, waving them back and forth. They did this to lure ships in to founder on the reefs and break up, and then they would claim the salvage rights," Poppy explained.

"Was that legal?" Skye asked. She thought they must have been awful people to have done that sort of thing.

Poppy shook his head. "Well, it's not legal now," he answered, "but back then it was. They made a decent living from their endeavors. The morning after the ships foundered, they would row out to the reef, save any survivors, and drag in as much cargo as their boats could carry. Once they got enough goods, they would load them into their small sailing skiffs and sail down to Key West to register their bounty with the Maritime Agency. For a while, it was a very lucrative business for them."

"That sounds mean and dishonest," Skye said.

"It was," Poppy said, "and that's why eventually the law changed." Poppy continued, "Around 1835, a man named Dr. Perrine moved his family down to Indian Key. He thought there were enough people coming and going for him to open up a medical practice. A little later the second of the Seminole Indian Wars broke out. Some people stayed, but many of the islanders, out of fear, left the island for the mainland."

"That would have been me," Skye interjected. "You wouldn't catch me down here with a bunch of wild Indians running around."

Poppy smiled at Skye and continued, "One night in 1840, a small band of Seminoles rowed over to the island, quietly sneaked up to the parameter of the buildings, and attacked the settlement. A gunfight ensued, and after all was said and done, five settlers and eleven Indians were killed. All the homes were destroyed except one. Dr. Perrine had hidden his family under the dock in the turtle cage, so they survived, but Dr. Perrine was killed." Poppy walked back to his stool and looked back down at the chart.

"Needless to say, the Indian attack was the last nail in Indian Key's coffin. All the survivors abandoned the island, and it's been deserted ever since."

"What about what Flapper said about the island?" Skye asked. "Has there been any gossip or reports from the local fishermen?"

"Not to my knowledge," Poppy replied.

Skye stood up and walked around the table to where Poppy was sitting. As she reached up to give her grandfather a hug, she said. "Well, I guess we'll just have to go and check this place out."

"Not on your life, little lady," Poppy said a little too sharply. "I'd better not hear about you two going over there. It's best to let it be. You two don't want to be on restriction again, do you?"

Trying to soothe Poppy, CJ said, "I'll bet my dad can check it out. He has government connections. All he has to do is make a few phone calls."

A slight smile crossed Skye's face. She knew that she would never be happy until she found out what was going on over there. *Now I have to convince CJ,* she thought.

———

Alexei Kovalchik and Anatoli Krasnoff stood at the water's edge and waited. The night was balmy with a warm southerly breeze blowing at eight knots. To the southwest, the Atlantic Ocean was as smooth as glass. The two men watched as oilers and freighters loaded with cargo lumbered up and down the Gulf Stream to unknown destinations. At that moment, Alexei wished he was onboard one of them. The night held too much uncertainty.

Alexei held a VHS radio in his right hand. With his left hand, he cupped the mouthpiece and whispered into the radio. "Alligator, this is Shark. Over."

Anatoli reached over and shoved Alexei's shoulder. "You idiot! Why in the heck are you whispering? There is nobody within two miles of here!"

Alexei looked over in the dark at his antagonist. He was glad that Anatoli could not see his face, which was red with embarrassment.

"Shark, this is Alligator. We are close," said the voice on the radio.

Reaching into his pocket, Alexei withdrew a laser light. He pressed its button and pointed it out into the night. A narrow green ray of light shot out into the darkness. The beam shone brightly in a wide arc, as it moved slowly back and forth. A moment later, it struck the side of the boat.

"Shark, we see your light. We'll be there shortly."

Alexei switched the light off. "Good," he mumbled, still embarrassed about the tongue-lashing he had gotten from Anatoli.

Minutes passed as the two men fidgeted nervously and waited.

A low rumbling sound slowly drew closer and closer. They did not see the large boat until it was almost upon them. Both men almost fell back as the boat's bow dug into the sand and came to a stop.

"Crap!" Anatoli shouted.

In the dim starlight, a man dropped from the bow of the boat down onto the narrow, sandy beach.

"One of you Anatoli?" he asked.

"I am," Anatoli answered. "Any problems with the Coast Guard?"

"Nope, the trip was uneventful," the man replied. "Are you ready for us to unload? The sooner we get out of here, the better."

"Yes, you're right, the sooner the better," Anatoli replied. With a deep sigh, Alexei said, "This will be a very long night."

"Go give them a hand!" Anatoli ordered.

Alexei didn't like the way Anatoli ordered him around. After all, they were equal partners. *He can be a real jerk sometimes. How would he like it if I talked to him the way he talks to me? I'll be glad when this job is done.*

Chapter 7

Most houseboats seen on Florida Bay were rentals. The ads read: *One-day rentals up to a week*. Tourists loved the boat's flat bottom. Renters could drive all around the islands without running aground. God help them, though, if a stiff breeze or thunderstorm begins to blow. They would be hung up in the mangroves with windows busted, and who knows what else. The marinas, however, loved it. Since they had each customer's credit card information, they thought the sky was the limit.

John Duncan was an exception. His houseboat was forty-eight feet long and fourteen feet wide. Four feet of draft held two decks above water. Twin Caterpillar diesel engines powered its massive hull.

John enjoyed spending his weekends and holidays cruising throughout Florida Bay. It was his escape. After five days of running his mega-corporation, Duncan Oil, fighting with the EPA, schmoozing politicians, and arguing with his beautiful young wife, Elizabeth, he needed a break. Boating kept him sane.

Occasionally, he brought Elizabeth along, but she usually had too many glasses of wine and became argumentative. He had had enough of his dysfunctional marriage, but his lawyers kept telling him it would cost him a small fortune if he divorced her.

John had met Elizabeth in a bar. That should have been his first clue. It was the Fourth of July weekend at the Ritz Carlton Hotel in Naples, Florida. He had just finished a round of golf. Hot, tired, and thirsty, he decided to get a cocktail before going up to his room to take a shower. The bar was crowded and noisy, not his usual kind of environment. He preferred a quieter place to drink and sulk over his golf score. His game today had been a disaster. He briefly wondered if he needed a new set of clubs. It never occurred to him that he should probably take up tennis instead.

John spotted a vacant stool midway at the hotel bar and hurried over before someone else could beat him to it. He felt relieved as he reached his destination. Hoisting his massive frame upon the stool, he was happy to know that he would have his liquid reward after a dreadful day on the course.

"Bartender, please give me a rum and Coke," he ordered loudly, over the rowdy noise of the crowd. His thick Texas drawl resonated throughout the room. Several people took notice upon hearing his command.

John Duncan could always get the attention of the crowd. He was a big man, six feet four inches tall, with a head full of deep brown hair and aqua-colored eyes. Not handsome in the traditional sense, he still had his share of women on his arm when he needed one for a corporate function, a dinner, or a show. Occasionally, he even took one of them on his boat for the weekend, but mostly he took the boat out alone. He enjoyed being on the water. It relieved the week's stress.

The first sip of his drink was like an elixir, calming his disappointment at having such a difficult day playing golf. Hot and tired, he leaned over the bar slightly as his broad hands placed the glass on a round piece of cork. A thick gold bracelet on his left wrist accentuated a one-carat diamond pinky ring on his finger.

John gazed around, not knowing that the next year would be one heck of a rollercoaster ride. At the far end of the bar, Elizabeth caught Duncan's stare. She was mesmerized, and neither wanted to break the visual bridge formed between them.

Finally, John rose from his seat, picked up his glass, and moved toward the beautiful woman. He worked his way through the crowd and stood beside her. *She is stunning. She has on a little too much makeup, but what the heck? She's still a looker.* He didn't bother to mask his admiration. Silky bleached blonde hair draped her soft shoulders. Spaghetti straps held up a beautiful black party dress, cut low in the back. The rest of the evening and night was a total shock for John Duncan.

Elizabeth was on the run. Three days before, while her husband was at the office, Elizabeth had packed her bags, gone to the bank, and withdrew twelve thousand dollars from their joint account. Her actions were "spur of the moment." Neither her husband nor her family knew where she was now. She had planned to call them in a few days. First, she wanted to put some space between her and them. Her life in the fast lane was ending. At least, that's what she thought.

Todd, Elizabeth's husband, was a party freak. His wealthy family, and his executive position in the family business, afforded him the money and resources to satisfy his desire for drugs, particularly cocaine.

Elizabeth enjoyed the abundance of money and confided in John about the wild parties in which they had both participated, but the drugs and partying had finally gotten out of hand. The lost weekends and terrible hangovers had affected their marriage to the point that Elizabeth detested her husband.

She told John that after less than a year of marriage, all she wanted was out, and this was the only way she knew to go about it. She would let the lawyers handle the rest. Though she didn't mention it to John, rehab was in the back of her mind, but here she was in a bar again with another rich man at her side. *Life is all about money*, she thought.

John unwittingly got sucked into Elizabeth's life. Initially, he felt sorry for her, and before he realized it, they were living together.

Six months later, after Elizabeth had reached a comfort zone, her true personality had begun to emerge. She became moody, slept late into the mornings, and started drinking heavily in the evenings.

When she drank, she became argumentative. She kept insisting that she and John get married.

John didn't know what to do. Elizabeth was certainly a beautiful woman. *Maybe if I marry her, things will get better. Maybe she will change. Our relationship can't get any worse, can it?* The decision to marry Elizabeth Carlton would haunt him for a long time.

This weekend he was alone. He was heading down to Gopher Key, located north of Islamorada. That afternoon, he had picked up his boat at Tavernier Creek Marina where he had had some mechanical work performed on his autopilot. Now he was headed south. The autopilot functioned flawlessly. He completely relied on his autopilot. The seventeen-inch monitor provided him with a moving chart that showed everything imaginable. All the information he needed to operate his boat safely was there. It showed all the channels, markers, islands, marinas, and even the docks extending out from peoples' homes. All he had to do was punch in the course, speed, and any waypoints needed to get to his destination, and he was there. It was hands-free boating at its best.

John left the wheel, walked over to the coffee table, and retrieved an illegal Cuban cigar. It was just one of the many vices he loved. He turned, stepped back to the captain's chair, and hoisted his tall frame into the luxurious comfort.

Even though lobster season was over, Gopher Key was loaded with them. All he had to do was roll his two hundred forty pounds over the side of the boat, spear gun in hand, and within minutes he would have dinner. His mind raced with pleasure at the thought of having boiled lobster with garlic and butter sauce. Of course, he knew he would have to be careful. The Marine Patrol was all over the place this time of year. He had devised an almost foolproof system. He would twist the tail from the lobster's body, drop the head to the bottom, put the tail into his dive sack, and tie it to the anchor line. Then he would surface.

His logic for tying the lobster sack to the anchor line was simple. If a Marine Patrol officer stopped by unexpectedly, and the odds were eighty-twenty that one would, the officer always inspected the bait wells and ice coolers. That was a good way to get busted for taking lobsters out of season, and he couldn't afford the publicity. The ticket was peanuts to him, but he didn't need the exposure. Keeping the lobsters on the boat was a bad idea. Later, when he was ready for dinner, he would retrieve his bounty from the anchor line and prepare a gourmet meal.

John looked down at his watch. *3:57 p.m. The sun will be setting in a couple of hours.* In his head, he calculated how much longer it would take him to reach an anchorage at Gopher Key. "Another hour or so," he mumbled as he pushed the throttles further forward. He glanced over at the GPS, which indicated 22.4 knots.

Red Marker 78A passed on the right side of the boat by a margin of barely ten feet. John continued his course of 250°, heading for his next marker, R80. Just ahead of the bow and a little to port, he noticed a school of dolphins playing tag as they skirted in and around the bow wake. He watched with awe as they effortlessly jumped in and out of the water. *God, what a beautiful sight!* Little did he know that soon he would have a personal experience with one of those intelligent and playful creatures.

Minutes later, John went past Marker R80 and changed direction for Steamboat Channel. Once through the channel, his last course change would be 270° for four miles to reach his anchorage.

Twenty-three minutes later, he reduced his speed and eventually stopped in eight feet of water about fifty yards off Gopher Key. Any closer, and he would have to contend with mosquitoes, and that was not something he wanted to do. The bite from those aggravating little pests made puffy red golf ball-sized welts on him that took two weeks to heal. He always covered himself with mosquito repellent outside, especially when he was close to the water.

Mosquito bites were not the only problem he had to worry about today. John Duncan had no idea that this day would be the worst day of his life.

Chapter 8

CJ's McKee Craft rested in the narrow channel at Little Rabbit Key. He stood on the bow of the open fisherman while working a Cabela's L-Tech fly rod and reel that his father had given him for his sixteenth birthday. It was designed specifically for him.

The breeze was light as the sun dipped low to the east. *No luck. No bonefish today,* CJ thought. He turned to face the rear of the boat and saw Skye bending over the live bait well, searching for another shrimp to thread onto her hook.

This year he had noticed a change in her demeanor as well as her physical appearance. On last year's visit, she still had been a girl. *She sure doesn't look like a little girl anymore. She's a young woman now. She is so gorgeous, but she doesn't even seem to realize it.* He was surprised as he felt a pulse of desire flow through his body. Skye was the only girl who had ever made him feel that way. He wondered how she felt about him, other than just being friends. *It doesn't matter. I'm too shy to ask. Maybe someday*, he thought. He reeled in his line, ready to cast it out in another direction.

"CJ, we're out of shrimp," Skye said flatly as she turned to face him.

Gosh, she's so pretty. If only she knew how I felt. Before I get the courage to tell her, she probably will be fully grown and married. CJ could not stop looking at her, and he was still unable to believe how much she had changed since last summer. "Why not try my rod?" he said, trying to take his mind off her gorgeous body.

"You know I can't work that thing, CJ. Besides, I'm too short. It works better for taller people."

"Well, just keep trying. You'll get the hang of it. It's pretty cool."

The lack of shrimp was forgotten as Skye sat on the center console bench seat. "It was so good to see Flapper this morning. Before you know it, he'll be back in the air. Those people at the rescue place do a wonderful job, don't they, CJ?"

"Yes, they do." CJ walked from the bow and took a seat next to Skye. He handed her his fly rod. "Here, give it a try," he urged.

Her mind was still on the pelican as Skye leaned over and touched CJ's shoulder. "I'm still so amazed that I can communicate with Flapper," she said, still a little stunned at what had happened.

CJ finally gave up asking her to try his new rod. He knew she wanted to talk about Flapper, and when Skye made her mind up she always got her way. *I'm just a wimp where she is concerned.*

———————

Earlier that morning, after Skye's repeated insistence, CJ had picked her up at Poppy's house to visit Flapper at The Laura Quinn Wild Bird Sanctuary in Tavernier. It was just up the road, a few miles from Poppy's house. They rode in silence as CJ's old Volkswagen Thing chugged along, each wondering what lay in store at the sanctuary.

Skye thought about the last time she had seen Flapper. She had seen the pain and anguish in his eyes. She quietly crossed her legs and fingers in an attempt to enhance her hushed prayer as they drove up the Overseas Highway.

Driving through Tavernier, CJ made a U-turn at Peace Avenue and headed south for a few hundred yards, arriving at the Sanctuary. He parked the VW next to the welcome sign.

Skye was out of the car before CJ could shut off the engine. As her feet touched the limestone parking lot, her brain was overwhelmed with the thoughts of hundreds of birds talking to her. Her head swam with the noise, unable to decipher any individual sound. "Stop!" she screamed.

CJ stopped dead in his tracks. *Gosh, what did I do?* He looked at Skye, who was standing still as though listening to something.

Please, I can only talk to you one at a time. She patiently sent the thought to the numerous birds calling for her attention. *Please, I'm trying to find Flapper.* Most of the birds got quiet.

I'm in here! Flapper sent the thought to Skye. Happiness rang in his thoughts.

CJ joined Skye at the entrance to the sanctuary, and then they walked inside the building.

Gianna Gianelli met them at the front counter. No older than eighteen, Gianna was new to the sanctuary. She was a beautiful young woman with long, wavy black hair pulled up into a ponytail. Her long-lashed deep brown eyes looked at the young couple with concern as she greeted Skye and CJ. Gianna had been working the counter for less than two weeks and was anxious to get out back and start working with the birds. She realized that she had to start at the bottom, and the front counter was the equivalent.

"Are you all right?" Gianna asked. "I heard a scream outside."

Skye just stood there, embarrassed, not knowing what to say.

"She's fine," CJ quickly answered for Skye. "The noise of all the birds took her by surprise, that's all."

"How may I help you?" Gianna asked politely.

"We'd like to see Flapper." Skye's voice quivered from excitement as she spoke

"Flapper? I'm sorry, we don't have a Flapper here," she answered, looking a little puzzled.

CJ answered, covering for Skye, "It's a pelican that was brought in here a few days ago. We nicknamed him Flapper after we rescued him. He had a broken wing with a fishhook stuck in it. We'd like to see how he's doing."

"Oh, yes, that one! Boy, did we have a time with him! He has a very nasty beak," she said as she laughed. "I thought we'd never get him sedated. But he's okay now, and he's an exceptionally good eater."

"Can we see him?" Skye's patience was beginning to wear thin. She could hear Flapper's thoughts. *I'm back here! I'm back here! I'm back here!* Through her thoughts, Skye responded to the bird, *We're coming.*

Answering their request, Gianna said, "Of course, you can see him. Y'all just come with me." CJ and Skye followed her.

They walked out the back of the building into a menagerie of local and exotic birds. Most were seagulls, pelicans, parrots, osprey, and other species of fowl.

I'm over here! Flapper shouted again in thought. Skye could feel his excitement in his thoughts to her.

Skye looked to the back of the bedlam. Most all the birds were free roaming, but Flapper was housed in an aviary about thirty feet wide and fifty feet long. Perched on an imitation stump, the poor pelican looked like a victim of a tough prize fight. His right wing was bandaged with white gauze, and a splint ran from the tip of his wing to his shoulder. All that was missing was a crutch.

"May we go in?" Skye and CJ chimed together. They looked at each other and smiled.

Gianna released the hasp and slowly opened the door, making sure no birds escaped. Life was so good on the inside that several ducks tried to enter. Gianna had to shoo them away.

Skye and CJ slowly entered the aviary, hoping not to frighten the residents. They slowly made their way to the stump where Flapper sat waiting for Skye.

Flapper tried to raise both wings as a sign of welcome, but he managed to move only his good wing.

Skye slowly knelt down beside him and gently closed her arms around the big bird. Her heart raced with joy as tears filled her eyes.

Flapper closed his good wing around her. His head tilted sideways to rest on her shoulder. Moments passed. Not a word or thought passed between them. There was only silence and joy at seeing each other again.

CJ and Gianna stood together, astounded at what they were witnessing. In her brief time working at the sanctuary, Gianna had never seen this kind of relationship. She remembered hearing her mother say that Ella Josephine, Gianna's great-grandmother, had told her that once in a while a rare person comes along who had a natural gift of communicating with animals. It was a special ability that was seldom mentioned, even among animal lovers.

Could this be what is happening? She wondered. *This pelican was out of control when he was brought into the sanctuary. Now he is the most docile, loving bird I've ever seen. It's as if the bird knows this young girl.*

Gianna loved birds too. She always had, but none had ever shown her the affection that this pelican was showing the girl. It was an astonishing spectacle to watch. She and CJ stood, watching in wonder and amazement. Gianna knew that she would never see this again in her lifetime.

Chapter 9

John Duncan had finally reached the spot where he was going to anchor his boat. He left the wheelhouse and moved forward to the bow. As the boat drifted in the light breeze, he put his left foot down on the power pedal of the Lofrans Falkon windless anchor. He had spent over seventy-five hundred dollars for it. After having congratulated himself on his recent purchase, he thought, *What a beauty! It was sure worth the price.* Duncan loved "toys" and tried to get all the newest ones, especially those for his boat.

He pushed the pedal to lay out anchor chain. At the exact moment that the anchor touched the water, the boat suddenly exploded. Both decks split into thousands of pieces of fiberglass and metal, flying hundreds of feet into the air.

Following the explosion, there was a giant fireball from the fuel tank. A shadow moved over the area as fire and black smoke rolled into the air. Duncan did not see it because he was unconscious.

His heavy frame was hurled over two hundred feet from the deck. As he flew through the air, his body was laced with shrapnel and scorched from the flames. What seemed like an eternity later, he hit the water.

———————

Fishing in CJ's boat, Skye and CJ heard the enormous explosion first, and then moments later they saw a fireball with black billowing smoke. Both were stunned into silence as they sat in their boat, mesmerized by what they saw. They stared in unbelievable horror, their minds unable to comprehend what was happening. "What was that?" they said in unison.

CJ knew the smoke was coming from the far side of Gopher Key, about four miles away. Mangroves almost totally blocked their view, but he knew that the explosion had to be from either a boat or an airplane.

Suddenly, he jumped from his seat, stashed his fly rod in the rod holder, and pressed the starter. Skye leaped from her seat at almost the same instant and headed for the anchor line.

Moments later, CJ spun the little boat around and jammed the throttle to full max. *Four miles at thirty miles an hour*, he quickly calculated. *Just under eight minutes.*

"What do you think it is?" Skye yelled above the noise of the wind and the engine.

"From the size of the explosion, I think it's either a boat or an airplane," CJ shouted back.

Skye held on to the railing that was attached to the center console.

As the boat drew closer to the channel, CJ spotted the red marker, Waypoint 74. As they almost grazed the marker, CJ twisted the boat over on its left side and lined up for the channel. The narrow waterway through the mangroves was about a mile long and thirty-five feet wide. CJ saw Waypoint 73 up ahead and yelled to Skye, "Hold on, we're going to make another sharp turn."

The closer they got to the fire, the larger and higher the smoke billowed. Waypoint 73 flashed past the boat, and again CJ laid the boat on its side. Two hundred yards ahead lay the remains of what appeared to be a boat. Black smoke and flames shot into the air from the melting fiberglass hull. CJ pulled back on the throttle, bringing the boat to an immediate stop.

Skye and CJ surveyed the scene, each wondering what they could or should do. "Where are the people onboard?" Skye asked CJ, wringing her hands. "We'd better call the Coast Guard," she suggested, her voice shaking.

"Yeah, you're right," CJ answered, and he reached for the mike on his VHF radio. He switched to Channel 16, which was the emergency channel for the US Coast Guard.

"Mayday, mayday, mayday. This is the motor vessel *Gator Bait*. Over." He waited for an answer, but his radio remained quiet.

Once more, CJ made his desperate call, and again there was no response.

Finally, a voice said, "*Gator Bait*, this is Islamorada Coast Guard. What is the nature of your emergency? Over."

"Coast Guard, this is *Gator Bait*. We are at the scene of a boat explosion, and the fire is down to the waterline. Our location is just south of Gopher Key. Over."

"Are there any casualties? Over."

"None that we can see. Over." Unexpectedly, Skye began to scream. "CJ, help me, help me! I'm going to pass out. I can't stand the pain! The noise is overwhelming."

CJ dropped the mike and lunged for Skye. Her knees were beginning to buckle as CJ grabbed her around the waist. He gently lowered her to the bench seat forward of the center console. He could hear the Coast Guard calling back. For the moment, he had to ignore the Coast Guard and tend to Skye.

Skye's eyes were beginning to roll back as CJ looked down at her. He had no idea what to do. Fear crossed his face. "Oh my God," he moaned. "Skye, wake up, wake up," he said and began to shake her. "Please wake up!" he commanded as he continued to shake her.

Skye finally began to move her arms, bringing her hands to her face. Suddenly her eyes started to focus, and she tried to lift herself into a sitting position. "It's happening again," she whispered. "I can hear a voice nearby."

"What voice?" CJ asked with alarm in his voice.

"Something is calling for help. It's becoming clearer now." Skye shakily stood and began to look around. She still felt disoriented and held tight to CJ's arm. Then she saw and heard it again at the same instant. She pointed toward the mangroves. CJ's eyes followed her pointed finger. Then he saw it too. Fifty yards or so from the mangrove there was a body bobbing in the water. Someone or something seemed to be pushing it slowly toward their boat.

Skye heard a voice, or what seemed to be a voice with intermittent squeaks.

Please, I need help, the squeaky voice said through thought.

CJ had already pushed the throttle slowly forward and turned the boat in the direction of the body.

"We're coming," Skye said to the squeaky voice. *This can't be happening to me again, can it?* She knew the voice wasn't Flapper because he was at the bird sanctuary. *What other 'thing' can be calling to me?*

As the boat drew closer to the body, Skye and CJ could see a dolphin gently pushing the body with its snout and trying to keep it on the surface. They watched as the dolphin moved its nose back and forth from the man's head to his mid-section, and then back again to his head, gently pushing the body toward their small boat.

————————

CJ's father, Michael Jansen, heard the emergency call at the same time the Coast Guard had answered. One of his hobbies was monitoring Channel 16, the Coast Guard's emergency frequency.

On one occasion, he had assisted the Coast Guard and the Sheriff's Office in rescuing a stranded jet-skier out on the flats north of Lignumvitae Key.

This time was different. He had heard his son's voice on the radio and had heard the name of CJ's boat, *Gator Bait*. He knew CJ needed help as he rose from his seat in front of the VHF radio. Michael's boat was at the marina for repairs, so the only way to get to his son was to use his Kawasaki Jet Ski. *It'll be fine. It's shallow water out there, and besides, it's just a few miles from home. The*

Jet Ski will be faster because I can cut across the shallows. Concerned for CJ and Skye's safety, he thought, *I need to get to them now!*

On his way out, he passed through the kitchen, scooped up his VHS handheld transceiver and two bottles of Zephyrhills water. Maria was out shopping, so he paused briefly to write her a brief note.

He slammed the back door on his way out. On the deck, he stopped for a moment to gaze out at the horizon and saw black smoke rising in the air. After running down the stairs, he hurriedly jogged down to the end of the dock where his Kawasaki Ultra 310LX waited. *It's a monster, and it's fast, thank goodness,* he thought.

The Kawasaki had three seats and a 310-horsepower engine. Michael liked his jet ski and enjoyed riding on it. He had made it a habit to always keep his equipment gassed and ready to go. It was a spin-off from his days with the National Security Agency. One always had to be prepared, especially living close to the water.

He jumped down onto the ramp, stashed his radio and the two bottles, and pushed the Jet Ski off the ramp and into the bay. After Michael had warmed the engine for a couple minutes, he blasted across the channel at top speed, leaving a rooster tail in its wake.

———————

"Coast Guard, this is the *Gator Bait*. We've spotted one victim in the water and are presently attempting a recovery. Over."

"*Gator Bait*, what is the status of the victim? Over."

"Coast Guard, *Gator Bait*. Not sure at the moment but will keep you advised. Over."

"Roger, *Gator Bait*, standing by."

Skye finally turned to the dolphin. "My name is Skye," she said to the dolphin. What's your name?"

"I don't have a name, the dolphin responded to Skye. We use

squeaks."

"Okay, I'll call you Squeaky if that's okay with you," Skye said. "How did you happen to be here when the boat exploded?"

"Yes, that's okay with me. My friends and I were following the boat. We were playing a game, and all of a sudden, the boat exploded. It scared all my friends away. I was leaving with them, and then I saw this big guy fall from the air and hit the water. I thought he might still be alive. I knew I had to try and help him."

"Skye," Squeaky said a little shyly, " I like the name you gave me. My pod will be jealous. None of them can talk with humans, and none of them have names."

As the boat got close, CJ put the engine in neutral and let it drift toward the body. Skye was shocked at what she saw. The man floated on his back, and his arms sank alongside his body. His body was black from the explosion, and he was severely burned. Blood seeped from his nose, ears, and eyes as he drifted naked in the tropical water.

"CJ, the dolphin says the guy's still alive!" Skye shouted. "Call the Coast Guard and let them know."

Jeez, thought CJ. *What's next?* He certainly couldn't tell them that a dolphin told Skye the man was still alive. Swallowing hard, he grabbed the mike. "Coast Guard, this is *Gator Bait*. Over."

"Go ahead *Gator Bait*. Over."

"We have one unconscious survivor, alive and severely burned. We need assistance right away. Over."

"Roger, *Gator Bait*; standby."

CJ dreaded what he had to do next. "Skye, I'm going in," he said, kicking off his boat shoes. "Throw the anchor over," he shouted as he plunged into the water.

As Skye heaved the anchor over the bow rail, the line became snagged on a bow cleat. She moved forward and began struggling with the taut line. Finally, she loosened it.

The water feels nice and warm, CJ thought as he reached the surface. Ten yards in front of him, he saw the dolphin struggling to keep the man afloat. Several strokes later, CJ's left hand grabbed the man's right arm just above his elbow. Small pieces of flesh floated away from the man's underarm.

CJ momentarily closed his eyes, and bile rose from his stomach. Shock raced through his body at what he saw. There was no hair on the back of the man's head. The constant rubbing of the dolphin's snout as he had tried to keep the man's head above water, along with the man's severe burns, had left an almost skinless skull.

He heard the man groan. *I have to get him to the boat.* He rolled over on his side and began towing the heavy human barge. Pulling almost twice his weight, CJ struggled toward the boat, his strength diminishing with each stroke as he drew closer.

"Skye, I need your help," CJ called out.

Skye stood at the edge of the boat near the transom. "I'm here!" she yelled.

Moments later, and out of breath, CJ reached the boat and grabbed the swim ladder with his free hand.

Skye stood over them, alarm on her face, wondering what she should do.

"Here, Skye, take his hand and hold him here while I get into the boat."

"Do I have to?" she grimaced. Just looking down at the poor, blackened and burned man made her stomach queasy.

"Yes, Skye, you have to help him. You have no choice," CJ urged her. "If we don't help him, he'll die."

Skye reluctantly reached down and took the man's hand.

CJ held onto the swim ladder, trying to relax for a bit and catch his breath. He said a brief prayer that the man would live.

Chapter 10

On his Jet Ski, Michael bore down on the black smoke at almost fifty miles an hour. He ignored the channels and sped across the flats, sometimes in less than eight inches of water. He took the most direct path to the fire as he dared, hoping that he wouldn't run aground. Glancing to his left, he saw an orange sun slowly setting on the horizon. He knew it would be dark in less than an hour.

Visions of the scene flashed through Michael's mind, and he wondered how Skye and CJ were handling their situation. *They are both too young for this, particularly Skye. Will she be okay? Yes,* he thought, *she's strong. She'll be okay, but CJ might be a different story. Like his mother, CJ is extremely sensitive and caring.*

When he was a child, Michael had watched him cry for two days after a car had hit his neighbor's dog. "I'll have to spend some quality time with him after this," he said aloud, above the roar of the Jet Ski.

CJ put his right foot on the lowest rung of the dive ladder and pulled his exhausted body aboard the craft. He saw Skye down on her knees holding the man's head above water. *She looks terrified*, CJ thought as he wiped the saltwater from his eyes. "I've got to call the Coast Guard," he said hurriedly, reaching for the dangling mike. "How's he doing?"

"He's still breathing. God, I hope he doesn't die. We need help," Skye said, her voice trembling with fear.

CJ spoke into the mike. "Islamorada Coast Guard, this is the *Gator Bait*. Over." It seemed to take forever for the Coast Guard to answer.

"Go ahead, *Gator Bait*," a young voice replied.

Speechless all of a sudden, CJ didn't know what to say. It took him a moment to gather his thoughts. "Coast Guard, we need a medevac. We have a victim who is unconscious and probably in shock. He has burns all over his body and apparent multiple injuries, and he's barely breathing. Over." CJ's voice was steady and firm, and he was in control again.

"*Gator Bait*, we've got a chopper coming to you out of Marathon. ETA is about twenty-five minutes. Just continue monitoring your radio. Over."

"Roger," CJ answered with a sigh of relief as he hung up the mike.

He turned from the center console and looked down at Skye, who was still holding the man's head above water. He could see the fatigue in her face and bent down to lend her a hand. *Please hang in there, mister. Don't die.* CJ didn't think Skye could handle it if the man died.

"Let's see if we can get him onboard," Skye groaned a few minutes later. After bending over the transom for ten minutes and holding on to the big man, Skye's back was starting to give out.

"Okay," CJ agreed. "You take his left hand, and I'll take his right." Maneuvering carefully between Skye and the engine, CJ tried to get into the right spot so he could grab hold of the heavy man's weight. Skye took the man's left hand, stooped down, and waited for CJ to get into position.

"All right, on the count of three," CJ said. "One, two, and three."

Skye straightened her knees and lifted with all her strength. CJ did likewise. They were able to get the man's body partway into the boat but could get it no further. His shoulders had jammed on the transom, and even though they were pulling with all their might, they couldn't budge him any further. They looked at each other, both realizing that the man was too heavy. Reluctantly, they eased him back into the water.

Thirty-two miles south-southeast of the fire, the US Coast Guard helicopter, HH-65 Dolphin, prepared to depart Marathon Airport to assist in the recovery of a critically injured boater who had been involved in a mysterious explosion.

"Where in the heck is our swimmer?" Captain Hoppe asked his co-pilot, Lieutenant Gavin Harbin, as they patiently waited in the cockpit for the remainder of the crew.

"No idea, sir."

Neil Hoppe had been a helicopter rescue pilot with the Coast Guard for five years. After extensive helicopter training in the U.S Army and two tours in Iraq, Hoppe returned to his home on Marathon Key.

A couple weeks later, an army buddy mentioned that the Coast Guard was looking for helicopter rescue pilots, and with his experience, it was a perfect fit for him. He loved his job, and he liked his crew. Flying was all he had ever wanted to do, and having the opportunity of saving lives made him feel like he was making a real difference.

With hazel green eyes, premature graying hair and a great sense of humor, twenty-eight-year-old flight mechanic First Class Tim Riddle stood thirty feet away from the chopper, just outside the whirl of the rotor blades. His left hand held a seventy-five-foot communications umbilical cord, which connected him to the helicopter. It was standard procedure for the flight mechanic to monitor all activity surrounding the chopper while preparing for liftoff. Moments before takeoff, Riddle would coil the wire as he approached the chopper, and then after he gave the "all clear" he would throw the cord into the craft and jump aboard the helicopter.

From the cockpit, Gavin Harbin looked to his far right and saw Corpsman Curt Shields running from the flight operations center toward the chopper.

Corpsman Shields was carrying his wetsuit and swim gear and had a self-conscious look on his face. "Crap! I'm late again," he mumbled. No matter how hard he tried, Curt Shields just couldn't be on time.

Shields hurriedly rushed past Riddle. Once Shields reached the craft, he threw his equipment into the chopper. Riddle immediately followed him.

"All clear, sir," Riddle said into his headset, slamming the sliding door closed.

"Roger that," Captain Hoppe replied.

Shields began removing his civilian clothes and replacing them with a wetsuit and other swimming paraphernalia.

Four thirty-nine-foot rotors, powered by two Turbomeca Arriel 2c2 turbo shaft engines, began revving up to their standard operating temperatures and RPMs.

Two minutes later, as the powerful craft left the ground, the captain said, "Gentlemen, let's go save a life."

As Michael Jansen turned his Jet Ski toward the accident, a shiver ran down the back of his neck. *About another mile and a half, and I'll be there.* He turned his attention to the fiery boat. The flames had reached the waterline and were burning fast. He figured it would sink within the hour, if not sooner. He began scanning the area and finally saw CJ's little boat anchored next to the mangroves. Michael changed course and headed for the *Gator Bait.*

Moments later, he pulled up alongside CJ's boat.

"Dad!" CJ yelled as he threw his father a line. "How did you find out about the fire?"

CJ tied off the line to the Jet Ski as Michael backed it down, coming to rest next to the boat. Michael reached over, grabbed the rail, and stepped down into the craft. He had not noticed Skye kneeling next to the transom.

Finally seeing her, and after surveying the situation, he moved over and patted her on the shoulder. "Good job Skye," he said gently. "Hang in there, okay?" His eyes moved to the man floating in the water. He could tell the man was barely alive. Looking at the burned skin on the poor guy, he thought, *It's a miracle he's not dead.*

CJ stooped down beside Skye. "Take a break, okay? I'll take over for a while. You need to rest."

Realizing he had not answered CJ's question, Michael said, "I was monitoring Channel 16 when I heard your distress call come into the Coast Guard. When you said the name *Gator Bait*, I knew it was you and Skye. My boat is at the marina for repairs, so I jumped on the Jet Ski. Thought I might be able to help until the rescue helicopter got here."

"I sure wish they'd hurry," Skye said with fatigue in her voice.

"Yeah, if they don't hurry, it'll be dark when they get here," Michael answered. "Any idea what happened?"

CJ shook his head. "No way of telling, Dad. We were fishing, and we heard an explosion, and then we saw smoke and flames. That's all we can tell you."

Michael looked over at the burning hull. He saw movement, and then the stern of the boat slowly began to drop beneath the water. "Look guys, she's going down," he whispered as if his voice had already sealed her fate.

They all watched as steam hissed in the early twilight. The sounds of cracking and expansion filled the air. It was as though they were witnessing a death. A few moments later, the boat was gone.

It was not the first time Michael had seen the death of high-tech equipment. He had been in Columbia, South America, and had seen a DC-7 crash. It had not been a pleasant sight. He shivered and brushed the thought away.

Silence fell over the little boat. They felt as if they were attending a funeral. All three of them waited. Waiting for the rescue helicopter to arrive and waiting for the big man in the water to die. No one said anything.

Skye was scared. She had never seen an injured person before, especially not one so close to death. She wished the day was over. She wanted to be home with Poppy, snuggled up between her clean sheets, waiting for the next day's adventure with CJ.

A light, southwesterly breeze stirred the once smooth water's surface. The *Gator Bait* began to swing in a large fishtail motion, making it difficult for CJ to hold on to the heavy man's head. His body needed to follow the boat, fishtailing as well. CJ should have been paying more attention as the man's head accidentally slipped under the water. CJ quickly grabbed for it and brought it back to the surface. The stranger started coughing and spitting blood from the side of his mouth. He stopped suddenly and was still.

CJ began to panic. "Dad, come quick! I need your help!"

Michael rushed over to where CJ was kneeling. "Son, I think he's stopped breathing. If we don't get him into this boat, he's going to die for sure. He needs CPR."

Michael kicked his boat shoes off and was in the water before CJ and Skye knew what was happening.

Chapter 11

Captain Meyer spoke into his mike, "Hey, Shields, you ready to go?"

Curt Shields had just finished putting on his swim fins and was adjusting his face mask. "Yes, sir, Skipper. I'm just waiting for the green light." Tall and trim with buzzed hair and aqua-blue eyes, Shields loved his job and was dedicated to saving lives, though he did need some serious work on his promptness skills.

The HH-65 Dolphin was cruising at one hundred eight-five miles an hour. Her crew had just finished going over their checklist when the captain's voice came over the intercom. "Stand by people. We'll be on target in two minutes."

Tim Riddle unbuckled his seat belt, stood up, and grabbed the lifting winch with his right hand while grabbing the door handle and twisting the latch. With a heavy tug, the main door opened. A frigid blast of air struck his body, forcing him to take a step back before he could regain his balance. He and his teammates had successfully practiced the procedure hundreds of times. In his mind, he hoped that this one would be no different.

First, they heard it, and a minute later they saw it. The HH-65 Dolphin shot out from over the tops of the mangroves no more than fifty feet above them. The *Gator Bait* shuddered from the roaring noise of the chopper's giant rotors as it passed over them. The three occupants in the boat crouched down as the vibration moved across the water. Bending over, Michael raised his head from John Duncan's mouth to look up at the giant machine. Skye was kneeling beside him as she rendered CPR to the injured man.

Shortly before the chopper arrived, John's blood pressure had dropped dramatically, followed by cardiac arrest. Michael and Skye had immediately moved into action, trying desperately to save his life. CJ stood next to the center console holding the radio's mike in his hand. He waited for the chopper's instruction. The helicopter significantly increased its altitude while making a steep left turn, slowing the craft for its final approach to the boat.

"*Gator Bait*, this is Coast Guard Helo. Over."

"Go ahead, Coast Guard," CJ said, his voice a little shaky. He hoped that the Coast Guard could save the injured man. When he had gotten up to go fishing with Skye earlier this morning, he had no idea of the events that would quickly unfold today, or that a man's life would hang in the balance.

"*Gator Bait*, switch to Channel 22. Over."

"Roger, Channel 22," CJ answered as he reached for the radio.

"What is the status of your patient? Over."

"He's not doing very well, sir. We're giving him CPR at the moment. Over."

"Roger, *Gator Bait*. We're going to put a diver in the water to assist. Over."

"Roger that," CJ replied. Looking over at the horizon, he thought, *Daylight is disappearing fast. It'll be dark soon.*

The HH-65 Dolphin was floating about thirty feet above the surface as it slowly made its way toward the boat. It stopped fifty feet from the *Gator Bait*.

CJ watched a man wearing a wet suit and swim fins step out from the doorway with his arms across his chest. His left hand held his face mask in place as he plunged thirty feet into the water. Seconds later, his head and shoulders popped out of the water. He looked around to orient himself and then began swimming toward the boat.

Thirty-eight strokes later, Corpsman Curt Shield's left hand touched the swim ladder on the *Gator Bait*. He reached up with his right hand, raised his mask and said, "Hi there, folks, my name's Curt Shields. How can I help you guys today?" A moment later, his swim fins lay in the boat, and he was lifting himself aboard the boat. CJ reached out to give him a hand.

Shields wasted no time moving to his patient. As Michael and Skye continued CPR, Shields slowly and methodically checked for cuts, broken bones, and any other trauma he could find.

After about a minute or so, Shields stood up from the patient and said, "We have to stabilize him before he can be transported. I need my trauma kit." He stepped over to the center console and took the mike from CJ's hand.

"Coast Guard, this is Swim Man. Over."

"Roger, Swim Man."

"We have a critical male onboard about fifty years old. I need a trauma kit ASAP!"

"Roger, Swim Man. Stand by."

CJ watched as the HH-65 Dolphin moved nearer to the boat. The closer it came, the louder and stronger the wind blew. Finally, it hovered twenty feet over them. It was all CJ could do to hold on with both hands curled around the center console rail. The noise and hurricane force wind were terrifying for the teens. Salt spray from the whipping wind soaked everyone.

Captain Hoppe flipped on the rescue lights located under the fuselage as First-Class Tim Riddle pushed out the lifting winch with a stretcher basket attached, and Shield's trauma kit secure inside. Riddle's gloved hand touched the down button.

CJ looked up and squinted at the blinding light. Saltwater spray magnified the light's intensity. As the stretcher passed through the beams of light, he was able to see it swinging dangerously back and forth.

"Don't touch it!" Shields shouted to CJ. "Let it contact the boat first. The static electricity could kill you! It needs to ground out."

CJ used the center console as a shield, trying to protect himself from the swinging electrode. He heard a loud thump as the basket bounced onto the deck.

Shields reached the basket first. He grabbed it and raised his right hand to signal the flight mechanic for more slack in the cable. As the basket settled onto the deck, Shields instantly went for the trauma kit.

"Hold on to the basket," Shields yelled to CJ. "Don't let it swing around. It's dangerous in this wind."

CJ secured the projectile. He shivered. The blowing wind from the medevac on the water made the salt spray cold.

Shields dragged the trauma kit as close as possible to where Skye and Michael knelt. He popped the cover off and pulled out a bag valve mask. He gently pushed Skye aside, placed the BVM over John Duncan's face and began squeezing the rubber bulb.

He glanced over at Skye. "Think you can do this?" he shouted as he demonstrated the technique for using the mask.

Skye nodded, reached down, and began squeezing the bulb.

Michael's face grimaced from fatigue as he continued pushing in on the injured man's chest.

Shields went back to his box and pulled out a bag of saline solution, along with an IV starter kit. He quickly inserted a needle into the injured man's limp arm and lifted the IV bag to get the fluid moving into his system. He did it quickly and expertly within a matter of seconds. "Let's see if we can get his heart kick-started."

Seeing the nervous look on the three faces, Shields smiled. He turned in a squatting position and extracted a defibrillator from the box. He unwound the wires attached to the unit, turned the monitor on, and made some minor adjustments. Last, he attached the paddles to the wires.

Michael looked a little concerned as Shields prepared the unit. "That thing isn't going to shock us too, is it? I mean, with all the water around?"

Shields looked up at Michael. "Not unless you're touching the patient," he answered.

"Stand back," Shields commanded as he placed the paddles on John Duncan's chest. "Clear!" he shouted.

Duncan's chest rose up a little for a second and then relaxed. Shields felt his patient's carotid artery. *No pulse*, he thought. "Crap," he whispered.

"One more try," he said to everyone, placing the paddles on the man's chest for the second time. "Clear!" he repeated again.

Duncan's chest again lifted slightly from the deck.

Shields thought he heard a soft moan. This time when he touched the man's carotid artery, he felt a weak pulse. "Yes!" he shouted. "Hallelujah!" He saw relief on everyone's faces.

"Thank you, Jesus," Skye said with a sigh of relief.

Exhausted, Michael still managed a big smile.

Looking a little pale from all the stress, CJ also offered a small smile of relief to the diver. His mind kept thinking about the way the critically burned man looked as he had towed him back to the boat. His stomach still felt a little queasy. *Man, saving someone's life isn't easy. What would I have done if it had just been Skye and me on the boat and the man had died?* Realizing that the worst was over, he relaxed a little.

Shields began to prepare the man for transport in the basket. First, he attached a brace around John Duncan's neck. Next, he wrapped his right arm to his body. "Guys, I need some help lifting him into the basket. He's a big guy."

Michael and CJ each took a leg while Shields lifted the man under his left arm. The maneuver was very awkward. Skye knelt down and leaned the basket onto its side. They had to roll him into the basket.

With John Duncan safely in the basket, Shields expertly strapped him in, placed the trauma kit next to his feet, and stood up. With his right hand in the air, he motioned to Riddle to begin the hoist. Tension snapped the cable tight, and the basket left the boat and disappeared into the blinding light.

No one could see beyond the intensity of the lights. They all stood around the center console and waited.

Michael was the first to speak. He reached out and began shaking Shields' hand. "Sailor," he said, "I want to thank you and your crew for a superb job well done. The man would be dead by now had it not been for you. Thank you so much."

Skye moved around the console and gave Shields a big hug. "Thanks," she whispered, exhaustion showing in her face.

"Just part of the job, miss," he answered, thinking how tired the young girl looked.

CJ, a little embarrassed at being so scared earlier, also reached out to shake the diver's hand. He wasn't one to show his emotions in public.

At that moment, a heavy-duty strap was lowered to the boat. Shields retrieved his swim fins and face mask, wrapped the strap under his arms, and with a wave to Riddle he was lifted into the air.

When Shields was ten feet above the boat, the chopper began to move away and up, leaving the small craft cloaked in darkness. The noise and wind immediately subsided.

Michael, Skye, and CJ stood in silence. No one spoke. They relished the quiet for a moment.

"That was quite a job, guys. I am immensely proud of you two," Michael said sincerely, looking at CJ and Skye. "Hey, we've got some steaks back at the house. Why don't you follow me home, and we'll grill some for dinner?"

"Okay," they said in unison. They were both starved. With the explosion and all that followed, they had never had a chance to eat Skye's delicious lunch.

Forgotten and realizing that Skye and the others were leaving, Squeaky began swimming back to his pod. *Boy, do I have a story to tell them. They're never going to believe it!* Hoping to see Skye again, Squeaky realized that he had made his first human friend.

Chapter 12

The day had been long and stressful. When the three of them were ready to leave the scene of the explosion, Michael had jumped on his Jet Ski and headed home.

CJ dropped Skye off at Poppy's boat dock and had driven his VW home. Skye had told him she was in desperate need of a shower and some quiet time with Poppy to sort out the events of the day, and then she would walk over to his house.

As she entered the house, she realized Poppy wasn't there. She called to him to be certain but received no response. *He must be at the movies,* she thought. *He loves movies.* She had very much wanted to share her thoughts with her grandfather concerning what had happened. She always felt better when she discussed her day with him. A weary sigh escaped her lungs as she headed for the bathroom.

A twenty-minute hot shower rejuvenated her sore muscles. It took another ten minutes to untangle her matted hair. *What to wear, what to wear?* she wondered, heading to the closet.

Fifteen minutes later, Skye left the house wearing a pair of slim white jeans, a sleeveless pink blouse, white Keds, and a tiny pair of pearl earrings her grandfather had given her for her fifteenth birthday. She pulled a tube of pink gloss from her purse, quickly smoothed it over her lips and was ready to go. Her blonde hair was drying in the soft breeze. Once again, there was a bounce in her stride as she walked the short distance to CJ's house. As she strolled along, her mind raced, thinking about the events of the last few hours. *I'll talk with Poppy in the morning. He was pretty shaken up when I told him about Flapper. Wait until I tell him about today. He's not going to believe it.* She smiled to herself, thinking about his reaction when she told him about Squeaky and the explosion.

———————

As Skye rounded the corner to the Jansen's multi-level home on the bay, the aroma of grilling steaks caused her stomach to growl.

The smell reminded her that the only food she had had today was a light early morning breakfast, and it was long gone. She was famished, and the thought of a big, juicy steak raised her spirits.

Mr. Jansen was standing next to his gas grill, tossing some green peppers on the side burner. *He looks handsome enough for his age,* she thought. With sandy blond hair, blue eyes and a dark tan, Mr. Jansen was the opposite in appearance of Mrs. Jansen. For a brief moment, Skye wondered what CJ would look like when he was his dad's age. She could not image either of them being Mr. Jansen's age. CJ had told her his dad was fifty, and his mother was forty-nine. *Man, that's old,* she thought.

Soft sounds of Jimmy Buffet emanated from Bose speakers hidden somewhere in the shrubs. The warm summer breeze felt refreshing in contrast to the cold, wet, hurricane-force winds generated from the helicopter earlier that evening.

CJ was slumped back in a fancy chaise lounge. His eyes were closed.

At first, Skye thought he might be asleep, but then she noticed that ever so often he would reach over and take a sip of Coke from a green glass bottle sitting on a small table beside the chair. His long, bony knees were up in the air, swaying to the rhythm of the late 70's music, which Mr. and Mrs. Jansen loved. Of course, Skye had always thought Jimmy Buffet was cool, too.

Mrs. Jansen was nowhere in sight. *She must be in the kitchen,* Skye decided.

Out of the corner of his eye, Michael saw Skye walking across the lawn. "Hey, Skye," he shouted.

"Hi, Mr. Jansen, something sure smells good."

Hearing Skye's voice, CJ raised himself up from his chair and walked over to greet his closest friend. *She looks so beautiful tonight. Of course, every time I see her, she looks beautiful. Just looking at her makes my heart do flip flops*

"How about a Coke?" Michael offered.

"Sure. Thanks, Mr. Jansen. I've been wanting one all day."

Skye heard the back-screen door close. She watched Mrs. Jansen walk down the steps. She wore a big smile. In white shorts, a sleeveless royal blue blouse and white, jeweled sandals, Skye thought she looked about twenty-five years old. Skye had always thought Mrs. Jansen was a real beauty. With a stunning figure, shoulder length, black wavy hair, and long dark lashes sweeping over beautiful brown eyes, Skye could understand why everyone said she was gorgeous.

"Well, if isn't my long-lost friend," Maria said as she walked over and gave Skye a big hug.

"You don't come around here often enough," Maria said sincerely. Her voice suddenly became serious. "I heard you three had a rough day, and I can only imagine what you've been through. My goodness girl, you and CJ seem to get into more trouble than Tom and Jerry."

Skye smiled as she thought of the cartoon characters and burst out laughing. Maria joined her, the seriousness of the day quickly forgotten.

"We're ready to eat, gang," Michael announced. "Everybody grab a plate and come on to the table."

Skye had a ravenous appetite, and the dinner was delicious. She practically inhaled her salad, and then she started on her steak with black beans and rice. All were chased down with a bottle of Coke.

Dessert was homemade key lime pie, which was Skye's favorite. Maria had gotten the recipe from her mother and had learned to make it after her family had fled Cuba and moved to Miami.

Watching Skye devour her dinner, CJ was always impressed with the amount of food she could consume. She ate whatever she wanted and never gained an ounce. He didn't know where she put all the food, but it sure hadn't put any weight on her. She was still very petite and weighed less than a hundred pounds. *Yeah, a hundred pounds of dynamite*, CJ thought, admiring Skye's spunk.

Satiated, Michael pushed his chair back and reached for his pipe. Smoking a pipe after dinner had become a ritual for him. He had a little tool with a flat bottom, and he took his time packing small amounts of tobacco into his pipe. He finally lit it, and the pungent aroma filled the air.

Skye loved the smell of pipe tobacco. It reminded her of Poppy. He always smoked a pipe when they were out on his boat fishing. It didn't matter to him whether they caught anything or not. He always said, "It's just plain old relaxing," as he puffed on his pipe.

"You know, I've been thinking about the explosion," Michael said. "It seems to me that the explosion was too big for just a twenty-five-pound propane tank. That was a big boat."

CJ perked up in his seat. "You know, Dad, I've been thinking the same thing. Do you think somebody may have intentionally tried to harm the guy?"

"It's possible, son."

Maria was starting to get a little agitated listening to the conversation. "You three listen to me," she said, a little bothered by the direction the discussion was heading. "There is no evidence there's any wrongdoing. You start poking your noses into other people's business, and you're going to get into trouble. It could be dangerous."

"But Mrs. Jansen," Skye interrupted, "if you had only seen the poor guy. Something or somebody almost killed him."

"What do you think we should do, Dad?" CJ ignored his mother's concern as he questioned his father.

"Well, I suppose I could give my old friend up in Miami a call," Michael responded, casting a glance at Maria.

"Michael, you leave Sonny Mitchell out of this!" Maria admonished.

"Sweetheart," Michael soothed, "you know Sonny has a lot of connections."

"Don't you dare sweetheart me, Michael Jansen! You know how I feel about Sonny. He's one of our best friends, and I've trusted him with our lives ever since we met him, but I don't want you to get him involved in this investigation, if there is one. He has connections all right, but some of them are less than desirable. I don't want you or the kids involved with people like that. Anyway, I've had my say. I know you're going to do whatever you want to do, regardless of what I say."

Skye moved from her chair to stand by Michael. "Mr. Jansen, I just had an idea. If there's no investigation, why don't we just salvage the boat? That way, we can let the sheriff's office take a look at it and see what they think. I doubt they'll raise the hull, but we could."

"Hey Dad, I think that's a great idea, don't you?"

Maria lowered her face into her hands and began shaking it back and forth. *Oh, Lord, not again,* she thought as she sighed.

Michael sat in silence for a few moments, contemplating their next move. "Okay, here's what we'll do..." Before he even shared his plan, he sensed the excitement in the faces of the teens.

Chapter 13

Alexei Kovalchik stood inside the tunnel with his hands on his hips. He surveyed the monumental piece of handiwork that he and Anatoli Krasnoff had just completed. They had received five boatloads of merchandise, and now it all rested on the thick wooden shelving they had installed.

He estimated more than half a million dollars retail of electronic equipment was neatly stacked and waiting, and more was yet to come. He could already see dollar signs. He and Anatoli had figured that along with the shipments they had already received, and several more that would be delivered, they would be able to retire and live the high life on Miami Beach.

Everyone wants iPhones, iPads, Xboxes, and televisions. They'll think the prices are cheap, and they won't even know that they're knockoffs. Anatoli and I will get rich peddling them to unsuspecting buyers. A true crook at heart, Alexei smiled, thinking about it.

They had invested over fifty-one thousand ill-gotten dollars on the sophisticated alarm system that their comrades in Miami had guaranteed not to fail. It included some of the newest electronic surveillance equipment available, all of which were remotely controlled from inside the tunnel. Some of the components were not even out on the market yet.

He wondered what effect the system would have on any would-be trespassers and what their reactions would be. The alarm system included fog and smoke machines, loudspeakers, holographic projectors, strobe and spotlights, and miniature cameras, all strategically placed around the island. The idea was to scare the wits out of anyone daring to come on the island. *Even Disney World would be impressed*, Alexei thought with pride.

Miami had insisted on no guns. It was one thing to get caught with illegal contraband, but an entirely separate set of charges for carrying a gun.

Tonight, they would begin transferring their goods to Miami via cargo vans.

Everyone was gathered around the ornate mahogany dining room table at Poppy's house. The entire front wall was Peachtree sliding glass doors. The spectacular view overlooked Florida Bay. Sheer white curtains that opened in the center were pulled partway open and framed the scenery. An early morning breeze swept in through a partially open slider, causing the curtains to sway gently.

After Skye had gotten home last night from the Jansen's house, she had told Poppy about the events of the day, giving him full details of the explosion and rescue. She also had told him about Squeaky.

Poppy believed what Skye had told him, even about the dolphin. After he had learned about Flapper, he readily accepted Skye's conversation with Squeaky. He still thought it was incredible, but he knew what she told him was the truth.

He had agreed with her that there was something fishy about the blast. He wanted to help in any way he could, so he spoke with Michael on the phone, and they decided to meet for breakfast at his house the following morning.

Since Poppy was hosting the meeting, he sat at the head of the table. Michael sat to his left, and CJ and Skye were seated to

Poppy's right. He had called it a breakfast meeting. The typical southern fare was served. Bacon, eggs, grits, and biscuits slathered with butter covered each plate with glasses of orange juice beside them. Jars of strawberry and peach preserves sat next to the biscuits.

After everyone had finished, Skye cleared the table and put the dishes in the dishwasher while Poppy and Mr. Jansen smoked their pipes on the deck. Finally, they had gotten down to the business of developing a strategy to salvage the boat.

"I called the Coast Guard this morning," Michael told the group. "They said that if I thought there was foul play that I should call the Monroe County Sheriff's Office, which I did."

Michael looked over at the teenagers. "They'd like for you all to go to their office sometime today and give them a statement."

Skye looked over at CJ, who nodded in assent. "Okay," she murmured.

CJ looked at Poppy and then at his dad. "How are we going to raise the boat?" he questioned.

"I've been thinking about that," Poppy answered. "Captain Anderson, an old friend of mine, is a retired lobsterman. I gave him a call early this morning. He has a work boat that we can use. In fact, he's willing to lend us a hand."

"Probably the best and cheapest way is to use fifty-five-gallon drums to raise the hull," Michael offered. "I've heard of other people using them. Supposedly, they work very well."

"Aren't they too heavy?" Skye wondered aloud.

"Not really," Poppy answered. "We can weld a shut-off valve in each end. If you want it to sink, just open both valves and let the water in. If you want it to float, just reverse the process and pump in some air. Actually, it's pretty simple."

"Okay," Michael said, "where are we going to get the divers? I hear salvage divers get big bucks."

CJ and Skye simultaneously left their chairs at the same time. "I'll do it!" Skye exclaimed. "Me too!" CJ added.

"Hey, hold on guys. I think this may be a little bit out of your league," Michael answered with conviction. *Those kids are game for anything. They're just not old enough to realize the dangers they could face.* Michael knew that look on their faces meant he would probably have to give in to them.

Poppy looked at the situation from a distinct perspective. He leaned back in his chair and reached into his shirt pocket to retrieve his pipe. "I don't know, Michael. These kids are expert swimmers, and besides, the water is only about twenty feet deep. It'll give them something to tell all their friends. Few teens ever get to experience something like this. We'll be right there, and you can even dive with 'em."

"Come on, Dad. Skye and I can handle it," CJ pleaded.

"If your mother finds out about this, she'll skin me alive!" Michael knew Maria would freak out.

"I promise Dad, we won't say a word," CJ smiled.

Skye was grinning. "When can we get started?"

"I know where we can get the drums," Poppy replied with a twinkle in his eyes.

Skye chirped in, "I have a friend who has a Brownies Third Lung. I'm sure she'll let us borrow it."

"And I have a friend in auto mechanics class that can weld," CJ said excitedly.

"Well," Poppy smiled, rubbing his hands together, "That settles it. We'll all meet here tomorrow morning around eight o'clock. Is that okay with y'all?"

Elizabeth Duncan staggered toward the phone carrying a half-spilled glass of champagne in her left hand. She had been celebrating since Friday evening. Finally, on the fourth ring, she reached for the phone and answered, "Yes?"

"Mrs. Duncan?"

"Yes," she slurred, "who is this?"

"Mrs. Duncan, this is Deputy Collins with the Dade County

Sheriff's Office. Your husband has been in a terrible accident, and I wanted to let you know that he's in the intensive care unit at Jackson Memorial Hospital."

Visibly upset, she said, "Thank you, officer," and she slammed down the phone.

"Crap!" she screamed. "Why isn't he dead? He's supposed to be dead. If he survives, he'll ruin all my plans." Taking a deep breath, she forced herself to calm down so she could think.

Chapter 14

The day before the dive to recover the injured man's boat hull, CJ and Skye had reported to the Monroe County Sheriff's Office Substation in Islamorada, Florida, as requested. They were both a little nervous about the visit. Skye had never had an encounter with the police, but that didn't ease her apprehension. CJ, on the other hand, had mixed feelings about it. On the one hand, he had no idea what to expect. Maybe they were going to grill them as if they were suspects in the explosion. On the other hand, he felt like a Crime Watch kid doing his part to help the community.

With CJ's Volkswagen Thing safely parked, he and Skye were about to enter the building. Skye shivered as they walked through the door. For some unknown reason, the air conditioning was freezing. *Maybe it's just me.* Goose bumps covered her tanned arms.

She took a fleeting survey of the room once she had recovered from the shock of the frigid air. The walls were painted yellowish beige. *Yuk!* Cheap plastic chairs lined one wall with a 16x20 inch photo of the current sheriff hanging in the center. The wall on the right had two doors. One said "Men" and the other said "Women."

Straight ahead was a four-foot-high counter stretching across the length of the room, except for a swinging door over on the right hand side. Skye assumed the door was for the officers to go in and out. An officer sat behind a desktop computer, typing something into the machine.

CJ took Skye's hand as they walked up to the desk. The policeman casually glanced over at them and continued his work. "What can I help you folks with?" he said, clearing his throat without looking up.

"We're here to give a statement," CJ answered nervously.

"What are the names?"

"Jansen and Somers."

"Have you been here before?" he asked.

"No, sir. We're here about the boat explosion yesterday."

"Oh, yeah, I heard about that. Quite a blast," he said, looking down at a notepad.

The officer pointed over toward the white plastic chairs. "Have a seat, and I'll have someone with you shortly."

Skye shivered as they waited for whatever was going to happen. *Maybe I'm just being silly, but I wish the butterflies in my stomach would go away. I hope they don't think we did anything wrong.*

Eight minutes later, a man dressed in a short-sleeved white shirt with a gray and blue striped tie, walked out from the back office toward them. "You Jansen and Somers?" he asked, looking down at the two teenagers. *They're a cute pair, but they look scared to death,* Callahan thought. He couldn't help but smile.

CJ and Skye both nodded and said, "Yes, sir."

The man waved his hand at them, motioning for them to follow him.

He waited until they reached the pass-thru on the right. Then he turned and casually said over his shoulder, "My name's Callahan. Detective Sergeant Callahan."

Of Irish descent, Sean Callahan was tall and well-built with thick black hair, light blue eyes, and very fair skin. His parents had immigrated from the West Coast of Ireland and were called Black Irish. Most people thought Irishmen were red-haired and freckle-faced, but in truth, less than ten percent of the population in Ireland was redheads.

The teens followed Callahan, negotiating around several desks, trash cans, and dilapidated chairs. The office wasn't large.

Callahan stopped at a door and motioned them in. He followed and closed the door to his office.

"Make yourselves comfortable," he directed, pointing to two straight back chairs positioned in front of his desk.

The detective walked behind his desk and took a seat. "So, I guess you're here to tell me about what happened with the boat, aren't you?" He could tell the two were extremely nervous.

"Yes, sir," CJ answered, his voice a little stronger and more relaxed than it had been when they walked into the sheriff's office.

Callahan relaxed in his chair, slumped back a little, and waited for them to tell their story.

Skye spoke first. CJ occasionally interjected or embellished on her version of the story. Callahan would interrupt at times, ask a question, and then make a note on a sheet of paper. He would then motion for Skye to continue.

Twenty-two minutes later, Callahan asked, "So, you two think there's foul play involved?"

"Yes, sir, we do," Skye said firmly. "That's why we're going to raise the boat."

"What do you mean you're going to raise the boat?" Callahan questioned as he rose from his chair.

"My dad thinks it's a good idea to take a look at her," CJ responded. "Maybe we can find some evidence or something."

Surprised, but trying not to show it, Sean Callahan couldn't help but smile at the hubris of the teens. "Young man, before you do that, you'll need a permit."

Chapter 15

Skye opened her sleepy eyes to the rumbling noise of a diesel engine. She glanced over at her bedside clock. "Oh, no!" she said, jumping from her bed. "It's seven-thirty! I'm so late!"

Her first stop before the bathroom was to check out the noise that sounded like it was coming from around the dock. Looking out of her bedroom window, she saw the ugliest boat she had ever seen. It looked about thirty feet long.

A twelve-foot piece of an old pipe protruded up from the deck and was attached to the wheelhouse. Black diesel exhaust belched from the makeshift muffler that was puffing like a steam engine.

She threw her hand to her mouth. "Oh, my goodness! That's our work boat?" she exclaimed aloud.

The boat's owner, Captain Anderson, was barely visible as Skye looked down at the ancient grime-covered window panes of the boat. The captain seemed to be having difficulty getting the transmission in reverse. The grinding of metal-to-metal pierced Skye's ears.

Skye crossed her fingers, hoping the captain wouldn't wreck Poppy's dock. She saw Poppy running down the dock at breakneck speed, hoping to intercept the oncoming blow. At the very last moment, Captain Anderson spun the wheel to the left, barely grazing a piling. The crusty old sailor walked out of the wheelhouse, grabbed a stern line, and tossed it to Poppy. The throw went wild, smacking

Poppy on the side of his face. "You old coot, can't you get anything right?" he grumbled. "I'll probably have a big bruise on my cheek. It's a wonder you didn't knock me out!" In spite of himself, Poppy couldn't help liking Mark Anderson. They had been friends for years.

Ignoring Poppy's comments as he always did, the captain responded, "Heck, yes, I can get something right! I'm here ain't I? Ain't it eight o'clock?" Sighing with resignation, he said, "I should sell this old piece of crap. Problem is nobody wants her. I guess I'm stuck with her."

"You sure this dilapidated old tub won't sink on us?" Poppy asked, with doubt in his voice. He had not seen the boat in more than five years. *It sure looks a lot different now. I hope it holds together,* he thought with uncertainty.

"Well, I reckon she'll do okay. She's been fine up until now," the captain said as he tied off the bow line.

Poppy looked up and saw CJ and Michael rounding the marker that led into his channel and up to his dock. The two of them burst out laughing as CJ expertly maneuvered the *Gator Bait* to the dock. Poppy figured they were probably laughing at the old piece of junk tied to his dock. *To be honest, I can't say I blame them.* He didn't want Cap to see him smile, but he couldn't help it. He felt exactly the same way about the beat-up old boat.

Not mentioning the condition of the boat, CJ shouted, "Hey Poppy, where's Skye?"

"She'll be down directly. She slept in this morning. I reckon she was exhausted from everything that happened yesterday. I heard her moving around upstairs right before I came down here to the boat."

Michael jumped from the boat onto the dock and then secured her bowline.

Nodding toward the wrinkled old sailor, Poppy made the introductions. "This here is Captain Anderson," he said as he introduced Michael and CJ to the old man.

"Just call me Cap," Anderson said as he offered his hand to Michael. Looking at CJ, he smiled. "Nice little boat you got there, son."

CJ's eyes lit up, and he grinned. "Thanks, Cap," he answered. "So, that's our salvage boat?" CJ said, pointing to the old lobster boat. "What's her name?"

"*Money in the Bank*," Cap chuckled. "Course, she ain't made a dime since I retired, and that was more than five years ago, I reckon."

Everyone turned toward the house when they heard the back-door slam. Skye walked briskly toward them with her usual girlish smile. She was carrying a large cooler stuffed with lunch. She wore a new pair of Sperry Topsiders, white shorts that showed off her tanned legs, and a light blue tank top that matched her eyes.

Even with the cloud cover, she knew the day would be sweltering, and she was prepared. Her swishing blonde ponytail was held high on the back of her head by a blue scrunchie. A touch of pink gloss covered her lips. The guys just stood there in awe. CJ wondered again if Skye ever thought about him the way he thought about her. Dismissing the thought, he grinned as Skye walked toward them.

"Good morning, everyone," she said as she reached the four men standing near the old boat.

Poppy introduced Skye to the captain. "Nice to meet you miss," Cap said, with a gleam in his eyes. "They tell me you two are gonna do the diving," he added, nodding at CJ.

"Yep, that's right," Skye answered excitedly. She couldn't wait to get started.

Poppy pulled a handwritten list from his pocket and handed a copy to everyone gathered around. "Cap, you take your boat up to Tavernier Creek Marina and pick up the drums. They should have the valves installed by now. Michael, you go with Cap, and I'll go with CJ and Skye over to Skye's friend's house and pick up the compressor. Then we'll go down to the hardware store and get the rest of the materials we'll need for the job."

"CJ, have you got the dive gear onboard?" Skye asked.

"Yep, all set. I've got four scuba tanks filled and ready to go.

You'd better get your dive gear and wetsuit. The water is a little chilly today."

With more than a little effort, Cap stepped down into his boat. *Can't move like I used to. Guess I'm getting old,* he thought, hearing his bones creak with wear.

Michael tended the boat's lines while Cap got the old Caterpillar started. It reluctantly coughed several times. Ten minutes later, both boats moved out of the channel. *Gator Bait* turned south, and *Money in The Bank* turned north.

Chapter 16

The *Gator Bait* was the first boat to reach the dive site. CJ had been on the CB radio with Captain Anderson and had requested their status. He had just begun to realize exactly how grumpy the old sailor could be. He thought the wrinkled old guy's gruff voice and foul language were inappropriate for a young girl like Skye to hear.

Though he had never used it, he had heard that kind of language plenty of times from the guys at school. CJ knew he couldn't change the old man's way of speaking, and he guessed that somehow Skye would have to contend with the obnoxious old lobsterman. In spite of Cap's trashy mouth, CJ hoped that maybe the old sailor would try to be more careful about what he said around Skye.

Cap and Michael were on their way with six fifty-five-gallon drums tied down on the stern of *Money in the Bank*. Their estimated time of arrival was about fifty minutes, more or less.

CJ, Skye, and Poppy found the submerged houseboat without difficulty. The water was clear, and a calm breeze left a glassy surface. Within minutes after their arrival, they had spotted it.

CJ backed the *Gator Bait* about twenty feet away from the dive site and then dropped a dive flag over the side. *This should be an easy dive. We're only in about twenty feet of water.* The day was clear and sunny, and CJ could see the bottom.

Skye expertly dropped the anchor overboard. Poppy fiddled with the Brownies Third Lung. He had read the instruction manual and began familiarizing himself with the compressor. The entire unit was designed to float on a large, heavy-duty rubberized inner tube. He was thinking about how far along technology had advanced since he was a kid. The unit could supply enough air for two people down to a depth of eighty feet. Instead of using scuba tanks for the dive, the compressor would have been perfect for the kids to use; however, this time the Lung would have to be used to fill the drums.

CJ and Skye began suiting up in their wetsuits. She chatted almost nonstop. She was nervous. Not afraid, just excited, and very anxious to visit the wreck. She sprinkled talcum powder down each leg of the pants, making it easier for her to wiggle into the rubber suit.

CJ did the same with his dive jacket. As he was zipping it up, *Money in the Bank* came into view. Its aging engine left a trail of black smoke over its wake.

Eventually, the *Money* moved up to the starboard side of *Gator Bait.* Michael threw Poppy a mooring line to mate the two boats together.

Cap shut the engine down and stepped out from the wheelhouse

"We'll use *Money* as the work platform," he recommended to the others.

"Okay by me," Poppy replied. "Hey, CJ, give me a hand with this compressor so we can get it into the other boat."

"I'll give him a hand, CJ. You finish suiting up," Michael offered.

"This sucker is heavy," Poppy grunted as he and Michael lifted the compressor to the gunwales of the boats. Cap grabbed hold of one side of the rubber float and held it balanced while Michael jumped into the *Money* to give Cap a hand.

"Instead of using it in the water, why not just leave it in the boat?" Michael suggested.

"Sounds good to me," Cap said, coughing up a wad of phlegm. "We'll feed them the lines from the stern."

"Hey, Dad," CJ called out. "Skye and I are ready to go."

"Hold on a minute, son. Let me get my mask and snorkel. I want to join you guys in the water."

Skye looked over at CJ, her eyes reflecting her impatience. Outside of the water, scuba tanks are heavy, particularly on the back of a petite girl like Skye. She moved over to the edge of the boat, turned, and rested the tank on the gunwale. CJ watched her take a deep breath and then relax.

Michael had his mask and snorkel strapped on his forehead and held his swim fins lightly between his fingers. "Okay, guys, let's go." He stepped up to the transom, and with one foot he stepped off into the water.

Skye followed him. Her heavy swim fins made walking awkward, but she managed to put one flipper up on the transom and pushed off into the depths. CJ was right behind her.

Initially, Skye was engulfed in bubbles. Within a moment, they were gone and were replaced with one of the most beautiful underwater scenes she had ever witnessed. Actually, almost every time she entered the water, she had the same feeling, but Skye preferred diving in the ocean.

Florida Bay had different underwater flora than the Atlantic side. The topography was flat with mostly sea weed and pockets of sand, unlike the ocean, which had coral reefs. The Bay lacked the vitality that was usually attributed to living coral and other forms of vegetation.

The forty-pound tank became weightless in the water as Skye floated effortlessly beneath the surface. With a stroke of her hand, she turned to get oriented.

CJ was positioned to her right about six feet away. He looked at her, checked her equipment, and then gave her a thumbs up. She saw Michael floating on the surface, looking down at her. He, too, gave her a thumbs up.

CJ estimated the visibility to be about twenty feet. *Perfect*, he thought as he bent forward, and with a flick of his fins moved to the bottom. He cleared his ears.

Skye mimicked his move and remained by his side. CJ turned

slightly to his left and saw what was left of the hull resting on the bottom. He heard Skye let out a loud squeal, letting him know that she had also seen the boat.

CJ's perception of the size of the boat was not apparent until they drew closer to the hull. He wondered about what had really happened on that fateful day. *Had there been other people on-board? If so, where were they? What had caused the boat to explode?* The thought of finding a body or bodies in the hull gave him the creeps. He wondered if Skye had given it any thought. Knowing her, he was fairly sure she had.

CJ glanced over to his right and saw Michael take hold of the transom. He paused for several moments to survey the wreckage. Twenty seconds later, he headed to the surface.

Skye had drifted about twenty feet away from CJ. She had just crossed the gunwale and was moving into the hull. CJ crossed the threshold at the same time. What he saw amazed him. Wreckage lay everywhere on the sand bottom.

Suddenly, he heard Skye scream into her face mask, motioning with her right arm, trying to get his attention. He moved quickly toward her. As he reached her side, she pointed down with horror-filled eyes.

CJ didn't see it at first. He moved in a little closer, and then he saw what Skye was pointing to under the hull of the boat. It was a person's burned, hairless arm sticking out from underneath the rubble. *Oh, my God*, he thought. Nausea churned in his stomach.

Chapter 17

Elizabeth Duncan woke up with a hangover. She struggled to get out of bed, but before the alcoholic fog cleared from her mind, she had to run for the bathroom. She barely made it to the toilet. As she lifted the seat, vomit spewed from her mouth. *Never again*, she promised herself. This time she really meant it. Of course, she always meant it until the next time and the next drink.

Drinking heavily since she was a teenager, she sometimes wondered why she kept abusing her body. With her ex-husband, it had been drugs and alcohol. *At least I'm not doing drugs anymore.* The thought made her feel a little better about herself. She knew she needed alcohol rehab, but she would wait until she got all of John's money.

Her visit to Jackson Memorial Hospital the evening before had been very upsetting, not to mention stressful. Her husband had been transferred to the hospital burn unit, where he lay in a coma, hooked up to a life support system. He was unrecognizable. Bandages covered his face and head, and a white linen tent covered his body.

An endotracheal tube had been placed in his nose to permit oxygen flow into his trachea and down into his lungs. The whole scene was disgusting to her. *Why couldn't he just die? After all my plans, he's still here. How in the world is he still alive? He's probably just hanging on to spite me.* Elizabeth Duncan was a cold, calculating woman. Always had been, always would be. After cleaning herself up, Elizabeth staggered back to the bed, sat down on the edge, and for the umpteenth time pressed the redial on her telephone. *Where in the heck is he?*

Skye reached the surface first. She spun around to get her bearings and realized she had surfaced next to Michael. CJ's head popped out of the water on the other side of Michael.

Fear covered Skye's face. She had never seen a dead person before. The injured man in the boat explosion was near death, but not dead and in pieces like the person under the hull. Hysterically, Skye shouted, "There's a body down there, Mr. Jansen!"

CJ said excitedly, "Dad, we need to get help!"

Michael could see that Skye's fear was almost out of control. He reached over and gently touched her arm. "It's okay, hon. There's nothing we can do for him. It's okay," he said soothingly.

The three swam to the boat. Michael boarded first. He took off his flippers and reached over the gunwale toward Skye. Motioning toward her, he said, "Give me your tank."

Michael hauled the tank aboard and reached for CJ's. A minute later, all three were onboard the *Gator Bait*.

Standing on the *Money* and seeing Skye's white face, Poppy asked with alarm in his voice, "What's going on?"

Michael's answer stunned Skye's grandfather. "We've got another victim below. Better call the Coast Guard."

Poppy turned and went into the wheelhouse to get on the radio, wondering what else they might find at the bottom. A moment of regret crossed his mind that CJ and Skye had witnessed such horrible things in the past couple of days.

Sean Callahan took the call from the Coast Guard. The caller reported that there was a body trapped inside the hull of a boat that had burned and sunk a couple days earlier. It was located near Gopher Key. Several boats were on the scene and standing by, waiting for instructions.

Callahan, the commander of the Monroe County Sheriff's Dive Team, rose from his chair. Aside from his position as Detective Sergeant supervising the Monroe County detectives, he and fourteen other detectives volunteered their time to serve on the dive team. He had been their leader for the past two and a half years. Their primary mission was to search and rescue, as well as to assist the US Coast Guard, Florida Marine Patrol, and Key West Police Department. Those who were on this team were a special breed of men willing to spend time away from friends and family in the performance of this service.

Callahan drove down to the Islamorada Coast Guard Station where he kept the county's boat. He met two other deputies at the end of the dock. "Ready to go, fellows?" he asked as he stepped down into the Angler 230B.

"Yes, sir," they answered in unison. "We've notified the Marine Patrol, and they'll meet us there."

Skye needed something to do to keep her mind off what lay below, so she busied herself serving lunch to everyone.

"Darn good sandwich. My compliments to the chef," Michael said to Skye, trying to take her mind off of what she had seen. She and CJ were both so young to have seen such tragedy; not only one, but two men, one of them critically injured and the other one dead.

Cap reached into his own cooler and pulled out a cold beer. "How's this going to affect our salvage work?" he asked.

"I'm not sure," Michael volunteered. "Our discovery sure puts things in a new perspective, doesn't it?"

"I don't know if I can go back down there," Skye murmured, staring down at the deck. It was clear to everyone that she had been very frightened. She looked wan and pale.

"Yeah, it scared the dickens out of me too," CJ said, trying not to make Skye feel so bad.

Instinctively looking out to the horizon, Skye saw a pelican swoop down to within inches above the water heading their way. She automatically stood and watched the bird. *It can't be, can it?* Skye wondered. "Flapper, that's you, isn't it?" A smile broke across her pale face when she heard him respond, a response that only she could hear.

"Yep, it's me," Flapper responded as he swooped in, circling low around the boat, looking for a place to perch. Finally, he landed on the roof of *Money's* wheelhouse.

"What the heck?" Cap reacted. For a moment, he thought the bird was going to attack.

"Flapper, what on earth are you doing here? I thought you were still at the bird sanctuary. How did you find us?"

The pelican waddled to the edge of the roof, waited a second as he looked around to see who was with Skye, and then settled down.

"They let me out this morning. Boy, it's sure good to have some fresh fish."

"How is your wing? Is it okay?" Skye questioned.

Poppy, Cap and Michael looked at the bird, then at Skye, and then back at the bird, not believing what they were witnessing.

CJ understood what was going on and moved over to stand beside Skye. He knew she would need the support from the looks on the others' faces. *Get ready for the questions, Skye,* he thought.

Flapper looked down on the group. "You sure are a hard person to find," he said. "I've been worried about you."

Sky looked into the bird's eyes. "Worried? Why*?*"

Flapper moved his beak back and forth as if he were thinking about what to say. "The word is out about your dolphin friend. Seems he and some buddies of his were over by Indian Key a few nights back, and they saw lots of boats going back and forth to a marina. Everything seems to be hush-hush. I just wanted to let you know. I don't think it's safe for you to go over there," Flapper warned. 'Those are bad people, and they are up to no good."

Cap couldn't stand it anymore. "Skye, what in the heck is going on?"

"Oh, I'm so sorry. Excuse me, please. Everyone, this is my friend, Flapper," Skye said. "Flapper, you already know CJ." Then, motioning toward the old sailor, she introduced him to the pelican. "This is the boat captain. Everyone calls him Cap." Pointing to her grandfather, she proudly made the introduction. "This is my Poppy. I stay with him every summer. Remember, I told you that when CJ and I rescued you that day?" Nodding toward Michael, she said, "This is Mr. Jansen, CJ's dad."

Flapper shook his head up and down in acknowledgment of the group.

Skye looked over to the three men, and in an apology she said, "Sorry to be so rude. Flapper's been telling me some stuff about Indian Key."

Cap still didn't understand. "How do you know what he's saying?"

"I'm not really sure, Cap. Let's just call it telepathy."

Cap just stood there shaking his head, totally confused. He knew what he just saw, but he sure couldn't believe it.

Michael just stood there with his mouth open, and Poppy stood there with a smile on his face. He had known all along that Skye was telling him the truth.

Chapter 18

After the introductions, Flapper said goodbye to Skye and warned her once again that it was not safe for her to go to Indian Key. Lifting his wings, he caught a momentary light breeze into the air.

Without the distraction of the bird, a somber feeling hovered over the boat as if shrouded in a foggy mist of darkness, even though the sun was bright and blazing hot. The group hunkered down on the deck of the *Money* waiting for the Marine Patrol that Poppy had called.

Everyone leaned against the bulkhead on the lee side of the wheelhouse, hiding in the shade to avoid the sweltering afternoon sun. The ninety-three-degree temperature and the humidity, along with no breeze, made the heat insufferable.

Cap tried unsuccessfully to nap, while the rest of the group gazed out across the glassy water, waiting for help to arrive.

Michael broke the silence. "Hey, Skye, what did that pelican mean about it's not safe to go to Indian Key?"

Skye leaned forward to make eye contact with Michael, who was sitting on the other side of CJ. "I'm not sure, Mr. Jansen. This is the second time he's warned me about going there. I guess it's because he knows CJ and I dive and fish in these waters, and we'll eventually end up over there. Why do you ask?"

"The only thing I know about the island is that there used to be a settlement there a long time ago, and some people were killed by the Indians. I think the pelican is right. You guys had better stay away from there."

Myriad thoughts about Indian Key were going through Skye's mind, but one thing she knew for certain was that she was going to find out what was going on over on the island.

Far into the distance, they heard the high-pitched sound of an outboard motor. It grew louder as a boat came barreling around the north end of Gopher Key, blue flashing lights rotating across the flybridge, giving away its identity.

CJ poked Cap in the side, startling him back to consciousness. Skye was the first to stand, and the remainder of the group followed.

Minutes later, they saw that it was a Florida Marine Patrol officer driving a twenty-three-foot Mako powered by a three-hundred-horse Evinrude engine.

It must be going at least fifty miles an hour, CJ thought as he watched the boat's antenna bending back in the wind.

The Mako sped directly toward them. It seemed as though its driver was oblivious to their presence. At the last moment, the officer pulled back on his throttle, and the boat skimmed to a stop after he had jammed the engine into reverse. The boat bobbed like a cork three feet away from the *Money*.

The young officer moved around the boat with the ease of a cat. He walked forward, bent down, and then picked up the boat's bowline, handing it over to CJ. He then moved to the stern, repeated the process, and gave Michael a line. The officer finally turned his attention to the *Money*.

"Captain Anderson, what brings you out here today?" he asked, glancing around at the others in the boat.

"Well, Officer Rogers, I thought I'd give these youngsters here a hand pulling up that wreck over there," Cap responded. "What are you doing 'round here?"

"Just keeping everybody straight, that's all. I understand you people found a body?" Rogers frowned as if doubting there was a body.

Corporal Daniel Rogers stood tall. In fact, he stood six feet three inches tall. He was slender but well built, with erect posture and piercing dark eyes. One could see almost immediately that he wasn't a particularly affable person. It was obvious that he was all business and no pleasure. His short military-style haircut, covered with a blue baseball cap with the letters FMP embroidered in front, reflected his serious attitude. The 9mm Glock 34 strapped to his right thigh solidified his authority.

"Whose McKee Craft is this?" he asked gruffly, looking at Michael.

Michael stared into Rogers' eyes defiantly as he nodded toward CJ. "It's my son's," he replied, wondering what was on the officer's mind.

Rogers turned to face CJ. "Let me see your registration young man," he commanded.

CJ stepped onboard the *Gator Bait* and began digging thru the glove box. His hands started to shake a little. He had never been intimidated like this before, particularly not from a law enforcement officer. *What did we do?* he wondered.

"Where's the body?" Rogers asked, looking up at Captain Anderson. Daniel Rogers didn't really believe there was a body. He thought it was some sort of prank orchestrated by the teens. He had heard that a badly-burned man had been taken to the hospital, but no others were on board the houseboat when it exploded.

Skye moved from the *Money* down into the *Gator Bait* to join CJ. She sensed his frustration with Officer Rogers. To her disappointment, she realized that not all law enforcement officers were the same. She might only be fifteen, but she could immediately see that this young lawman had some serious difficulties with his people skills.

Cap looked down from the wheelhouse and answered Rogers' question. He pointed over into the distance. "Over there, about twenty feet deep."

Rogers automatically looked around, seeing nothing in the water.

There was no boat and no body. His suspicious mind was sure now it was a trick. Looking at Cap, he asked, "Who told you there was a body down there? Those kids?"

Cap chuckled to himself. He knew Rogers. He had always reminded Cap of a little boy trying to play grownup. "Yes, the teens told me, but the young man's father was down there too."

CJ finally found his boat registration, moved over to the side of the boat, and handed it to Rogers. Rogers studied the document for a moment. "Son, this registration has expired," he said a little harshly, looking over at CJ. *Typical punk*, he thought, *always breaking the law*. Rogers had forgotten all the laws he had broken as a teenager. The minor infraction gave Officer Rogers exactly what he wanted; a reason to search CJ's boat.

"You got any lobsters onboard?"

"No, sir."

Rogers waved his arm at CJ, motioning for him to move to the other boat. "You folks wait over there," he ordered, letting everyone who doubted it know that he was in charge. His attitude reminded Michael of Jackie Gleason in the movie *Smokey and the Bandit*. At Rogers' instructions, CJ and Skye reluctantly climbed onboard the *Money*.

Officer Rogers left his boat and climbed aboard the *Gator Bait*. He immediately walked to the cooler and opened the lid. All he found was ice and several containers of Gatorade. He slammed the lid shut and moved on to inspect the rest of the boat. He took his time going through all the compartments hoping to find some illegal contraband, perhaps a spear gun or some marijuana, anything to enhance the ticket he was going to enjoy writing this young punk. *I'll show him about breaking the law,* he thought.

Stunned, everyone onboard the *Money* remained quiet.

CJ looked over at Skye, then to his dad who slowly shook his head, warning him to keep quiet. He felt violated by this arrogant officer as he rummaged through his belongings. He knew his registration had just expired. He and Skye had been so involved with the explosion, the injured man, and the statement to the police

88

detective, that he hadn't had time to have it renewed. It expired the day after the explosion. *What kind of priorities does this guy have, invading my privacy while there is a dead man at the bottom of the bay? He's piddling around on my boat, and there's a corpse in the water that needs to be retrieved so he can be identified and his family can be notified. What kind of officer is he anyway?* The more CJ thought about it, the madder he got.

"I'm going to write you a ticket," Rogers said as he jumped from the *Gator Bait* to his boat.

"A ticket?" Michael asked, trying to hold back his anger. "Why in the world would you write him a ticket?"

"Yep, a ticket," he said, snapping at Michael, "for an expired registration." Roger reached for his ticket pad.

"Can't you cut the kid some slack?" asked Cap. "These kids have been through enough these past couple of days."

"Sorry, but no can do." Rogers smiled, but his steely eyes reflected satisfaction at the task. He thought his personality made him look tough, but in fact it made him look like a bully.

What a jerk! Cap could not believe Rogers could be so unreasonable.

Off in the distance, Michael saw more blinking blue lights. He noticed they were becoming brighter as the boat approached. *Good, it's the sheriff's office. Maybe they'll run this guy off,* he thought.

"Oh, Mr. Jansen, you'll need a state permit if you plan to mess with that boat," Rogers said smugly. "This is a state-controlled park. You can't remove anything without a permit."

We'll have to see about that, won't we? Michael looked at the officer and shook his head. Thinking the same thought about the officer as Cap had, he decided the guy was indeed a real jerk.

Chapter 19

A frustrated Elizabeth Duncan was saying, "I just want to know what my options are."

She sat in her attorney's office, located on the corner of Southwest 8th Street and 27th Avenue, in the heart of Little Havana in Miami.

Rafael Diaz sat behind his desk listening to the rants and ravings of his client. She had been sitting in front of him for over an hour, and his patience was beginning to wear thin. What he really needed was a shot of Cuban coffee and a cigarette. Then he thought about the hourly rate he was charging her and began to relax.

Elizabeth was asking, "What happens if he stays in a coma for the next five years? What the hell am I going to do?"

Rafael couldn't feel sorry for Elizabeth. He knew she was a kept woman. *Now she's crying like a spoiled brat, not seeming to care that her husband could die at any moment.*

"Well, Elizabeth, we'll just have to wait and see if his condition improves. In the meantime, I'll make sure ten thousand dollars is deposited into your account on the first of each month."

Elizabeth frowned. *Ten thousand dollars! I don't want a measly ten thousand dollars; I want five hundred million dollars. If John was already dead, I would be sitting in this shyster attorney's office, smiling as I listened to the will being read, making me a rich woman.* Elizabeth Duncan had no idea that her husband had changed his will two months ago, leaving his entire fortune to his widowed sister and her three children.

As Detective Callahan pulled up to the scene, he saw three boats tethered together. He recognized Corporal Rogers, who was writing out a ticket.

He slowed and brought the Angler around to the port side of the *Money* where Cap was waiting to tie them off. Greeting the old man Callahan asked, "How 'ya doing Cap?" He had known him for years.

"Can't complain, Detective. You doing okay?"

"Wife's getting ready to have a baby," Callahan smiled proudly. Turning to one of the men in the boat, he said, "John, you'd better suit up. I'll find out what's going on." He climbed aboard the *Money.*

Callahan made his way across the lobster boat and stopped at the railing to look down at the other two boats. Rogers was writing the kid a ticket. *What is that about?* He knew Rogers could be a real butt-head sometimes.

Callahan looked over at Michael. "I'm Detective Sergeant Sean Callahan," he said, offering his hand to Michael. "I think we spoke on the phone."

Michael shook his hand firmly. *Friendly enough,* he thought. "Detective, you remember my son CJ, and Skye, a friend of ours," Michael nodded toward Skye.

"Yes, we've met."

Callahan shouted over to Rogers, "Seems like you got the word fast enough! How long have you been here?"

"About half an hour," Rogers answered. "Are you here to recover the body?" He was surprised that there really was a body, but he knew there must be if Callahan and his dive crew were here.

Callahan shook his head. "Not me. My crew will bring it up." "Which one of you found the body?" Callahan asked casually.

Skye timidly raised her hand. Directing his attention to Skye, as well as CJ, he said, "Well, one of you has to show me where the boat is, and then one of my guys will do the dive. Is there anything you two want to add or say?" Callahan asked.

"No, sir," CJ answered, looking questioningly over at Skye.

"By the way," Michael said as he looked over at Callahan. "Do you have any word on the guy the Coast Guard helo took to the hospital?"

"As a matter of fact, I do. His name is John Duncan. He's some kind of oil guy up in Miami. They say he has big bucks."

Skye interjected, "Is he going to make it?"

"Don't know yet. He's in the hospital in a coma, and it doesn't look very good."

Callahan turned and walked toward his boat. "Let's get this show on the road," he said over his shoulder.

CJ and Skye looked at each other. Each silently asked the other which of them was going with Callahan. Finally, CJ reluctantly shrugged his shoulders and moved toward the lobster boat.

His trepidation was obvious to Michael. *I guess he might have to face things like this eventually*, he thought, *but I sure wish he didn't have to face them now.*

CJ stood in the bow of the Angler while Callahan steered the boat in the direction CJ had pointed. As Callahan steered, CJ strained his eyes, trying to spot the boat. The water was clear but very still. It was like looking for a tiny pill on a vast dark carpet. "There it is!" CJ shouted, waving his hand.

Callahan drove the boat forward very slowly and looked down into the water. *Yep, there it is.* He dropped the gearshift into neutral and coasted to a stop. The Angler had floated just past the wreck when Callahan said, "Go ahead and drop the anchor."

Callahan's two dive team friends had suited up and were ready to go into the water. They stood still, waiting for Callahan's go ahead.

CJ leaned against the railing, nervous about what was going to happen. He didn't want to see the corpse. It gave him such a creepy feeling. Still, he had no other choice but to stay put and wait for the outcome. He looked over at the *Money* and saw Skye leaning against the bulkhead, hugging herself with both arms. He heard two splashes, looked toward the noise, and watched the divers disappear below the surface.

———————

Squeaky, the dolphin who had helped save the burned man, had patrolled around Indian Key all during the night. He had seen several boats pull up to the beach. They would load boxes onboard and then make their way inland. He wasn't sure where they went, but maybe tonight he would have one of his friends follow them. He knew they were not nice people and were up to no good. Besides that, they talked funny.

Chapter 20

CJ paced around the boat, waiting to see what was happening below. Frequently, he looked over the side and watched the divers' bubbles gurgle to the surface. *There's no current*, he decided. He was glad of that. It made it a little easier to see. It was still difficult to see the divers clearly as they moved around, twenty feet down. *How much time has passed since they entered the water?* he wondered.

Thoughts of the gory scene below upset him. He could feel the nausea rising in his throat at the idea of the burned body being removed and brought to the surface. *Who was the other person on the sunken boat? Was he a friend of the critically burned boater that was in the hospital?*

The divers eventually found the remains of the dead man. Wood from the main deck covered the corpse, except for the left arm. Debris littered the hull. It took them nineteen painstaking minutes to free the body.

After being in the water for two days, the corpse was fully bloated. Gases formed from decomposition had caused it to double in size as if it were an inner tube fastened to an air hose. Even though the divers had seen the same thing many times before, they never got used to it. That was a part of the job that none of them liked.

How do you handle a bloated corpse in deep water? That was the first question a new diver trainee always asked. It was only about twenty feet deep, but the dead man was underneath the beams and wreckage, so it would take some maneuvering to extract him.

After moving the debris around, the divers freed the corpse. To prevent the body from floating to the surface unattended, the lead diver prepared to attach a weight belt around his torso.

The second diver was holding the dead man on the bottom by one leg and one arm. As he adjusted his hold, the diver's flipper became entangled under a cross beam, distracting him from his task. Reflexively, he let go of the man's remains to free his foot. As he let go, the body quickly began to rise, and before the diver could react, it was free. Within seconds, it was out of reach, rising faster and faster.

Detective Sergeant Callahan and CJ saw the body rising. Small trickles of bubbles escaped its mouth as it rose. As it hit the surface, it exploded. Guts, fecal matter, and stomach contents sprayed the area as if a bomb had gone off. CJ's legs became peppered with the gruesome material. The horrible stench slapped Callahan and CJ in the face, knocking them backwards as if the gloved hand of a boxer had hit them at eighty miles an hour. CJ vomited. Callahan held his hand over his mouth and leaned over the side of the boat, but to no avail. His breakfast spewed down the side of the craft and into the water of Florida Bay.

In shock, CJ stared down at his legs. Realizing he was covered with the gruesome contents of the man's insides; he turned and ran for the other side of the boat. In a split second, he was in the water.

Free of its bloat and contents, the corpse slowly began to sink to the bottom.

Skye stood watching CJ swim toward the *Gator Bait*. *What's he doing?* she wondered. Then she grabbed her mouth.

Pale and still standing in the Angler, Corporal Rogers bent forward and leaned over the side. His stomach released its contents into the water.

Michael said something to the effect of, "Oh, my God!" His stomach churned like an angry sea, but he didn't throw up. Cap ran for the stern of the *Money*. No one saw him again for several minutes.

Within a brief time, a small breeze had swept the stench into the mangroves. For some unknown reason, the local fowl had cleared the area. Michael wondered if they could also smell the rank odor.

With his stomach empty, Callahan was recovering from the dry heaves as the lead diver broke the surface.

"Hey boss, I need a body bag," he said, matter-of-factly. "The body's in bad shape," he said as if those on topside had no idea.

Callahan staggered to a locker near the transom and dug out a black body bag. He stumbled over to the side and handed it down to his deputy. His stomach was still queasy.

CJ was finally able to climb aboard the *Gator Bait*. He lay there for several moments trying to catch his breath and willing his stomach to stop rolling.

Corporal Rogers ripped his tether lines from the *Gator Bait*. With his stomach still churning, he started his engine and slowly backed away. In a couple seconds, his boat was at full throttle heading for parts unknown. He wouldn't easily forget what he had just seen. The ticket in his hand got caught up in the wind and was forgotten.

CJ made his way over to the *Money*. Michael reached down to give him a hand as he climbed aboard the boat. "What a rank odor," he groaned.

Skye went immediately to CJ's side. She was silent, glad to be with him. She knew he needed her close after what he had just been though.

The four of them remained alongside the railing, waiting for the divers to bring the deceased man up to the boat. Soon, they popped up from the water with the body bag in tow. Callahan reached down, took hold of one corner, and waited for his two deputies to climb aboard and give him a hand.

They took their time peeling off their tanks and swim fins and eventually climbing into the boat. They rested for a moment and then made their way back to the stern where Callahan impatiently waited.

The four in the other boats heard the count of three and watched as Callahan and the diver's drug the limp bag onboard. One of Callahan's team went forward to tend the anchor line, and moments later Callahan started the engines. He eased the boat forward, made a sharp right turn and headed for the *Money*.

Alongside the *Money*, Callahan yelled over to Michael. "Mr. Jansen, give me a call tomorrow."

He eased the Avenger out, and with full throttles forward, he headed for the Islamorada Coast Guard Station.

Chapter 21

Sean Callahan parked his boat at the Islamorada Coast Guard Station at 6:43 p.m. He looked to the east and saw dark angry looking clouds hiding the sun. Sweat on his brow and the ninety-five percent humidity announced the oncoming thunderstorm. It was a daily occurrence during the summer months. The storms wreaked havoc with the local boaters.

Callahan's crew had just finished tidying up the boat when the Monroe County EMS truck pulled in next to the boat dock.

No flashing lights this time and no need to rush with this one, Callahan thought, shuddering as he remembered his experience earlier in the afternoon. It was something he never wanted to go through again, nor ever see again for that matter. Transporting the deceased would be an easy trip into the Dade County Medical Examiner's office. He made a mental note to call their office tomorrow for the autopsy report. He had given it a lot of thought on his way back in from the scene of the explosion. *For such a large fire, this guy has relatively few burns on his body, except for his right arm.* Callahan knew that was very strange. *It will be interesting to find out the cause of death. Maybe the kids are right. Maybe it was a larger explosion than a twenty-pound propane tank would make. If it was foul play, the ME's office in Miami will certainly figure it out.* It was his opinion that they were the best in the world.

Both somber, the EMS driver and his attendant slid from the

truck, walked around to the back, opened both doors, and retrieved the stretcher. It was folded flat. As they took it out of the truck, the front wheels dropped down into position and locked. The back wheels mimicked the front. The two men effortlessly wheeled the gurney to the edge of the boat. The divers lifted the body bag up onto the gurney. Finally, the attendants rolled the gurney back to the truck for transport to the Miami Medical Examiner's office.

———————

Michael Jansen made the call from a service phone next to the Tiki Bar in Islamorada. As he dropped the coins into the slot, he was reminded of a few years ago when he and Sonny Mitchell were with the National Security Agency and raising hell with the Cubans.

He listened as the phone rang on the other end. He needed help, and if anyone could help him, it was Sonny. Sonny had more clout and more contacts than anyone Michael had ever known. Of course, his years with the NSA had afforded him the opportunity of meeting people from all walks of life, some less than reputable.

"Mitchell," Sonny answered. Nearing sixty-one, he had decided it was time to retire, relax, and enjoy life on a sandy beach somewhere. Michael had made the move not too long after CJ was born.

"Hey Chubby, it's me," Michael said, calling his friend by his nickname. Sonny's friends had always called him Chubby.

Sonny relaxed after hearing Michael's voice. He was glad to hear from him. "What's up, my man?"

"I guess you heard about the boat explosion down here?"

"Yeah, what happened? It was on the news."

"Well, CJ and his friend Skye were out on the boat, and they witnessed the entire thing. It looks to me like it was deliberate. The owner is at Jackson Memorial in critical condition, and today we recovered another body from the same explosion."

"So, what can I help you with, Michael?" Sonny asked.

"I was wondering if you could set up a meeting with the Medical Examiner's office in Miami and go there with me. I'm curious about what killed the guy and who he was."

"For you, my friend, I'll see what I can do. Let me make some calls, and I'll get back with you. Okay?"

"Thanks, buddy. I appreciate it."

Michael hung up the phone and stood there gathering his thoughts.

"What am I getting myself into?" he mumbled to himself. Maria would have a fit if she knew he was becoming involved in what could be a murder investigation.

Skye sat at a picnic table next to Burger King in Upper Matecumbe Key. It was late in the evening, but she wasn't concerned about the time as she waited for CJ to arrive. The thunderstorm had quickly passed, and the evening air relaxed her, particularly after having one hellish day out on the water. The events earlier had disturbed her. She was having difficulty sorting out the sights and smells she had witnessed from the boat. CJ was perceptive and analytical, and he would help her understand and rationalize her fears. She trusted him implicitly.

When she had arrived at Poppy's house earlier, she had headed straight for the shower. She felt dirty and needed to wash away the salt and foul odors that permeated her skin. Scrubbing until her skin was almost raw, she still felt unclean as thoughts of what she had seen rushed through her mind.

Thirty-five minutes later, Poppy served dinner, which consisted of a delicious plate of paella, along with a loaf of hot, crusty Cuban bread. Full and totally exhausted, by eight o'clock Skye was in bed.

She tossed and turned, but sleep evaded her. Images of the day flashed across her mind in a kaleidoscope of colors. The longer she lay there, the more stressed she became. Eventually, she tossed off her covers, reached for the phone and called CJ, who had agreed to meet her. Next, she called a taxi.

Squeaky made his way under the bridge at Channel Five just south of Lower Matecumbe Key. His pod had settled down for the night at Old Dan Bank north of Long Key. Taking advantage of the opportunity to be alone, Squeaky had decided to get away and check out what was going on at Indian Key. He was a little scared, but he wanted to see for himself if there were ghosts there like everyone said. All his friends were too afraid to get close to the island at night.

The night was beautiful. A warm northwest wind blew off the Gulfstream at twelve knots creating smooth rollers that were perfect for surfing. Squeaky took a westerly tack, moving parallel to the Overseas Highway, which most people called US 1. He made his way past *Roamer*, a sunken schooner in about fifteen feet of water, and then on up to Indian Key Anchorage.

He hung around the area for a few minutes, waiting for the cloud cover to move out, revealing a strikingly bright full moon. He moved into shallower water, hugging the two-foot shoals surrounding Indian Key.

Fifty yards from the beach, Squeaky paused and heard the voices of a strange language he had never before heard. He could see that the people were humans and not ghosts. They didn't talk the same way his friend Skye did.

Easing closer to shore, and with the help of the moon, Squeaky saw the outline of a boat parked with its bow on the beach. About twenty yards from the boat, he saw four men loading boxes forward of the wheelhouse. Their words were different from any he had heard. Moments later, he heard the engine start, and then three men jumped from the boat onto the beach.

Squeaky moved back from the boat, careful not to get caught in its propeller. The propeller wash created a cloud of silt and sand as the captain revved the engine. He turned the wheel and steered the boat toward Indian Key Channel.

It's odd that there are no lights, Squeaky thought, following the boat at a safe distance and a comfortable speed of about ten knots. He wanted to see where the boat was going. He needed to warn his friend Skye that there weren't ghosts on the island, but there were some strange-talking humans.

The boat passed under the bridge and followed the channel, staying between the red and green markers. It was obvious to Squeaky that the captain had practiced this route many times, particularly in the dark. The craft passed Shell Key on the left, and the Intracoastal lay dead ahead. At Steamboat Channel the captain turned north, followed the Intracoastal to Cotton Key, turned right, and steered directly toward the Overseas Highway. Eventually, the boat pulled into a nondescript boat ramp at Windley Key.

A black cargo van with dark-tinted windows waited with its lights out. Squeaky couldn't see inside, but he wondered what had been loaded on the boat and where the van was taking the boxes he had seen those strange-speaking humans load. It was a mystery. He had to warn Skye and her friend CJ not to go to the island. They could be in danger. *Those men don't look like nice humans,* Squeaky thought.

Chapter 22

Sky heard CJ's Volkswagen before she saw it. *He should get a new muffler*, she thought. She couldn't understand his passion for his Volkswagen Thing. Of all the cars he and his parents had looked at, he had chosen the 1973 Thing. It wasn't her taste in cars, but of course, it was a classic.

Recently, her parents promised her that when she reaches sixteen, they will buy her a car. Like CJ, she also loves classics, and especially sports cars. Her favorite is the 1984 Nissan 300ZX 50th Limited Edition. She had been searching the Internet trying to find one in good condition at a price her parents would be willing to pay.

She would own a car next summer when she came back to Poppy's, but her parents had already told her she couldn't drive it from Connecticut to Florida. They said it wasn't safe for a teenage girl to travel alone. At first, she had thought they were being overprotective, but after what she had seen earlier today, she was more inclined to trust their judgment. For now, she was happy to ride alongside CJ in his Thing.

CJ zipped his car into the parking lot and brought it to a stop in front of Sky's picnic table. His long, stork-like legs came out of his car first, followed by his head, and then he finally unwound the rest of his lean body. Oddly enough, the roof of the car was even with his chest. In five steps of his long stride, he stood next to Skye. "Thanks for coming," Skye smiled, looking up.

"For you, anything," CJ grinned, as he looked longingly down into her sparkling blue eyes. He seated himself next to her. *If only I could tell her how I feel, and if only she returned my feelings, I would be a happy guy.* Unfortunately, he lacked the courage to tell her.

"What a day," CJ said as he tried to focus on the reason she had asked him to come instead of on her beautiful face. *I could get lost in her beautiful blue eyes. Boy! I really have it bad.*

This summer, since she had gone from being a little girl to a young woman, he had thought about her constantly.

The thought occurred to him that maybe he had also gone from being a boy to a young man. That was the only way he could describe the strange feelings he had every time he saw Skye.

Again, he tried to focus on what Skye was saying to him.

"I couldn't go to sleep, CJ. My mind kept racing, thinking about that body and the awful stench. Goodness, I never thought a person could stink like that!"

"I'm sorry you're so stressed out," CJ said, trying to console her. "I could never be a rescue diver or an EMT. The thought of having to deal with situations like that freaks me out too."

"By the way, what about what Flapper said? That was a big surprise, wasn't it?" CJ questioned.

Skye placed her elbows on the table and put her hands under her chin. Then she leaned over and touched her best friend's shoulder with hers. "What Flapper said has been bothering me. Something strange is going on over there, and I think we should find out what it is."

"Hold on just a minute! Don't you remember what Dad and Poppy said? We're not to go there. Even Flapper told you not to go."

"I know," Skye said, as she stood and put her hands on her hips. "I've been thinking, CJ. Maybe we could sneak over there at night, and nobody would know. What do you think about that?"

"Are you crazy? What if there really are ghosts, or who knows what else over there?" CJ argued back.

"Then we call the police."

"Oh, just like that," CJ snapped his fingers. "In the meantime, we may end up dead!" CJ didn't often defy his parents' wishes, but lately it seemed like he was always with Skye when he did.

"Don't be so dramatic. I think you're just an old scaredy cat," Skye joked.

"Maybe so," CJ smiled. "I just don't want to get into any trouble, unlike you."

"C'mon partner. We'll be all right. We can swim over to the island after dark and just check it out. That's all. We'll be back in no time."

"Let me think about it. By the way, Dad says he's going to see the medical examiner tomorrow. I hope they can ID the guy. Oh, and Captain Anderson wants to go ahead and get the hull up. Maybe we can learn something from it."

————————

Squeaky hung around the boat ramp until the cargo van was loaded and left the area thirty-five minutes later. He had watched the entire event. Headlights still off, the van backed close to the dock. Two men got out of the vehicle, walked down the dock, and began helping the captain secure the boat. One man jumped aboard the boat, and the other remained on the dock. No one said a word. Each man instinctively seemed to know what to do. The man aboard the boat began handing down boxes, one at a time, while the man on the dock placed them into the back of the van. This went on for a half hour or so. Eventually, the boat was emptied, the cargo doors locked, and the captain and two men climbed into the vehicle and sped off.

I'd better get back to the pod. I'll find Skye tomorrow. I need to tell her what I saw, Squeaky thought.

"What do you mean you'll have to think about it?" Skye argued. "It's a no-brainer!"

"Yeah, well maybe for you it's a no-brainer, but as for me, I think you're insane!"

"Look, if you don't want go with me, then fine. I'll have to go by myself!" she said with more bravery than she felt. Skye was a curious young lady, but she wasn't crazy enough to swim over to the island without CJ. If there were ghosts on the island, she certainly didn't want to face them alone.

Testing CJ, Skye stood and started to leave.

CJ jumped up and took her by the arm. "Okay, okay, darn it. I'll go with you, but we'd better not get into trouble."

Skye turned, reached up, and gave him a big hug. She usually got her way with CJ, and now they would finally get to see exactly what Flapper was talking about. CJ's face turned a little red at having Skye so close to him, but he liked the way she felt in his arms. Sadly, for CJ, she seemed totally unaware of his feelings.

This girl should be a politician. She sure knows how to manipulate a guy. Maybe I'm just a sucker for petite girls with big blue eyes.

Chapter 23

The early morning ride to Miami had been uneventful except for a breathtaking sunrise. Low, wispy clouds had cast dancing shadows across glassy emerald water as CJ's dad, Michael, had driven north on the Overseas Highway into Homestead, where he took the Florida Turnpike into Miami. His breakfast meeting with Sonny Mitchell was scheduled for eight o'clock at the Rancho Luna Restaurant off 22nd Avenue, just a couple of blocks south of Southwest 8th Street.

Michael glanced down at his Rolex watch. The watch was a special treasure that Maria had bought for him when he worked with Sonny at the National Security Agency. *Those were the days,* he thought, *undercover with a life full of excitement, money, and danger, all thanks to the NSA.*

Shifting his attention back to the turnoff into the restaurant parking lot, he thought, *I'm right on schedule, and I sure hope Sonny's on time because I'm starved.*

He pulled into the rear parking area of the restaurant and saw Sonny's blue Bronco parked on the side.

Rancho Luna brought back vivid memories of the times he had brought Maria, her parents, and CJ here for Sunday morning breakfast. His mouth watered just thinking about it. He relished the flavor of the fresh toasted Cuban bread spread with melted butter. Rancho Luna was one of the most popular Cuban restaurants in the area. They served generous portions, and the food was delicious and reasonably priced. Maria was from Cuba, and between hers and her mother's delightful dishes, Michael had come to love Cuban food.

Walking through the back door, Michael spotted Sonny sitting at a table for two. *Thank goodness he's alone*, Michael thought. He wasn't sure if Sonny's contact would be with him or not. He hadn't seen Sonny in a long while and wanted to spend some time catching up. He knew Sonny was thinking about retiring in a couple of years and wondered what he planned to do if he did retire. He couldn't imagine him as a civilian. He had loved the excitement of the NSA and had been the best at his job. They had both been undercover, which added to the excitement, and the danger.

The dining area was warm and welcoming. Spanish tile covered the floor, and plate glass windows exposed the street side traffic. Ten or maybe fifteen people occupied the room, most of which were speaking Spanish. Waiters dressed in black slacks and white long-sleeved shirts moved about the room, serving Miami's finest Cuban cuisine.

Sonny looked up from his menu and saw Michael approaching. He raised his hand, gesturing Michael to come sit down. "Hey, Bro, long time no see," Sonny said as Michael pulled out a chair and seated himself.

"It's great to see you, Chubby. How are you doing?" Michael asked as he slid his chair under the table.

Sonny smiled, "I'm good. It's just been business as usual, trying to keep America safe. How are Maria and CJ? I sure miss her and the kid." Sonny liked being called Uncle Sonny by CJ. He had no children of his own, and CJ was as close to being a son as he would ever have.

"We're all good, thanks."

Seriously, Sonny looked Michael square in the eyes. "You know we need to stay in touch more often. You guys are the only family I have down here. They keep trying to convince me to move to DC, but I hate the weather up there." With a twinkle in his eye, Sonny continued, "Besides, the women down here are much better looking."

"You'll never change, will you?" Michael laughed. As part of his cover with the NSA, Sonny had spent a ton of money on entertaining and women. Women were Sonny's favorite budget item. Michael had never discussed any of that with CJ. Michael smiled as he pictured CJ's response if he was told about his Uncle Sonny's women. Heck, if CJ knew, he might even think it was cool. *Teenage boys and their raging hormones,* thought Michael. *I sure remember those days.*

Sonny studied the menu as Michael motioned to the server.

Michael knew the list of food by heart and had already decided what he wanted to order.

"Buenos Dias," the young man said. "How may I help you?"

Sonny ordered black coffee, and Michael ordered café con leche.

"Tell me what's going on in your neck of the woods," Sonny asked as the server stepped away.

"I need your help, Sonny. You already know that a few days ago, there was a boat explosion with one severely burned survivor. The following day, CJ, his friend Skye, and I were diving on the sunken wreck and discovered another body in the wreckage about twenty feet deep. I think it was sabotage, but so far there is no evidence."

Hesitating, Michael said, "I'd like for you to go with me to the medical examiner's office and get their report. Maybe it'll shed some light on identifying the corpse and help determine why he was on board the boat. The Monroe County Sheriff's office thinks it was an accident, but I don't agree."

"Sounds like you're missing the excitement of your old job, Michael? Is civilian life too boring for you?" With a questioning look on his face, Sonny smiled.

"Not on your life, old man," Michael responded firmly.

Sonny had to laugh and finally said, "I'm one step ahead of you, partner. We have an appointment at nine-thirty with Dr. Fernandez. He's the head honcho."

Knowing he had always been able to count on Sonny, Michael felt relieved and said, "Great! Now, let's order. I'm starved."

————————

Skye sat on the edge of Poppy's dock. She was enjoying the early morning sun and sipping a cup of hot cocoa. The cool, early daylight temperature felt wonderful as a light breeze swirled about the bay, but Sky knew that it would be another sweltering day. *That's life in the Keys,* she sighed.

After meeting with CJ the night before, Skye finally went back to Poppy's, and to her surprise she fell asleep the moment her head touched the pillow. Seven hours later, and nightmare free, she felt refreshed and was looking forward to another day on the water. The events of the day before were slowly fading.

She thought about her and CJ's conversation the previous night. His reluctance to go to Indian Key bothered her. *Certainly, it can't be as bad as some people think.* She didn't believe in ghosts and spirits and all that mumbo jumbo. Or did she?

Of course, she hadn't believed that people could talk to pelicans and dolphins either until it happened to her. Trying to be logical, she halfway admitted to herself that ghosts and spirits might possibly exist. *If they are on Indian Key, I sure don't want to go over there by myself.* Thinking of it made her shiver. *Is CJ's lack of enthusiasm really fear?* she wondered.

After thinking about it, she decided that was not the case. *CJ has always been fearless in our escapades, both on his boat and in the water. Of course, he was as white as a sheet when the body on the sunken wreckage floated unattended to the surface of the water and exploded. But admittedly, none of us were in particularly good shape. We all upchucked, except Poppy and Michael, and they looked pale as ghosts. What a yucky mess*! she thought. Just thinking about it again briefly caused nausea to tug at the pit of her stomach.

Her bottom was slowly going to sleep from sitting on the hard-wooden dock. Changing positions, she eased a little closer to the edge. Suddenly, just below her feet, Squeaky's head popped out of the calm water. Another one of her new communicating friends, he seemed to have a smile on his face every time he saw her. He let out a few high-pitched squeaks, raising himself up out of the bay and throwing himself over backwards.

Still thinking about ghosts, the movement startled Skye. As she tried to catch her breath, she scolded the dolphin. "Squeaky, you scared the dickens out of me! I almost had a heart attack."

Squeaky eased back to the dock and looking up at Skye, he nodded his head up and down as if agreeing with her. Since meeting Skye, he sure didn't want to lose her friendship. He loved being able to communicate with her through their thoughts.

"I followed the boat last night," Squeaky said.

"What do you mean followed the boat? What boat?"

"I went up to Indian Key, and there were strange talking, mean-looking people putting stuff on a boat. I followed it to Windley Key."

"So, what happened?"

"Nothing happened. They took the boxes off the boat, loaded them into a van, and left."

That confirmed it for Skye. Whether there were ghosts or not, she had to go to Indian Key and find out what was going on over there. Her curiosity had to be satisfied.

CJ had always teasingly called her Nancy Drew, a young detective girl in the old Nancy Drew Mystery books.

But today, however, she had to meet CJ at Cap's boat and go to the sunken wreck. Indian Key would have to wait a while, but not too long.

Looking down at the dolphin, Skye said, "Thanks, Squeaky. CJ and I will go check it out."

"No!" Squeaky said. "Don't go over there! All my friends think there are ghosts on the island. They said there are ghosts of Indians that lived there a long time ago, and they don't like people coming to the island."

Squeaky continued, "A friend told me that some people disappeared over there a couple years ago. I don't know whether or not there are ghosts on the island, but it's not safe for you or your friend. Even if there aren't ghosts, there are still bad people over there that could hurt you. I'll keep a check on the island and let you know what is going on if the bad people are still there."

"Thanks, Squeaky, but I think we'll be okay," Skye answered, knowing full well that now she absolutely had to investigate the island. She had always been very curious, and this was a mystery she was going to solve, but she sure hoped there weren't any ghosts. Swallowing at the thought, she gave Squeaky a brave smile.

Chapter 24

Michael said, "It's not a nice area to work, is it?" as he and Sonny approached the Dade County Medical Examiner's Department at 1851 NW 10th Ave. The three-building, multi-story facility housed some of the latest technological forensic equipment in the world. Many law enforcement agencies around the globe relied mainly on the expertise of the scientists working in the building, whose reputations were second to none.

This downtown area of Miami was old and dilapidated. Haitians and Central Americans were slowly taking over this section of the city, bringing with them drugs and crime. The murder rate had increased by twenty-percent over the past three years.

Sonny parked his Bronco under one of the few banyan trees. His decision to park there came with mixed feelings. He wondered whether or not the shady parking spot was worth the additional bird poop that would probably be on the roof and hood of his car when they returned.

Michael opened the passenger door and stepped out onto the hot pavement. Sonny slid out of his seat and locked the doors. A loud beep from his alarm system followed. "Welcome to Miami," flashed through Michael's mind.

Air conditioning cooled them as they entered the building. A nondescript odor, probably formaldehyde, permeated the offices. Several uncomfortable, straight back chairs discouraged visitors from remaining too long.

Sonny took the lead as they walked to the reception desk. He whisked out his National Security Agency identification card and handed it to a full-figured, attractive, professional-looking, young Cuban woman who was busy at the computer. Sonny guessed her age to be somewhere around twenty-five or so. Aymee was on her name tag. Her long legs flattered the tight-fitting dress that was a little too short. Sonny got the feeling that she didn't appreciate the interruption.

"Good morning," Sonny said with a broad smile. "We're here to see Dr. Fernandez, please."

"Do you have an appointment?" she asked a little curtly.

"As a matter of fact, yes, we do." Michael could tell that Sonny didn't like her attitude.

Aymee touched a speed dial number. "Dr. Fernandez, there's a Mr. Sonny Mitchell here to see you. After a slight pause, she said, "Yes, sir."

Looking at Sonny, she waved her arm toward the elevator and said, "Second floor, first door on the right." Abruptly, she returned to her computer.

Ignoring the snub, Michael said, "Thanks," and poked Sonny in the ribs, guiding him toward the elevator. *Aymee must have had a late night.*

The Morgue Bureau had been established in 1955. Five coolers provided capacity for five hundred fifty-five bodies. The twenty-three thousand square foot building housed eight departments making up the ME's domain. Sonny and Michael were interested in only one, Records and Transcription.

After a slow ride in the antiquated elevator, Sonny knocked on the door that read 'Dr. Fernandez.'

"Enter," a Spanish-accented voice replied.

Sonny opened the door to a surprisingly beautiful and spacious office. High recessed lighting fixtures provided indirect lighting, and rich beige carpeting covered the floor. A conference table made of solid pecan was placed on the right side of the room. Dr. Fernandez sat behind an oversized oak desk almost completely covered with myriad papers.

As the two men entered the room, Dr. Fernandez stood to welcome his guests.

Michael noticed one long wall covered with diplomas. Each was professionally framed. *It's probably an ego thing*, he decided.

"Good morning, gentlemen," Dr. Fernandez said and smiled courteously in greeting as he stretched out his hand. Sonny glanced down and saw long slender fingers with clean manicured nails. His manners suggested that he was from an upper-class family. He had almost completely lost the accent of his native country.

Studying the doctor for a split second, Sonny decided he was the perfect likeness to Antonio Banderos. Appearing to be around five nine and about a hundred seventy pounds, the doctor was very handsome with wavy black hair and dark eyes. *He could pass for Antonio Banderos' brother,* Sonny thought as he concluded his assessment. Michael and Sonny shook hands with the doctor.

Dr. Fernandez waved a hand at the beige leather chairs in front of his desk.

Sonny handed him his business card before seating himself.

As the doctor read the card his eyes grew larger, displaying a subtle curiosity.

"How may I help you gentlemen?" he asked quietly. "May I offer you some espresso?"

Both men declined.

Sonny took the lead. "Doctor, a corpse was brought in yesterday from the Keys. He was pulled from Florida Bay and apparently was the victim of a boating accident. However, we have reason to believe there was foul play involved. I'd like to see the autopsy report and any identification that you may have on him."

Dr. Fernandez studied Sonny for a moment and then looked over at Michael. "May I see some identification, sir?"

Sonny leaned forward in his chair. "He's my associate," he said with authority.

Dr. Fernandez seemed to relax a bit. He reached for the phone, pressed a button, and leaned back in his chair. After a moment, he entered a few numbers into his computer and waited.

"Hey Jose, would you please bring me the file on case number 2936-451?" He placed the receiver back in its cradle.

"It will only be a minute," he said politely.

The three men sat in comfortable silence and waited. Forty-one seconds later, there was a knock on the door.

"Come in," Dr. Fernandez called out to the closed door.

Michael assumed it was Jose that walked into the room carrying a thick manila folder.

The man nodded to the guests as he handed the folder to the doctor. He turned and quickly left the room.

Dr. Fernandez laid the folder on his desk and began shuffling papers, studying each page.

Sonny took out a small notepad from his pants pocket and readied himself to take notes.

"Let's see," Fernandez mumbled. "At 6:33 p.m. yesterday, the victim was brought in, and processing began at 7:28 p.m. Initial diagnosis for the cause of death was trauma from a major concussion, most likely an explosion. The subject suffered second-degree burns on the anterior portions of his body, but they were not the cause of death. Death occurred before the burns."

"Any ID, Doc?" Sonny asked.

"Hmmm, let me see. Here we are," Fernandez answered. "His name is Roscoe Bertolli, age thirty-five. No current address." Fernandez scanned on down to the bottom of the page.

"According to this, he spent three years in the U.S. Army as a demolitions expert and two years in federal prison for automatic weapons possession."

"Is there a phone number listed anywhere?" Michael questioned.

"No, I don't see one," Fernandez said.

"One last question, Doc. Has the Monroe County Sheriff's Office contacted you about this case?" Sonny asked.

Dr. Fernandez looked at Sonny questioningly. "Not to my knowledge."

"Thank you, Doc. I think we've heard enough," Sonny said, rising from his chair. "We appreciate your time." He reached out to shake the doctor's hand.

Chapter 25

Perspiring, Skye mumbled, "The sun is already getting hot."
She rose, wiped the sweat from her brow with her shirttail, and then
placed a white tennis cap on her head to shield her eyes from the
glaring sun. Dressed in pink shorts and a white tank top, she was
prepared for the sweltering Florida heat. Settling back on the dock,
she continued to wait for CJ.

Squeaky had left a little earlier, wanting to get back to his pod.
He mentioned something about having a mullet roundup, whatever
that meant. She figured he was talking about food. She smiled to
herself as she thought of her new friends, Flapper and Squeaky. She
was still amazed that she could communicate with them. They both
seemed so protective, and it made her feel happy that she had met
them.

She had been thinking about going back out to the wreck but was
having reservations about the dive. *What if there's another body
down there that we missed? I suppose the sheriffs' divers did a
thorough search, and CJ will be with me.* Just thinking about CJ
made her smile. *He is the best friend I have ever had.* She knew
she could always count on him for help and advice and to participate
in her adventures. Still smiling, she pictured CJ at the cookout at
his house a few days ago.

*Even though he is tall and on the skinny side, he is still a very
good-looking guy and has finally started to fill out a little. All the
girls will be running after him.* Thinking of CJ with another girl,

Skye felt a twinge of jealousy. *What am I thinking?* She snapped back from her reverie. *CJ would never think of me that way. He just thinks of us as friends, doesn't he? He's never indicated any interest in me other than as friends.* She knew there was no way she would ever bring it up to CJ. It would be too embarrassing. At that same moment, Skye had no idea that some of the same thoughts were going through CJ's mind.

Clearing her head, she heard the whine of CJ's McKee Craft, and as she looked up she saw it round the mangrove. Moments later, the boat was resting against the dock. Skye drug her cooler loaded with sandwiches, Gatorade, and homemade chocolate chip cookies to the edge of the dock close to the boat.

CJ picked up the load and placed it carefully in the Gator Bait. *Skye is always prepared. She constantly asks me to join her in her crazy schemes and adventures, but she does feed me good.* Just thinking about Skye and her delicious lunches made CJ smile.

Glancing at CJ, Skye asked, "What?" She wondered what the smile was about. When CJ didn't respond, she asked, "Where's Cap?"

"He's going to meet us at the site."

"Are you sure you're okay with this?" Skye questioned.

"Let's go find some ghosts." CJ was definitely onboard with her. Of course, he always was, for more reasons than one.

———————

Cap had just dropped anchor when he heard the McKee Craft. He went about unleashing the fifty-five-gallon drums and checking the valves that had been installed on each end. *Six total*, he thought. *That should be enough to raise the sunken craft.*

Several minutes later, CJ came alongside the *Money* and heaved to until Skye readied the lines to moor the boats.

"How are y'all doing?" Cap asked, smiling down at the young couple. *I really like those kids. Most kids would never have dived again after what these two saw the other day. They both have a lot of guts.* Cap admired the teens' courage and would do anything to help them.

"We're good, Cap. How about you? You ready for a big day?" CJ was glad that Cap had agreed to help them. The thought crossed his mind that even though Cap was a grumpy old sailor, he was still a nice old guy, kind of like a cantankerous, elderly grandfather.

"Yep, I'm ready. Let's get saddled up!"

Skye started to undress, revealing a two-piece dark blue bathing suit that was at least one size too small. *Man, Skye sure has filled out this year,* CJ thought, feeling a little guilty for staring, but he couldn't help himself. He glanced up at Cap, his face red with embarrassment. Cap looked back at CJ. Both smiled at each other. Each knew what the other was thinking.

"Before you guys suit up, jump onboard and let's talk about how we're going do this."

Both men sat in silence as Sonny drove back to Rancho Luna from Miami. Michael had left his car there so he could ride with Sonny to the medical examiner's office. It was lunchtime when Sonny pulled into the restaurant parking area, and to his surprise the lot was full. He pulled next to Michael's car in the only empty space, threw the Bronco in park, and turned toward Michael.

"Well, old partner. Where do you want to go from here?"

Michael rubbed his chin in thought. "I'm not sure Chubby. What are your thoughts?"

"Here's the way I see it. Apparently, the guy in the morgue was shady. He was a munitions expert, and the boat blew up. The question is, why was he on the boat, and what was he doing?"

Michael considered what Sonny had said. "From what the detective said, Duncan is a wealthy guy. His wife has a lot to gain if Duncan is dead. Maybe she hired this Bertolli guy to blow him up. There would be little evidence left, particularly if it happened in Florida Bay," Michael stated. The more he thought about it, the sounder the idea seemed.

Nodding his head at Michael's assessment, Sonny agreed. "That's a possibility. Maybe Bertolli was on the boat doing his thing when Duncan came onboard. Maybe he panicked and had nowhere to go except to hide somewhere on the boat."

"Now it's beginning to make sense," Michael agreed. "The guy must have been hiding in the bilge out of sight when the explosion occurred. He probably had the explosives set on some kind of timer and couldn't get off the boat in time. More than likely, that's why he only had a few burns."

Sonny looked over at Michael. "Now all we have to do is find a link between Mrs. Duncan and Bertolli and connect the dots."

———————

After they had confirmed the dive plan with Cap, Skye and CJ hit the water at the same time. It took a couple of seconds for the bubbles to disappear and for them to get their bearings. The water was about eighty-three degrees and crystal clear.

It looks like a bathtub full of clean water, Skye thought. She heard the sound of CJ's regulator and then the sound of her own. Her eyes focused on the bottom, and there it was. The hull lay directly below them. It seemed to appear different today. Maybe it was the clarity of the water. She relaxed a little as they drifted down. *Good, no ghosts and no more bodies so far.* Cap had insisted they wear gloves.

The edges of the drums were weathered and uneven. "A safety precaution," he had said.

Moments later, they were resting on the sandy bottom in twenty feet of water. They both cleared their ears. Their first task was to survey the perimeter of what was left of the hull. They needed to find a place to attach at least four drums; two on the starboard side and two on the port side. They moved to the stern for a closer look and to check the damage. CJ pointed to a cleat still attached to the port transom and gave Skye the okay signal. She nodded her head in agreement.

Next, they moved to the starboard side. Again, they were in luck. The cleat looked okay, so they moved on to the bow, which they discovered was a completely different story. There was no place to tie a line for the drum. The fire had burned beyond the railing. The port side of the bow was no different. They would have to come up with some other way to attach the drums. CJ motioned the up signal to Skye. They both headed for the surface.

Cap was waiting when they broke the surface. He was leaning over the starboard side of CJ's boat, hanging out about two feet above the water.

Skye reached up and grabbed the side. CJ followed.

"What do you think?" Cap asked.

"The stern is okay," CJ replied, taking deep breaths.

Skye looked relieved to be on the surface. Catching her breath, she added, "Cap, the bow is the problem. There's no place to tie a line."

"Well, get those tanks off, and let's talk about it. We'll just have to figure it out, won't we?"

Chapter 26

Mile Marker 81.2 has been a landmark in the Keys since 1947. Today, people passing by would not recognize it. No longer an old nostalgic place for locals, it had been replaced with a new face and a new building.

Back in mid-1940, when supper was over, the tables and chairs were moved aside, and the local revelers would start their music and party into the night.

After Hurricane Wilma in 2005, the new owners had to rebuild. Still, the menu was vast and the food delicious. The Green Turtle Inn & Restaurant had morphed into a new era.

Anatoli Krasnoff and Alexei Kovalchik wouldn't have known that being foreigners. They couldn't appreciate the history on which they sat, and they wouldn't have cared if they had known.

Anatoli Krasnoff sipped his drink. He preferred fine Finnish vodka instead of his native Russian vodka. He felt as though it gave him a feeling of internationalism. He considered himself worldly and sophisticated, but in truth, he and Anatoli were just small-time hustlers who worked for the Russian mob. They reminded the Russian mob boss of two of the three stooges.

"So, my friend and comrade, are you pleased with our progress?" Anatoli asked, taking another sip.

"Yes, very pleased. No, mostly pleased," his partner Alexei answered. He would be happier if they got rid of the cargo of electronics and made a boatload of money.

"We are well on our way to being millionaires," Anatoli smiled broadly, seeing visions of suitcases full of money.

"There must be a way to increase our production. The boats are moving too slowly. The captains are all pansies. A little rough weather and they refuse to leave their safe haven. They are all wimps!" Alexei said, in exasperation. his voice growing louder. "This operation will not last forever! We must make the most of it while we can."

Awakened by the ringing of his cell phone, Michael looked at the alarm clock. It was 10:47 p.m. He had just gotten to sleep. *Who in the heck could be calling so late*? He reached over and picked up his phone. The name on the caller ID said Sonny Mitchell.

"Hey, Chubby, what's up?" Michael whispered. Marie lay sleeping next to him, and he didn't want to wake her. He eased off the bed and gently closed the bedroom door behind him.

"I put a couple of my guys out on the street after you left, and guess what? They found out the name of Bertolli's girlfriend and her address. He's been living with her for the past month or so."

"That's great, Chubby," Michael whispered as he headed for the kitchen. to write down the name of the woman with whom Bertolli was living. CJ and Skye would want to know the latest on the dead man, and he planned to tell CJ when he came downstairs in the morning.

Chapter 27

Getting up early to go pick up Skye, CJ half staggered down the stairs, not fully awake. The odor of coffee already permeated the air, and he heard the rattle of silverware in the kitchen. *It's 6:30 in the morning. Who else could be up so early?* he wondered. At the bottom of the stairs, he rounded the corner to see his dad standing next to the stove holding a spatula in his right hand.

Michael heard the patter of bare feet on the wooden floor, turned, and saw CJ standing next to the island, rubbing his eyes.

"Morning, son," Michael smiled.

"Hi, Dad, what are you doing up so early?"

"Oh, I just thought we'd have a little quality pal time, that's all. Have a seat. Your eggs will be ready in a minute."

CJ walked to the coffee pot, poured himself a cup of hot coffee, and then took a seat at the island.

"Did you get a call late last night?" CJ asked. "I thought I heard you down here talking to someone."

Michael dipped up CJ's fried eggs and then placed the plate in front of him. "Yeah, it was Sonny. He's making good headway on the case. He located Bertolli's girlfriend, and now he's trying to get a search warrant for her phone records."

"Boy, it'll be great if we can bust this case wide open," CJ grinned. He knew the news would also make Skye happy, and he loved to make her happy. He wished he dared to talk with her about his feelings, but he knew he couldn't. Telling her how he felt might hurt the close friendship they had, and he didn't want to lose her. *Maybe I should talk to Dad about it. No,* he decided, *Dad will probably tell me to talk with Skye, and there is no way I can do that. She'll probably think I'm pathetic.*

"So, what are you guys up to today?" Michael asked, leaning over the counter in front of CJ, holding a fresh cup of coffee.

Clearing his mind, CJ thought for a moment as he took a bite of egg. "Yesterday, Skye and I surveyed the wreck. There are only two places we can attach the drums, and that's at the stern. There's no place at the bow. I just hope Cap comes up with some ideas. Today, we're going to meet Cap at the site and see what we can do."

"Mind if I meet you there?" Michael asked.

"No, Dad, of course not. In fact, we can use all the help we can get."

"Great!" Michael smiled. He walked around the island, stood next to CJ, and put his arm around CJ's shoulders. "Son, I just want you to know that your mom and I are very proud of you."

CJ hung his head, a little embarrassed at the praise, but he was pleased to hear what his father had said.

———

All three left the stern at the same time. CJ floated down first, leaving Skye and Michael on the surface. Cap reached down and handed the rope to Skye. She turned and followed CJ to the bottom. Cap handed Michael the nozzle end of the hose, and then he submerged.

Cap had suggested they wear wet suits. They would be working on the bottom, and the sand and muck would most likely cut their knees to pieces. Gloves were also a necessity. As Cap looked down, he could see the three of them moving about in the clear water. Three streams of bubbles floated lazily to the surface.

When Skye reached CJ on the bottom, she gave him a thumbs-up. She was happy to be with him no matter what they were doing, especially when they were in the water. She reached out and handed him one end of the rope. CJ moved off toward the bow, pulling and unraveling the line as he went. Skye waited for Michael.

As Michael drifted to the bottom, he was suddenly overwhelmed with emotion. Working and sharing this day with CJ and Skye was every father's dream. The events of the past few days had brought him and CJ closer together than ever before. He only wished that Maria could be here to share this experience. Maria wasn't especially fond of boats or being in the water.

After she and her family had left Cuba and moved to Miami, she had almost drowned in the water off Miami Beach. She was a teenager and was with three of her friends who were sunbathing. She went into the water to cool off, and a big wave sent her spinning. She hit her head on the bottom, knocking her unconscious. After losing consciousness, she was pulled from the water by the fast actions of a lifeguard, who happened to notice the waves throwing her around. Since that day, she had stayed out of the water, unless it was for a shower or to get in the hot tub on the deck.

Michael eased up close to Skye. She had been resting on her knees in the shallow sand as he approached. Their eyes met through face masks. Michael could see the smile in her eyes. He took the rope she was holding and began tying the line to the nozzle of the hose. Moments later, he pulled hard three times on the hose and waited.

Cap felt the tug, reached over to the water pump, and opened the valve. The hose wiggled as if a snake had come alive. High pressure air forced water toward the other end of the hose.

Michael looked up to see the snake-like hose moving toward them at high speed. He was surprised when the water erupted through the nozzle. It took a major effort on his part to hold onto the hose. He looked across the hull and saw CJ waiting for his signal to start pulling on the rope.

Cap stood up from his handy work and looked out across the bay.

He couldn't hear anything except the whine of the generator and electric pump. Something told him to look up. "There's that dadgum bird again!" he muttered.

Flapper, circling overhead, looked down to watch what was going on in the water. He finally headed toward the boat and landed gracefully atop the wheelhouse.

Cap shouted up at the bird, "What do you want?"

Of course, Flapper couldn't understand a word he said. Skye was the only human with whom he had ever been able to communicate. The bird just looked down at the old man with indifference.

———————

Squeaky had gotten the word through some of his friends that there were people at the wreck. He broke off from his pod and headed that way. *Ten minutes and I'll be there.* He figured it might be his friend Skye and the boy, CJ. *I hope that pelican's not around. He's always so grumpy,* Squeaky thought.

———————

CJ saw the signal and began pulling on the rope. It was harder than he had imagined. At first, nothing happened. Then slowly, he felt it give a little.

Skye and Michael watched as the hose began to move forward, a little at first and then faster. The force of the blasting water began to stir up sand and silt. Within forty seconds, a cloud of silt floated over the hull. In another minute, their visibility was down to less than ten feet.

CJ looked up in surprise. He couldn't see Skye or his dad, but he continued to pull on the rope.

Moments later, Skye and Michael appeared beside him. Michael took hold of the rope to assist CJ. Three minutes and thirty-three seconds later, the world seemed to come apart. The high-pressure nozzle shot out from underneath the hull. It whipped back and forth as if were a snake's head searching for prey. *If the nozzle hits anyone, a major injury could occur,* Michael thought in alarm.

Sand and silt covered the water. Visibility suddenly went down to two feet. It was difficult to determine which way was up and which way was down.

CJ began experiencing vertigo and nausea. Suddenly, his body was jerked by an unknown force he had never felt before, left, and then right as he was being pulled away from the wreck. His right knee twisted as pain shot up through his leg. He involuntarily screamed as he was pulled swiftly through the water.

Michael heard the scream but could not see CJ. His heart pounded as he shot to the surface. Rising twenty feet was taking forever. Michael hit the surface shouting. "Turn it off! Turn it off!"

Cap looked over and saw Michael gesturing. He couldn't understand what he was saying, but he realized what he meant. Cap ran over to the water pump, closed the valve, and pressed the stop button on the generator. There was silence. He turned and saw that Michael had disappeared. *What was happening down there? Was one of the kids hurt? Why had Michael shouted something and disappeared?*

As CJ was being pulled swiftly through the water, his visibility improved a little. *What is that awful pain in my foot?* Terrified, he finally managed to look down toward his foot. Blood was everywhere. To his horror, he saw a huge grey shadow. *What is that?* His heart began racing, as fear overcame him as he let out another scream.

In all the commotion, CJ heard a loud thump, thump, thump. With each thump, a flurry of bubbles began to rise to the surface.

Abruptly, the intense pressure on his foot was released. The water still was not clear. As he looked down, he saw something big and light gray darting in and around the shadow. Moments later, the shadow was gone.

CJ could see blood floating toward the surface. *Is that my blood?* he wondered. As he made a slow, sluggish ascent, Squeaky's face popped up in front of CJ's mask, startling the already frightened CJ. His heart felt like it stopped. "Squeaky!" CJ screamed at the dolphin. A fresh rush of adrenalin made his heart race like a freight train.

When Michael reached the bottom again, Skye and CJ were nowhere in sight. He still couldn't see anything in the soft silt, and he was terrified that something had happened to CJ. *Where is he? Is he okay? God, please don't let anything happen to my son.*

Moving around would only stir up the bottom worse. At that moment, he saw a small current slowly moving the silt cloud away from the site. A minute passed, and then he saw CJ, Skye, and Squeaky at the surface.

Michael quickly made his way to up to join them. When he was about eight feet from the surface, he noticed CJ's flipper was half torn off, and quite a bit of blood was coming from his foot.

With an alarmed look on his face, Michael broke the surface and asked, "Oh, my God! What happened?" His heart was pounding in fear for his son.

"Dad, you're not going to believe it!" CJ gasped. "A huge shark had me and was carrying me off. If it hadn't been for Squeaky driving it away, I'd probably be dead by now."

Squeaky poked his head up between the three of them and nodded as if agreeing with CJ. Skye thanked him, and CJ patted him on the head. "Thanks, partner," CJ said as the four of them made their way toward the boat. CJ would have to have a few stitches, but at least he hadn't lost his foot, or worse, his life, to the shark.

Chapter 28

Sitting at his desk with a lukewarm cup of coffee in his hand, the phone rang. Sean Callahan answered on the first ring. "Detective Sergeant Callahan," he said with authority.

"Detective, this is Sonny Mitchell, Michael Jansen's friend with the NSA. I think you may have a case on the boat explosion. We've been able to connect the telephone numbers of Roscoe Bertolli to Elizabeth Duncan. I thought you'd want to know as soon as possible."

"That was quick, Mr. Mitchell. I'm impressed. I'll get the Florida State Attorney involved and see if he will agree to an attempted murder charge. Thank your guys at the NSA for me."

"My pleasure, detective," Sonny said and hung up the phone. His next phone call would be to Michael.

A week later, with his sutures dissolved, CJ, along with Skye and Michael, joined Cap on the *Money* once again. All three were below the surface as Cap watched them in the clear water.

Flapper, sitting on top of the wheelhouse, saw the whole incident that happened next. Cap had been leaning on the side of the *Money* when Squeaky popped up by the edge of the boat. It scared Cap so badly that he lost his balance and fell into the water.

Flapper couldn't help but laugh. He'd never seen such a funny sight, particularly when the old man came to the surface. He was screaming his head off, but Flapper didn't have any idea what the old guy was saying. He could only understand Skye. From the way the old man was yelling, Flapper figured the words that were coming from his mouth weren't nice ones. *My goodness*, he thought. *He sure is upset.*

Nodding his head up and down, Squeaky continued to squeak as Cap tried unsuccessfully to climb onboard.

Swearing like the old sailor he was, Cap clung to the side of the boat and glared at the dolphin. Squeaky stayed close by to make sure he was okay. *After all, the old guy is ancient, and he is a friend of Skye's. I don't want anything to happen to him. A friend of Skye's is a friend of mine, and besides, I didn't mean to make him fall. I only wanted to surprise him.*

Noticing the commotion above, Michael was the first one on the boat. "Let me give you a hand, Cap," Michael offered as he reached for the gunwale.

Cap's pride wouldn't let him have anything to do with Michael's offer of help. "I can manage myself, thank you very much," he mumbled, forgetting for a moment how old he was. "That darn dolphin scared the pee out of me. If I get my hands on him, he's dinner on the table, I promise you that!"

CJ and Skye had just popped to the surface and heard Cap grumbling about Squeaky.

"Oh, Cap, don't be that way," Skye scolded. "Squeaky was just playing."

"Hey, Skye."

Skye looked up and saw Flapper sitting atop the wheelhouse.

"Hey, Flapper," she responded. "What are you doing here?"

"Oh, I thought I'd stop by and see all the action. I heard there were people at the sunken boat, and I figured it must be you and CJ."

"Well, there sure has been lots of action," Skye said as she removed her face mask.

Cap finally pulled himself aboard the *Money*. To say the least, he was not a happy man. "Crap," he grumbled, "I ain't got any dry clothes."

Skye turned to stare at Squeaky. "I ought to spank you," she scolded, but she could not help smiling at him.

"I was just having a little fun," he squeaked. "I didn't know he would fall in the water."

Michael interrupted the conversation. "Hey guys, we've got work to do today."

Squeaky followed the three back down to the bottom. He wanted to make sure they would be safe.

"Can I help with anything?" Squeaky asked Skye.

Skye responded, "Thanks, but I think we'll be okay."

Looking closely, but not seeing any danger around them, Squeaky said, "Well then, I'll get back to my pod. They're probably wondering where I am."

"Thanks again for saving CJ from the shark last week. I owe you big time. I think you know how much he means to me."

Squeaky nodded and squeaked his goodbye to Skye. He loved having her as a friend and would do anything he could to help her.

Twenty feet below, Michael handed CJ the end of the hose that goes to the pump and motioned for him to return topside.

CJ kicked off for the surface.

Cap was waiting when CJ came up. Cap was still in a foul mood. He had changed into an old bathing suit he had found in a locker. He was dry again, but his disposition sure had not changed.

Seeing Cap's ghostly body in his swimsuit almost hurt CJ's eyes. *Man, the old guy sure is white.* From years in the sun, Cap had what was called a "farmer's tan. He never took his shirt off in the sun and was deathly white everywhere except his face, neck, and arms just above his elbows and down to his hands. Those areas were weathered, brown, and speckled with age spots.

CJ noticed that Flapper had flown away. *No time to waste*, he thought and headed back down. *The process will be the same, except this time the propellers might be a problem*, CJ thought.

He worked his way back down to where Skye was waiting with Michael. He took the end of the line and made his way around the stern. He stopped at the transom and worked the rope down and under the hull as well as he could. Then he made his way to the far side of the hull, where he dropped the line and headed back up to the surface.

Seeing Cap standing close to the side, he said, "Ready when you are, Cap." At seeing Cap's nod, he flipped forward and kicked for the bottom.

Michael waited for the hose. He looked up and saw it coming. He braced himself, put his weight into it, and pushed it forward. Slowly, it penetrated the silt and began to move underneath the hull. Silt started blowing out of the hole as CJ began pulling the line. Skye and Michael moved around the stern to join CJ. Michael wanted to give CJ a hand with the line.

They had pulled the line about twelve feet when all of a sudden it stopped. *Man, oh, man. It must be stuck either on the shaft or the propeller,* CJ thought. He looked over at Michael for guidance, thinking his dad may have some idea. Michael looked back and shrugged his shoulders. *No help there.*

CJ put up his hand in a stop motion. He dragged it back around to the stern and began pulling as hard as he could. Finally, he felt it move. He stopped pulling and moved it back to its original position. Again, he started pulling and felt the tension release. Silt began to cloud the area. Visibility got down to four feet. Michael motioned to Skye to go ahead and surface.

CJ continued pulling on the rope. The cloud of silt was so thick he couldn't see the hull. He kept pulling until the nozzle finally broke through from where it was stuck. The snake's head began thrashing about. *Good!* he sighed with relief. He let go of the rope and headed for the sunshine.

The process came to a standstill. Cap stopped the pump, disconnected the hose, and handed it down to CJ. Everyone waited for the cloudy silt to move. CJ decided that raising a sunken boat was not an easy task.

Chapter 29

Detective Sergeant Callahan sat at his desk pondering his next move as he fumbled through his ten-year-old worn-out Rolodex cards. Sighing, he thought, *I've got to get a new one. This one is on its last leg.*

He'd been saying the same thing for the past two years. How he found anything baffled him, but somehow he did. The outer edges were tattered and torn, and business cards were taped over old ones. It was definitely a mess. His mind raced as he slowly fingered through his Rolodex.

Thinking about Elizabeth Duncan made Callahan think about jurisdiction. He called jurisdiction the good, the bad, and the ugly. The good is that it limited law enforcement authority to within a confined area. The bad is that in order to pursue a felon, one had to contact other jurisdictions and get their permission to go into their area. The ugly is that many times, lone-wolf policemen ignore the practice, resulting in many cases being thrown out of court.

I have to go by the book with Mrs. Duncan. Logically, he knew he had to, or his case could get thrown out.

"There it is," he said with a sigh of relief, picking up the card for Detective Ralph Martinez, Miami-Dade Police Department.

He stared at the card, gathering his thoughts about what to say to the Miami Detective. He had met him several years ago at a police officer's conference in Tallahassee. "Probably won't remember" he mumbled, reaching for the phone. Waiting impatiently, the phone rang and rang.

Twelve rings later someone said, "Yeah, Martinez here."

Callahan had remembered that he was Spanish. "Good morning, Detective Martinez."

"Yes, how can I help you?" Martinez answered hurriedly.

"This is Detective Sean Callahan with the Monroe County Sheriff's Office. We met several years ago at a police conference in Tallahassee."

"Yes, detective?" What can I do for you?" Martinez sounded rushed and impatient. He didn't remember Callahan.

"I'm investigating a boat explosion that occurred about a week ago."

"Yeah, I remember reading something about it in the *Miami Herald*."

"There's a woman of interest who lives in Miami, and I'd like to ask her a few questions. That is if you don't mind. She happens to be the wife of the survivor. Also, there was one other victim that didn't make it. The bottom line is I we have a homicide on our hands."

"When do you want to interview her?"

"If your schedule is free, maybe sometime tomorrow morning at your office?"

Callahan heard what sounded like papers being shuffled about.

"How about eleven o'clock?" Martinez asked.

"That'll be great. I look forward to working with you."

"We'll see," Martinez replied.

Callahan heard a click and then a silence that left him alone on the phone. *Not the friendliest cop, is he?*

———

Biscayne Bay looked like a sheet of glass. Not even a small breeze moved a sail. As the thermometer reached ninety-five degrees, everyone scattered for shade, including Elizabeth Duncan.

Everyone called the view spectacular. The mansion overlooked some of the most expensive real estate in Coconut Grove. Elizabeth Duncan did not appreciate it, though. She had gotten used to the bay's view just like everything else in her life. She was a victim of familiarity.

She lay on a chaise lounge in the shade of a large gazebo, which had recently been built by her husband, but only after she had demanded it over and over. Elizabeth was working on her third martini when the phone rang. "Margaret!" she shouted. "Please bring me the phone."

A middle-aged woman of Latin origin wearing a blue uniform, shuffled from the kitchen carrying a remote phone. With no expression on her plain face, she walked over and handed Elizabeth the phone. She then turned and followed the path back to the kitchen.

"Hello," Elizabeth said, irritated by the interruption.

"Mrs. Duncan?"

"Yes, who is this?" she demanded.

"Mrs. Duncan, this is Detective Sergeant Callahan. I'm with the Monroe County Sheriff's Office."

Elizabeth almost dropped the phone. Her hands began to shake.

"Yes, what is this about?" she asked, trying to control the quivering in her voice.

"Mrs. Duncan, there are a few questions I'd like to ask you regarding your husband's accident."

"I don't think there's anything more I can offer, officer. I already spoke with the Miami Police Department when my husband was brought to the hospital. I was shocked about the accident, but there's nothing I can add to what I've already told the Miami police officer."

"Well, there are a few things I think you can help us with. I would appreciate it if you would meet me at the Miami-Dade Police Department tomorrow morning at eleven o'clock," Callahan paused and continued, "I think it will be in your best interest for you to show up."

Elizabeth's mind was racing. *What could he possibly know? Where the heck is Roscoe?*

"Detective Callahan, is this absolutely necessary?" She squirmed in the chaise lounge, and her heart began racing.

"Yes, Mrs. Duncan, it's necessary. Otherwise, I'll have to leave it up to a grand jury."

The word grand jury was the power word Callahan had used many times in the past. It seemed to work wonders on most people.

Elizabeth's heart almost stopped. She had to get this guy off the phone, so he wouldn't hear the quivering in her voice.

"Very well, officer, if you insist. Tomorrow at eleven." She hung up the phone and took a deep breath to try to calm her nerves. It didn't work.

Elizabeth lay on the lounge chair shaking uncontrollably. She was nearly hysterical. *What kind of trouble has that idiot gotten me into? Should I take my lawyer with me? Should I just ignore the detective's threat?* She wondered why Detective Callahan told her it was necessary. *Does he have proof that I was involved?* She would have to wait until their meeting tomorrow to find out.

Chapter 30

The foursome met early at the wreck. Sea conditions were similar to the day before, except maybe a little warmer. The project had turned out to be more than for what they had bargained. Skye looked tired, but CJ was his usual self. Cap was still cranky from his fall into the bay, and Michael seemed distant. Despite their differences today, they all had one thing in common. They wished this entire horror was over.

Skye struggled to put on her tank. CJ had barely finished working his way into his wetsuit. Michael was talking with Cap at the bow. Cap already had one barrel floating in the water with a strap lashed around the center.

Michael returned to the stern to give Skye a hand with her tank. "Thanks," she smiled.

Michael had decided to sit this one out. He would let the kids perform the tasks of the day. They were in better physical condition than he. An old back injury had nagged him all night from the previous day's dive, and sleep had been fitful. After all, he had just celebrated his fiftieth birthday. He had resigned himself to the fact that he was getting older. He didn't like it, but aging was an unpleasant fact.

Cap made his way back to the teens in the stern. "Y'all be careful," he warned. "These here barrels are heavy and awkward. Whatever you do, don't get under one." C J and Skye eased into the water, swam over to the barrel, and looked up at Cap for further instructions.

"Y'all gotta let the air out real slow; both ends at the same time. What you want is neutral buoyancy. That way you can move them around without killing yourselves. Understand?"

Skye and CJ both nodded yes.

Cap reached down to the barrel and began showing them how the system worked. The valves were fitted opposite each other in each end. Cap rolled the barrel with the high valve up while the low valve stayed underwater. He opened each valve, and water began flowing in from the bottom valve. Slowly, the barrel began filling with water. They could hear the air escaping from the top valve.

CJ looked up at Cap and said, "Cool."

Cap said, "Remember, if you want more air in the barrel, you have to do the opposite. The air goes in from the top valve, and it forces water out of the bottom valve. Now, y'all please be careful."

Skye and CJ played with the valves for a few minutes before they got the hang of things.

CJ looked over at Skye. "Ready to try it?"

"Yep, let's go."

As the barrel filled with water, it began to sink. Moments later, the kids were heading toward the bottom.

———

Detective Callahan was thirteen minutes early for the interview with Elizabeth Duncan. It always irked him when people were late. That's why he had made it a habit to be on time or early.

The drive up from Islamorada had been uneventful until he got on the Palmetto Expressway. Two cars had crashed, leaving one of the drivers in critical condition. Traffic had been backed up for seven miles, and when it moved, it crawled at a gopher's pace. At one point, he almost panicked, thinking he was going to be late.

He finally pulled into the Miami-Dade Police Department

parking lot just off 91st & NW 25th streets in Doral, Florida. He remembered coming here as a kid to see the great golf players while they competed at the Doral Country Club. His dream of golf eventually turned to police work. To this day, he wondered if he had made the right decision.

On his way up from the Keys, Callahan had given a lot of thought to the questions and strategy he would take with Mrs. Duncan. He knew there had been forty-seven phone calls made back and forth between Mrs. Duncan and Roscoe Bertolli. He had no idea what the content of those calls could have been. *Were they of a romantic nature or a conspiracy? What exactly was their relationship? What was Roscoe doing on Duncan's boat?* He hoped today's meeting with Elizabeth Duncan might shed some light on his questions.

Callahan sat in his car until 11 a.m. As he put his hand down to open his door, he saw Mrs. Duncan turn into the parking lot. The scowl on her face told him that it was not going to be a pleasant interview. He watched as she exited her BMW, walked behind the car, and headed for the front door. Callahan got out of his car and followed her inside.

Detective Martinez stood at the front counter and watched Elizabeth Duncan enter the office. He just stared at her. *Wow! What a gorgeous woman*! Callahan entered right behind her.

Martinez walked out to meet Elizabeth Duncan before she got to the counter. He reached out his hand and said. "Mrs. Duncan?"

Elizabeth hesitated for a moment, wondering how to respond. Her sweaty hand shook his. "Good morning, officer."

Callahan stopped beside the two and introduced himself.

"Would anyone care for some coffee?" Martinez offered, trying to break the ice.

Elizabeth Duncan shook her head and said, "No, thank you." Callahan also declined the offer.

"Well then," Martinez said. "Please follow me this way," as he waved them forward.

A metal door next to the counter stopped them. Martinez nodded his head to an officer. There was an immediate buzzing sound, and the door popped open.

The walls were painted a nondescript shade of beige.

Callahan noticed Elizabeth Duncan looked tense as they walked down the hall. Several doors on the right had signs that read "Interview Room." Martinez led them to the second one.

Elizabeth Duncan froze at the door when she saw the room. *Oh, my God, I'm going to faint.* Callahan nudged her forward.

The room was bare except for a cheap metal table placed in the center of the room with chairs on opposite sides facing each other.

Elizabeth Duncan looked around and saw a video camera next to the ceiling. A large, framed mirror was on one wall.

"What is this?" she gasped.

"Have a seat, Mrs. Duncan," Martinez suggested, pulling out a chair.

"Am I under arrest?" she stammered.

Both men looked her square in the eyes. "That depends, Mrs. Duncan. Is there any reason why you should be under arrest?" Martinez asked

"Well, no," Elizabeth Duncan's voice quivered as she spoke.

Callahan took a chair in front of Elizabeth Duncan. He leaned forward, put both elbows on the table, and looked at Elizabeth Duncan. In a soft voice he asked, "Mrs. Duncan, what is the relationship between your husband and Roscoe Bertolli?"

"I don't know," her voice shook. "I've never heard my husband mention him. Who is he?"

Without answering her question, Callahan continued, "Okay, then, what is your relationship with Roscoe Bertolli?"

Elizabeth Duncan's face turned beet red. "I don't know Roscoe Bertolli!" she stammered.

"All right, then please tell us why you and Mr. Bertolli have been exchanging phone calls. Forty-seven calls to be exact."

Elizabeth Duncan's mouth opened, and she pulled her purse close to her chest as if it would give her comfort. She just stared at Callahan without answering.

"Mrs. Duncan, did you know that Roscoe Bertolli is dead? He

died on your husband's boat!"

Elizabeth Duncan swayed in her chair. Her eyes clouded as a teardrop slid down the side of her nose.

Shaking, she whispered, "I want to see my lawyer."

Chapter 31

After Elizabeth Duncan had left the Sheriff's office, Martinez and Callahan decided to go to lunch. They chose a Denny's restaurant just down the street from Martinez's office. It was twelve-thirty in the afternoon, and business was brisk. The air was filled with Spanish-speaking customers. The atmosphere was jovial, which was quite different from the interview room they had just left.

Martinez sipped on an unsweetened iced tea, and Callahan nursed a cup of hot coffee.

"That woman is guilty as hell," Callahan was saying, "but the way I see it, we have to get more evidence before we can indict."

"Yeah, I think so too. She sure was nervous, and when she asked for her lawyer, I figured she knew she was caught. Maybe we can get some forensics on the cause of the explosion when those kids you told me about bring the boat up. If your department needs some help, I'll be happy to lend a hand."

———————

The foursome met on Cap's boat just before noon to finish putting the drums in place to raise the hull. Since it was close to lunchtime, they decided to indulge in the delicious lunch Skye had prepared for them. Cap loved her lunches. He was usually a picky eater, but Skye had won his heart with her mouth-watering fare. He was positive her lunches couldn't have been any better if they had been prepared by a chef in a fancy restaurant. *That kid sure has a knack for cooking, especially for someone her age.*

His eyes moistened as he remembered the delicious meals his wife Nicole had prepared for him for thirty years before she died in a traffic accident four years ago. Skye's potato salad and coleslaw reminded him of Nicole's cooking. Since she had passed away, he had eaten a lot of bacon and eggs and bologna sandwiches.

Each found a spot on the shady side of the *Money* to have their lunch. Cap had rigged up a temporary makeshift awning to shade everyone from the sweltering heat.

Skye had packed a lunch large enough to feed an army. Ham and cheese, roast beef, coleslaw, potato salad, and chips, along with her special, homemade, double chocolate walnut brownies that she had made the night before. To chase it all down, she had included Coke, iced tea, and Gatorade.

She served everyone, and they ate until they were about to pop. Cap estimated it would take the rest of the day to put the remaining drums in place, and he figured that tomorrow they would be ready to lift the hull. Later this evening, he would have to find a pump large enough to empty the hull before it could be towed to a safe haven. Arrangements for a tow would also have to be made.

"Michael, would you mind finding a pump? I'll take care of the tow. I'll make arrangements with the *Sea Tow* if they're not too expensive. If they are, I'll find somebody else."

"Not a problem, Cap," Michael agreed and smiled. "By the way, I need to call Sonny Mitchell and find out where he thinks we should tow this thing. I know the police will want to look at it."

"If the police want to look at it," Cap scowled, "let them pay for everything."

"That's a good idea. I'll speak with Detective Callahan about it," Michael answered.

Cap groaned as he stood. *Getting old isn't any fun. In fact, it stinks.* He knew his aches and pains would get worse as he aged.

That was an unpleasant fact of life.. "Okay, guys, time to go back to work."

Skye stood and stretched out the kinks. CJ opened his eyes from a shallow slumber. Rising, he mumbled something unintelligible and slowly moved aft.

Cap had the third drum in the water and ready to go.

Skye donned her tank with CJ's assistance and slid into the water. CJ followed.

CJ opened the valves, slowly filling the drum with water. Moments later, CJ and Skye followed the drum to the bottom. The two divers made a great team. After the first two drums had been placed next to the hull, each diver sensed what to do next while waiting for the other to perform his or her task. They moved about their work effortlessly, and within forty-eight minutes, they were ready to return to the surface.

As the two divers reached the boat, Michael was seated in his Sea Craft, ready to stop for the day.

"Hey guys, I'm heading for the house," he called out. "Skye, if you would like, stop by for dinner. Cap is going to join us. I'll give Poppy a call too."

Skye looked over at the Sea Craft and gave a thumbs up.

Chapter 32

At thirty-five hundred feet, Flapper could see for miles. He had just passed Indian Key and was heading out over Florida Bay. Off in the distance, he saw four boats tied alongside each other, anchored at the site of the boat explosion. He had a twelve-mile-an-hour tailwind and was clipping along at breakneck speed. He would be at the site in no time flat. *What's going on down there? Maybe Skye is on one of the boats.* He loved having Skye as a friend.

Directly overhead, Flapper banked hard to the left. The maneuver did several things; it slowed him down, and he lost altitude. Forty seconds later, he landed on the *Money's* wheelhouse.

Skye and CJ were nowhere in sight.

Nobody seemed to notice Flapper's landing. He sat there in solitude, watching what was going on with all the boats. He noticed a different boat parked here today. It looked similar to Cap's boat, but it was painted yellow with black lettering on the side. Flapper didn't know how to read, but there were two words on each side. He wondered what they meant.

There were three men onboard the *Money*. He recognized Cap and Michael, but he had never seen the other man. Cap was manning the air compressor while the other two stood around talking with each other.

Twenty feet below the surface, Skye knelt on her knees. She was on the port side, and CJ was on the starboard side of the bow. They were forcing air into the drums to displace the water. It had to be a coordinated effort. Each drum needed to have the same buoyancy; otherwise, the hull wouldn't lift properly. Skye noticed the line attached to the drum had drawn tight. She looked over toward CJ to see how his drum was doing. A small cloud of silt began to rise from the bottom of the hull. She motioned to CJ to stop his air. *One more drum to go.* Skye breathed a sigh of relief. She was ready for this job to be over and done.

CJ swam around to join Skye. He reached down and lifted the drum several inches from where it rested. He then looked at Skye and gave her a big okay, circling his thumb and forefinger. Skye reciprocated with a big smile.

CJ motioned for her to follow him as he kicked off for the stern. Skye dragged the air hose as she followed him. He helped her connect her end of the hose and then went back to the bow to retrieve his. He motioned for Skye to surface. When Skye reached the boat, she heard a "Hello." She ripped her face mask off and looked around. *There he is in all his majesty,* she thought, smiling. Flapper stood atop the wheelhouse, holding his wings out in a welcoming fashion. That was as close as he could get to hugging her right now, which is exactly what he felt like doing.

"Hey, Flapper. It's so good to see you again."

Flapper lowered his wings and then took a seat. "What are you doing down there?" he asked.

"Raising the hull of the boat that exploded," Skye answered.

CJ broke through the surface and stroked over next to Skye. "We need to change tanks and talk about how to coordinate the raising of the *Titanic*," he joked.

Michael stepped aboard the *Gator Bait* and reached down for Skye's tank. She put her right foot onto the dive ladder and heaved herself onboard. CJ followed.

Cap had temporarily shut down the compressor and was looking up at Flapper. "That dadgum bird is back," he grumbled. "If he or that dolphin messes with me today, they'll be sorry," he continued. Still embarrassed by his fall into the bay the other day, he decided he had better stay away from the side of the boat.

The stranger stood at the rail onboard the *Money*, looking down at the teenagers, first at Skye and then at CJ. *They are awfully young to be undertaking such a big job,* he thought. He took a second look at the girl and decided she was extremely cute for someone her age. *Man, she'll be a knockout in a couple more years,* he decided. Michael looked down at the teens. "This is Captain Bill Wilson. He's the skipper of the *Sea Tow*."

Skye and CJ looked up and gave Wilson a wave.

"Glad to meet you," he smiled. "I've heard nothing but great things about the two of you from these guys," pointing to Michael and Cap. "Even the police department is raving about you. They said you are determined to find out what happened to the man in the hospital and the dead man under the debris in the hull. They told me they would have ruled it an accident and closed the case if you hadn't decided to play detective. I hear you're a regular little Nancy Drew, young lady," Wilson said with a smile.

"She sure is," CJ said, still holding his swim fins. Laughing, he added, "She bribes me into going along with her schemes with homemade chocolate walnut brownies. I guess I'm just a sucker for brownies." Taking a seat next to the center console, he addressed the group. "We need to discuss what kind of approach we're going to take raising the hull. I think if we're not careful we may screw this whole thing up."

"Yeah," Skye added, "it looks a little dicey."

Cap, grunting and groaning, worked his way aboard the *Gator Bait*. "Yep, I think you two are right. If you're not careful, the hull could flip. Then we'd be in big trouble."

Michael looked over at Captain Wilson. "Bill, you've had some experience at this. What do you recommend?"

Bill Wilson thought about the question for a moment as he leaned over the rail. "Well, each end of the hull has to come up at the same time. Otherwise, the lines might slide out from underneath. That's the real danger. The way I see it, there are four drums, and they all have to be filled exactly the same as buoyancy increases. If they're not, it'll get out of balance, and when that happens there's no way to stop it. You'll have one big mess on your hands."

Cap seemed to be studying the situation. "Even if we had four guys down there, it'd be impossible to know what the buoyancy is in each drum. We need to devise a way to fill all four drums at the same time and at the same rate."

"We could use a four-way split from a single hose and connect them to the drums," Bill suggested. "But if we did, you'd have to be able to shut each outgoing valve off at the same time."

CJ raised his hand as if he were in school. "I could be at one end and Skye at the other. When the hull comes off the bottom, we could shut the exit valves off manually as fast as we can."

Bill asked, "How long will it take you to swim from one drum to the other?"

CJ cocked his head. "I'm not sure, maybe ten or fifteen seconds."

"Well, son," Cap interjected, "go jump in the water, and let's find out. The sooner we get the hull up, the quicker we'll find out what really happened on the boat. Your dad said that Detective Callahan talked with the wife of the guy in the hospital yesterday, and he thinks she was involved."

Chapter 33

Nathaniel Brown looked down at his speedometer which showed he was going eighty-five. He glanced down the highway and in the rear-view mirror to make sure there were no state troopers racing to catch him.

The old Continental's ride is smooth even at this speed, Nate thought proudly. His grandfather had given the car to him as a graduation gift the day he graduated from the University of Florida. Along with the car, he also had included a ticket for a one-week cruise aboard Royal Caribbean's *Liberty of the Seas*.

He had looked up the ship on the Internet before he left home. He thought it was awesome, and he couldn't wait to begin the cruise. It originated and was leaving from Tampa, Florida, but he had missed the boarding date. He was making a beeline for Key West, the next stop on the ship's itinerary. He had to be there by the following morning.

The drive down Florida's Turnpike lulled him into a hypnotic stupor as his foot got heavier with each passing mile. North Miami came into view, and he passed Joe Robbie Stadium. He followed the road around the stadium and onto the turnpike extension. Its dead end was in Homestead. After paying the toll, he headed west toward the Florida Everglades.

Four and a half minutes later, he looked into his rear view mirror and saw flashing blue lights directly behind him. *Oh, crap!* Nate slowed, eventually pulling over on the shoulder of the road, coming to a halt.

The Florida State Trooper pulled in behind him and stopped. He sat there for a minute or so talking to someone on the radio. *Calling in my tag number*, Nate surmised. Nate kept his hands on the steering wheel like his grandfather had instructed. He didn't want to get accidentally shot because a skittish cop thought he was going for a gun.

The trooper finally got out of his car and slowly walked towards Nate's car. He remained in Nate's blind spot as a precautionary move. The officer's movements were trained, eyes moving about, taking a visual picture of his surroundings.

Midway to the car, the officer stopped, turned, and looked back at the oncoming traffic. Satisfied, he walked alongside the back of the Continental up to Nate's window.

Leaning forward, he moved his head next to Nate. "Young man, do you have any weapons in this car?" he questioned.

"No, sir, I don't," Nate stated.

"License, insurance, and registration, please," the trooper asked politely with a Southern drawl.

"They're in the glove box, officer," Nathan said as he motioned toward it.

"Go ahead."

Nathaniel leaned over, opened the box, and pulled out an envelope with all his paperwork. He sat back, riffled through the contents, and handed the papers to the trooper.

"Know how fast you were going, son?"

"No, sir."

"The speed limit here is seventy. I'd let you slide to eighty, but you were going eight-five. What's the hurry?"

Nate's voice began to quiver. "Well, sir, I'm going on a cruise tomorrow morning out of Key West; the Royal Caribbean *Liberty of the Seas.*"

"You keep speeding, and you might not make that cruise. "You hear?"

"Yes, sir. I'm sorry."

"You might wanna put some air in that back right tire, next time you stop."

"Yes, sir."

"Mind if I have a look in the trunk?"

Nate's grandfather had told him to always cooperate with the police, especially if you have nothing to hide.

"No, sir. Go ahead."

"Pop the trunk."

"Yes, sir."

Nate reached down and pressed the trunk button.

The trooper turned and walked back to the trunk, raised the lid, and moved some of Nate's suitcases. A moment later, Nate heard the trunk slam closed. Then the highway patrolman stepped away from the car.

"I'm gonna call ahead and tell my friends to keep a lookout for you," his voice rose slightly. "If they catch you speeding, you'll probably miss that cruise. Have a nice day, 'ya hear?"

"Thank you, sir." Nate took a deep breath and tried to relax. *That sure was a close call! Thank you, God.* With his part-time job, he couldn't afford a ticket, and he didn't want to have to ask his parents for the money. They had a way of not letting him forget that he was dependent upon them, at least until he started his new position as an underwater archaeologist with the Florida Department of State, Division of Resources.

The trooper got into his car, backed up a little, pulled out onto the highway, and began cruising down the road, looking for his next lawbreaker.

————————

CJ set his tank aside and dove into the water. In the past, he had snorkeled down to forty-five feet while spearfishing and had free-dived seventy-two feet with no problems. This would be a piece of cake at only twenty feet.

When he reached the first drum, he looked at his dive watch, waited until the big hand got to twelve, and then pretended to turn off the outgoing valve. Exactly nine seconds later, he was at the second drum and pretended to shut off the outgoing valve.

As he surfaced, he shouted out, "Nine seconds."

Cap looked over at Captain Wilson, who nodded his head in the affirmative.

With a smile on his face, Michael stood there, proud of his son. Free diving twenty feet was impossible for some people, and he knew CJ had gone a lot deeper in the past.

Skye's face lit up when she saw CJ. He smiled back at her.

CJ breast stroked over to the boat. "Let's meet here in the morning, and I'll have the four-way valve ready to go."

The closer Nate got to the Keys, the more he thought about the seismic readings he had discovered. He didn't know why, but he had brought along a copy of all the coordinates. The epicenter was exactly at Indian Key. Why anybody would be using explosives in the middle of the night on a deserted island baffled him. For some reason, his mind just couldn't shake the idea.

Key Largo was in his rear-view mirror, and Islamorada loomed ahead. At Mile Marker 86.6 he saw a sign on the right that said Monroe County Sheriff's Sub Station. Seeing the sign, Nate spun the wheel to the right and pulled into the parking lot. He had waited long enough. He had to tell somebody.

As Nate pushed open the glass doors into the building, Detective Sergeant Callahan left his office and stopped at the front counter.

I hope they don't think I'm nuts. Gathering his courage, Nate walked over to the counter and introduced himself to the officer.

"Good afternoon," Nate said, looking at Callahan. "I'd like to speak to an officer."

"What can I do for you, son?" Callahan questioned, sizing up the young man who seemed extremely nervous.

"My name is Nate, uh, Nathaniel Brown, sir. I just graduated from the University of Florida with a degree in archaeology. I've been working part-time at the Seismic Center at the Disney Wilderness Preserve." Nate pulled out the copies of the seismic coordinates and handed them to Callahan.

Callahan's impatience became apparent. "So, what does all this have to do with the Sheriff's office, Nate?" He questioned.

"Well," Nate continued, "somebody's been using dynamite in the middle of the night on Indian Key. I thought I should tell someone. It's making pretty deep tremors underground, all the way up the state."

Chapter 34

This morning's weather is a little unusual, Cap thought, as he wrinkled his already wrinkled brow. At seventy years old and being in the sun and on the water for the past fifty years, he was the epitome of what the locals called an "old salt."

A thirty-two-knot wind blowing from the north raised white caps over two feet high across Florida Bay. Barometric pressure had steadily dropped during the night, and the weather bureau was now saying that a small tropical depression was forming. "Hope it don't get any worse," Cap mumbled.

It was hurricane season, and anything could happen. The *Money* was the first boat to anchor at the site. Cap's anchor was holding fast as he stood in the wheelhouse drinking his sixth cup of coffee of the morning. It took at least eight cups for him to wake completely up and feel human. He waited for the rest of the boats to arrive. Radio traffic had been light, probably because of the weather, and few boats were on the water. Visibility was diminishing. He wondered if there would be any diving today.

Cap had spent most of the prior evening working on fabricating the four-way split for the air hoses. He had to solder several pieces together, and he wasn't sure if the splices could hold up to the air pressure.

Talking to himself, Cap said, "I suppose I'll find out soon enough," hoping they would be okay. "Those kids want to get that hull off the bottom, and I'm going to do everything I can to help them." Cap really liked both of them. He felt sort of like a second grandfather to them.

"*Money,* this is *Gator Bait*; over." Cap's VHS radio crackled. The radio startled Cap. "Go ahead *Gator Bait.*"

CJ's transmission was loud and clear. "How's the weather out there?" he asked.

"Not too good."

"Do you think we should wait another day?"

"I don't know. I hope it'll just be some high wind. We can give it a try if you're up for it. It's up to y'all."

CJ looked over at Skye and shrugged his shoulders. "What the heck," she said. "Let's give it a try."

"Okay, Cap. We're on our way out. Is the *Sea Tow* there?"

"Wilson is on his way," Cap replied.

———————————

Detective Sergeant Callahan drove his squad car south on the Overseas Highway. His vehicle occasionally shook from unexpected gusts of wind. Before he left the station, the weather announcer said that the winds were at thirty miles an hour. *It'll be worse on the bridges,* he thought. Dark skies to the north created an ominous and surreal atmosphere surrounding the highway. He briefly shivered in the ninety-three-degree heat.

As he left Upper Matecumbe Key at Mile Marker 80, he looked over to his left and saw Indian Key. It was a lonely speck of an island, forgotten long ago.

He had spent some time last night thinking about what the kid, Nate, had said. *It's just a stone's throw from the highway. I need to check it out and find out what is over there. I'll take care of it tomorrow.*

Deciding to wait another day to investigate the island, he decided tomorrow would be a better time because he had too much to do today.

———————

Captain Wilson pulled the *Sea Tow* up alongside the *Money*, threw his engine in reverse, and stopped expertly next to Cap's boat.

"Think your anchor will hold us both?" Wilson shouted above the wind.

Cap looked down, nodded his head, and then stepped back into the wheelhouse. "Let him tie his own boat up," he grumbled. "I'm too old to be catering to those young whippersnappers."

Minutes later, after tying his boat off, Captain Wilson stood in the wheelhouse with Cap. "Got any more coffee?" he asked politely.

"I always have coffee," Cap answered. "On a cold night, it's better than a good woman, at least from what I can remember."

"Well, I don't know about that, but if you say so. I'm sure you're more experienced than I am."

Wilson, a tall, handsome man, with sun-bleached hair and green eyes had a kind manner. Still unmarried at thirty-one, he was constantly looking for Ms. Right in his spare time. His divorced and re-married brothers kept teasing him about being single. But he had decided several years ago that when he married, it would be to a woman he wouldn't mind waking up to for the rest of his life. His parents had been married for more than fifty years and still doted on each other.

They heard the sound of a motorboat. Cap stuck his head out of the door. CJ was roaring up from the distance.

"Here they come," Cap sighed. "Guess we'd better see if the four-way split will work. C'mon, let's get this over with."

Captain Wilson stepped out from the wheelhouse and threw the remainder of his coffee out into the wind. *Taste like crap anyway,* he thought, making a face. *How does he drink it?*

Cap thought the wind had increased, but he wasn't sure. He looked down into the water and wasn't happy at what he saw.

Visibility appeared to be getting worse. He couldn't see the bottom.

CJ and Skye pulled up alongside the *Money*.

"You'll have to anchor off a bit," Cap shouted. "My anchor wouldn't hold everybody."

CJ heard Cap and moved his boat a little forward of the *Money*.

At CJ's nod, Skye threw the anchor out and waited for it to take hold. She gave CJ a thumbs up and slipped the anchor line around the bow cleat. She let the wind move the boat into position and then slowly eased the line out, little by little until the *Gator Bait* was just a few feet from the *Money*. They could jump from one boat to the other. Satisfied, CJ shut his engine down.

Skye grabbed her dive gear, wet suit, swim fins, and mask and moved to the stern.

CJ grabbed his gear and followed. "Man, I hope this wind doesn't get any stronger," he yelled to Skye.

She nodded her head in agreement. Her hair was blowing wildly. Most of her ponytail had come loose, and though the temperature was already over ninety degrees, the wind caused her to shiver a little.

Cap met them up at the bow. He reached down, took Skye's hand, and pulled her aboard. CJ followed.

The wind blew harder. It was much stronger than they had expected. Bracing against the force of the wind, they had to bend low to keep from being blown overboard.

Jeez, are we going to be able to do this? CJ wondered. He reached over and took Skye's hand.

It won't be this rough down at the hull, she thought. She wanted to get this project over with so she and CJ could investigate Indian Key.

The wheelhouse became their refuge. CJ slammed the door behind him. The wheelhouse was warm, and it shielded them from the elements. The smell of fresh coffee flooded the small space. CJ's nostrils flared with the rich aroma, but he didn't know if he should take the time to drink a cup now. He and Skye had to get down in the water in case the impending tropical depression worsened.

They each threw their gear in a corner and just stood there, trying to get their bearings. The boat was rocking back and forth.

"Cap, do you think we're going to be able to do this?" CJ asked.

Skye held on to the wheel as she acclimated herself to the claustrophobic surroundings.

Cap reached over for a mug, filled it with black coffee, and handed it to CJ. The warmth of the dark brew in the cup was much better than the taste. Cap certainly would never be known for his java.

"It's up to you guys. If you don't think you can do it today, we'll wait until tomorrow."

CJ thought about Cap's statement for a moment. "The longer that thing stays in the water, the less chance of evidence the forensics people will be able to find. Let's do it."

Chapter 35

"Y'all just remember that the air will be going into all four drums at the same time," Cap said. "That means there'll be equal buoyancy in all four drums. Theoretically, the hull should float up from the bottom evenly."

Arriving just after the *Sea Tow*, Michael had concerns about the strong wind and CJ and Skye getting into the water. He knew it had turned into a mystery that the kids wanted to solve, but he wondered if they should postpone the dive until the weather improved.

Glancing over at the teens, he asked, "Are you sure you don't want to wait a couple of days until this weather has passed?"

"No!" They both shouted at the same time. Then more calmly, CJ said, "Dad, it won't take long, and Skye and I both will be careful. We'll be back on the boat before you know it."

Michael still had his doubts, but he told them to go ahead and be cautious.

Skye spat into her face mask as Cap continued with his instructions. He wanted to make sure they understood, but he droned on and on. She spread the spit around in the mask, then reached down into the water and rinsed it out. Her patience had run out. All she wanted to do was get into the water and get the hull to the surface. She placed the mask on her face and slid into the water.

Knowing he was as ready as he would ever be, CJ followed Skye into the water. Visibility was a little better than he had anticipated.

Probably twenty feet at best, CJ estimated. He could barely see Skye. She was just a dark image slowly moving. As he reached the drum, CJ made two strong tugs on the hose and heard air rushing into the drum, making a gurgling sound. He waited in anticipation, not knowing how the drums were going to react.

CJ placed his hand next to the outgoing valve. He felt water rushing from the drum. *Looks like it's working*, CJ decided, breathing a sigh of relief.

Skye knelt on the bottom, watching for the drum to break loose. *A watched pot never boils*, she thought. Poppy had said that many times. She smiled thinking of Poppy. She wished he could be here to see them bring up the hull of the boat, but he hadn't felt well for the past couple of days. "Summer cold," he had told her with his eyes watering and his nose running.

All of a sudden Skye saw movement. "There!" she yelled into her mouthpiece.

Slowly, the drum began to break free as sediment clouded around it. Skye made a mad dash for the opposite drum. She had to hurry and shut the other valve off. Just as she reached the drum, it too had broken free from the bottom and begun to rise.

CJ followed the hull as it rose to the surface. Seconds later, it broke free of the water. He looked toward the bow and saw Skye's head next to the drum. "We did it!" he yelled. She smiled at him through her face mask.

A quick survey showed the hull was barely two inches out of the water.

Captain Bill Wilson was moving the *Sea Tow* toward the hull. He gently eased the boat next to the hull, jumped to the stern, grabbed a hose, and threw it into the hull. Within seconds, he had the auxiliary water pump running. Next, he reached over, grabbed a drum, and tied a line to it, securing it with a fast-release knot, just in case he had an emergency. He didn't want the hull dragging him underwater if the drum failed.

Skye joined CJ next to the *Sea Tow* and waited. A thirty-five-knot wind still blew from the north and occasionally blew white cap foam onto their face masks. "The wind is getting stronger," she shouted. The storm must be getting closer. Lightning flashed far in the distance. They knew they had to get out of the water soon.

They watched as the hull gradually gained height in the water. The drums were no longer of any use. They floated freely alongside the hull.

The two swam over to the *Sea Tow* next to where Captain Wilson stood. He looked down at the two divers. "Great job, you two! I think we're past the critical point. I'd appreciate it if you'd give me a hand. We'll hook a line to the bow, and then I'll tow her into the Coast Guard Station."

CJ looked at Skye. "Go ahead and get in the boat with Cap and Dad," he urged. "I'll take care of this," he smiled and began moving forward. He saw the lightning flash again and knew he had to finish up and get out of the water. Water and lightning spelled danger.

"They're going to blame this whole damn thing on me," Elizabeth Duncan screamed at her attorney, Rafael Diaz.

"Elizabeth, now don't go getting yourself all worked up. They don't have any evidence, at least none of which we are aware." At that moment, he wondered if she had indeed hired this Bertolli character to kill her husband. *I wouldn't put it past her.* He wanted to ask her, but a lawyer is never supposed to ask his clients if they are guilty.

"How in the world am I gonna explain all the phone calls? The only excuse I can come up with is that we were lovers. And, who in the world is going to believe that? Me, sleeping with that ugly troll! For God's sake, no jury will believe that!"

"Look, Elizabeth," Rafael appeased. "You're making a mountain out of a molehill. This will never come to an indictment. I guarantee it." *She must be guilty if she is trying to justify the calls. She just admitted they weren't lovers.* Rafael wasn't the most honest of lawyers, and that's probably why she chose him. But there was no way he would ever get involved with killing someone. Elizabeth Duncan sank into her chair, and tears poured from her eyes.

––––––––––––

CJ got the tow line attached to the bow cleat and then moved out of the way as the line took on tension.

A powerful nudge to his back startled him. "What the heck?" he mumbled as he turned and saw Squeaky staring into his face mask. CJ reached over and patted him on the head. "What are you doing here, buddy?" CJ asked, knowing the dolphin wouldn't understand him. *I'd better get Skye*, he thought.

CJ reached up and took hold of Squeaky's dorsal fin and then pointed toward the *Money*.

Squeaky seemed to understand and began pulling CJ through the water toward the boat. *This is a lot of fun.* CJ smiled, not realizing that Squeaky had been watching from a distance. He sensed that CJ would be in danger if he didn't get back on the boat. He had seen two sharks close by, stirred up by the impending weather heading their way.

As they approached the *Money*, Squeaky began slapping his tail atop the water, squeaking as loud as he could, and making as much noise as he could.

Skye stood in the wheelhouse talking with Cap when she heard the ruckus. She stepped out of the wheelhouse and saw Squeaky pulling CJ through the water. A big grin crossed her face, and she began to laugh.

"Boy, you two make a nice couple," Skye laughed harder.

Cap stepped through the door to find out what was happening.

CJ let go of Squeaky as they reached the boat.

"To what do I owe this pleasure?" Skye asked Squeaky.

Squeaky shook his head up and down as if acknowledging her greeting, and then he responded, "I saw some bad sharks close by, and I wanted CJ to get back on the boat before they decided to make a meal out of him like that one tried to do the other day."

Skye gasped. "Oh my gosh! Thank you so much, Squeaky, for everything you've done for us! I would die if anything happened to CJ." Telling Squeaky in thought how she felt about CJ made her feel better, and CJ would never know her thoughts to the dolphin.

"You like him a lot, don't you?"

Smiling, but changing the subject, she said in thought, "How are you and your friends doing?"

"Everybody is good," Squeaky responded. "I see you got the boat up."

"Yeah, and it was a huge job, much harder than we had anticipated. I sure wish you'd been here to help."

"Not me. I'm not mechanical," Squeaky responded.. "Oh, by the way, those bad men are still moving stuff off the island."

"Well, now that we've got the boat up, and as soon as the weather clears, we'll take a run out to the island to see what's happening over there."

Squeaky knew that warning her again not to go would not help. She was like a girl detective, and she would not stop until she solved the mystery. He would just have to stay close and watch out for her when she and CJ went over there.

Chapter 36

Captain Wilson finally saw the lights at the Coast Guard Station in Islamorada just after nine o'clock that evening. He had more trouble than he had bargained for with a strong wind a good part of the way. His boat has rocked and swayed for over half of the trip. He was afraid he would lose the boat's hull and himself with it. *What a bumpy ride. I don't want to do that again.*

Finally, sea breezes had dropped down to under twenty knots, which had eased the stress on the tow lines, enabling him to make it safely with his boat and the burnt-out hull intact. *Sea Tow*'s water pumps worked continuously throughout the voyage, and by the time it arrived at the Coast Guard Station, the boat hull was riding three feet out of the water.

The captain called the Coast Guard station on his VHS for assistance in mooring the hull. As he slowly approached, two young seamen ran out of their barracks and down to the dock. He carefully eased the boat next to the dock where the two men waited. Ten minutes later, the boat was secure. Wilson spent the rest of the night alongside the dock, pumping out the remainder of the water.

———

At eight o'clock in the morning, the forensics team arrived. Several dump trucks and a lightweight crane went through the gate.

Three men got out of a cargo van and began suiting up for the job ahead. They put on white coveralls over their regular work clothes, followed by rubber gloves that covered the ends of their sleeves. They were all professionals and wanted to know what had happened to cause a man to be in the hospital in critical condition and another to be dead.

Captain Wilson watched in fascination as the men went about their business. First, they stood on the dock surveying the situation, seemingly deciding how to go about the collection of evidence.

The hull was full of debris. Whatever had not burned had fallen into the bilge, leaving two-thirds of the boat filled with junk. Electrical wire lay everywhere. A refrigerator, ice makers, mattress springs, anything metal, and whatever wouldn't burn lay in the lower part of the boat.

One team member climbed aboard the boat and then motioned to the driver of the crane to move forward. *Going through all this is going to take forever* went through his mind, and he was not looking forward to the job.

The remainder of the team split up. One went to the bow while the others went to the stern. They climbed aboard and began meticulously digging through the wreckage, moving trash aside, and making a path to their destination.

The crane moved to the side of the dock and stopped, and the driver lowered the hook down to the man standing amidships. He wrapped a strap around the refrigerator and gave the operator a thumbs up. The first dump truck moved into position, ready to receive the first of the load.

An hour passed before the majority of the sizable items were loaded onto the trucks and readied to be sent to the lab.

Occasionally, a team member would reach down, study an object, and place it into a bag. They carried all sizes of bags, from quart-size containers to garbage bags. Once filled, each bag was carefully placed at the side of the dock and would be collected later.

The *Sea Tow* captain knew the pump hose was starving for water when it began shaking, indicating the bilge was dry. He reached down and shut off the engine. "Well, that's it for me," he said aloud as if someone was there just to hear him. He walked aft, untied his stern line, and walked forward, repeating the process. Moments later, with his engine purring, he pushed off from the dock, waving goodbye to the forensic team. He was exhausted. It had been an exceedingly long night.

As his boat picked up speed, he thought about the teens, CJ and Skye. *Those kids sure had spunk to do what they did.*

While they were down preparing the hull to be brought to the surface, Cap had told him that CJ had been dragged away from the sunken boat by a large shark. A dolphin appeared and fought the aggressive fish until it let go of the boy. CJ could have been killed. Thanks to the dolphin, he had only suffered a bite on his foot that earned him a visit to the emergency room and twelve stitches. It sure took a lot of courage for both of them to go back down again. From what Cap had told him, he had a strong feeling that Skye was the adventurous one and CJ would do anything she asked. *If I were his age, I would probably do anything for a girl that looked like Skye too. Ah, young love.*

———————

CJ drove his Volkswagen through the gate at the Coast Guard Station in Islamorada. Skye sat beside him drinking a small vanilla Coke from a transparent plastic container they had bought at a local deli. The air was crisp and fresh, unlike the day before had been.

As CJ pulled into a vacant parking space, the crane operator was securing its boom as the two dump trucks, diesel engines clanging and clattering, were making one heck of a noise.

The harsh clamor annoyed Skye to the point that she had to walk away from the deafening racket. She looked around the closest dump truck and spotted the *Sea Tow* leaving the little harbor. She had hoped she would be able to thank Captain Wilson for all his help. *Another time*, she thought.

CJ walked directly to the man standing in the middle of the boat, looking like he was a young man on a mission.

"Hey, I'm the guy that got this thing floating!" he shouted with authority.

The man standing in the center looked over at CJ with a questioning look.

"How can I help you?"

"I was wondering if you could tell me what blew this thing up."

"Can't say yet. It might take several days to figure it out. Who did you say you are again?"

CJ detected a little sarcasm in the man's voice but responded firmly, "We're interested because we've been working with Detective Callahan."

"Well, son, you'll just have to wait and talk to the detective. He'll get our report. This is a crime scene, so you'd better step back. We can't let you contaminate the evidence."

Skye stood beside CJ, gently pulling on his arm. She was young, but she knew when to withdraw.

CJ looked down at Skye, shook his head in resignation, turned, and began walking with her toward his car.

"Everybody thinks we're kids. Seventeen is almost an adult, and you and I did something that no one else had even thought of doing. Heck, we're entitled to be involved." CJ decided he would contact the detective. *I am going to find out one way or another, what happened on that boat. After all Skye and I have gone through and risked, we have a right to know.*

Chapter 37

Skye lay by the pool at Poppy's house. She had forgotten her beach towel, and the plastic straps of the chaise lounge had begun cutting into her back and legs. Her Tommy Hilfiger swimsuit barely covered her trim figure. *It must be shrinking*, she thought. Skye had no idea how much her body had changed since last summer. Of course, unknown to her, CJ had certainly noticed.

Drenched with sweat from the mid-morning sun didn't improve her disposition much either. Two days had passed since she and CJ had gone to the Coast Guard Station to try and find out what had caused the explosion. There was still no word from Detective Callahan, and on top of the sweltering heat, she was also irritated that they still knew nothing. *What's taking them so long? Maybe the saltwater destroyed all the evidence. Maybe CJ and I were wrong, and there was no foul play.* She couldn't stand waiting to find out.

Getting up from the chaise, Skye adjusted her skimpy bikini, walked to the side of the pool, and dove in head first. Holding her breath, she swam underwater until she touched the end of the pool, flipped under, and kicked off with her feet heading for the other end.

Too much chlorine, she thought as her eyes began to sting. Her hand touched the side of the pool, and she kicked for the surface, having no idea what awaited her. As her head broke the surface, she took in a large gasp of air, opened her eyes, and to her horror she saw the ugliest looking prehistoric creature she had ever seen.

Flapper's long twisted beak was just inches away from Skye's face. Startled, she let out a loud scream. Flapper was taken aback by her shriek. He was more startled than Skye.

"Oh, my gosh, Flapper!" Skye shouted, "Don't ever do that to me again! You scared the wits out of me."

Momentarily, Flapper regained his composure. "I'm so sorry, Skye. I didn't mean to scare you."

"Well, you certainly did."

Skye reached up with both arms and rested her elbows on the edge of the pool, still trying to catch her breath.

Flapper waddled closer. "My friends told me you got the boat up from the bottom of the bay. What are you going to do now?"

Finally, calm and a little ashamed for yelling at her friend, Skye cocked her head sideways and gave Flapper a little smile. "It's good to see you, my friend. How's your wing?"

"Good as new, thanks," he said a little stiffly. His feelings were still hurt, and it showed in his response.

Still sorry for her outburst, Skye answered Flapper's question. "Yeah, we got the hull up. We're still waiting on the forensic report. It's taking forever to find out anything."

Finally placated, Flapper gave Skye the information he had come to tell her. "I ran into that dolphin you call Squeaky the other day. He said bad people are taking stuff from Indian Key at night and moving it ashore."

Skye perked up as Flapper described what was happening, even though Squeaky had already told her about it.

"They're loading boxes into vans and then driving north," he continued, "and maybe you should have the Marine Patrol check it out."

Skye reached over and fondly rubbed Flapper's head. "Yeah, Squeaky mentioned it to me, and CJ and I talked about it. I think maybe one night we'll swim over and check it out."

"No, don't do that! My senses tell me there's danger there. You could get into bad trouble. Please tell me you won't go." Flapper couldn't stand the thought of something happening to Skye or her friend CJ. Skye was the first human friend he had ever had, and he wanted to keep her in his life.

Skye looked deep into the concerned pelican's eyes. "We'll be okay, Flapper, I promise. Don't worry."

—————————

When he got the call, Detective Callahan had just passed Plantation Yacht Harbor at Mile Marker 87 on his way to the Tavernier Dive Shop to pick up some dive tanks he'd dropped off to have refilled.

"Yeah," he answered, a little annoyed at the interruption while he was driving.

"Good morning detective. It's Martinez."

No longer irritated by the call, he replied, "Hey, Martinez, thanks for calling." Callahan closed his window so he could hear what Martinez was saying. "Did you get the results?" he asked.

"As a matter of fact, yes, we did, and Elizabeth Duncan is in big trouble. Traces of ammonium nitrate were found on some of the engine parts, as well as bits of blasting caps."

Callahan smiled, "That great news. What's next?"

"My guys found a bartender at the Skyway Inn over on 36th Street. He identified Mrs. Duncan and confirmed that she was there with Bertolli on several occasions. The bartender didn't think there was anything romantic between them. He said it just looked like conversation to him. He said the guy was too ugly for a woman that looked like Mrs. Duncan."

"There's our connection," Callahan replied.

"I'm bringing her in for more questioning. You want to be here?"

"Nah, that's okay. Y'all can handle it better than I can. I'm just a small-time conch cop."

Smiling at Callahan's description of himself, Martinez said, "Whatever you say. Take it easy." He hung up the phone.

Michael got a call from Sonny Mitchell just past one in the afternoon. He had just entered the house when the phone rang. Maria had treated him to lunch at the famous Chesapeake Bay Seafood House at the north end of Upper Matecumbe Key. Michael ran for the phone and snatched it up on its last ring.

"Hello," he said hastily.

"It's me, Michael," Sonny said. "What were you doing? You sound out of breath."

"Hey, buddy. Maria and I just walked in from lunch," Michael said as he smiled. He was always glad to hear from his friend. "What's cooking your way?"

"I just received the forensic report. Ammonium nitrate and pieces of blasting caps were found on the hull."

"The kids were right," Michael answered. "They'll be glad to hear that. CJ's been bugging Detective Callahan every day about it."

"When are you guys coming up for a cookout?" Sonny asked. "I've missed seeing Maria and the kid. Tell him he can bring that little cutie with him," he laughed.

Michael had told Sonny that he thought CJ had noticed how much Skye had changed since last summer. It was hard for Michael to admit that his son was becoming a man.

Michael thought, to himself, *Sonny will never change.* Responding to Sonny's invitation he said, "Chubby, we all want to see you too, but it's been pretty hectic around here lately. Let me get back with you on a date, okay?"

"Anytime, old friend," Sonny answered and hung up.

"Skye, you are crazy," CJ groaned. "We're gonna get into trouble for sure." *Not again, please, not again*, he thought.

"Why, CJ?" Sky asked as they sat at a round table next to the pool. "We'll be fine. If there's a hint of trouble, we'll just high-tail it out of there, okay?"

CJ scooted his chair over a few feet to take advantage of the shade from the umbrella and took another swig of his Coke. Sighing, he finally said, "All right, we'll go tonight." *Why can't I say no to Skye once in a while? It's been that way since the first summer she came to stay with her Poppy.*

CJ smiled slightly as he remembered being put on restriction for a week when Skye had talked him into fishing off the Seven Mile Bridge after dark. His parents had freaked out when he had told them where he and Skye had been. He knew he would probably be put on restriction for the rest of his life if they found out that he and Skye swam over to Indian Key alone at night.

"What time?" asked Skye, excited at the thought of another adventure. For a moment, she shivered, briefly wondering if it would be safe for them. Deciding the risk would be worth it, she pushed her fear aside.

Chapter 38

CJ drove his Volkswagen south, just under the speed limit on the Overseas Highway. Skye sat beside him, and for a change she was silent. CJ didn't have much to say either.

Man, it sure is dark, she thought, looking out the window. For the second time since they had begun the drive, she felt a shiver of fear go up her spine and down her arms. A light warm southerly breeze blew in through her window.

Distracting herself from what they might be facing on Indian Key, Skye turned her thoughts to the history of the Overseas Highway. She loved the past and was like a sponge when her grandfather talked to her about the history of the Keys.

Poppy had told her that railroad tracks had been there before the road had been built. Most of the bridges they crossed had been built for trains, not cars.

Henry Flagler, for whom Flagler College in St. Augustine had been named, had spent his fortune building the Overseas Railroad. Whether it was fate or just misfortune, eventually the elements had won the battle.

The railroad finally did make it to Key West, only to be short-lived. Two major hurricanes were the thieves.

Flagler began to rebuild after the Okeechobee Hurricane of 1928, but couldn't withstand the devastation of the Labor Day Hurricane of 1935, which destroyed the Florida East Coast Railroad and killed five hundred people.

Poppy had told her that two hundred of those killed had lived in Islamorada, which had been almost completely destroyed.

Later, the Florida Keys became the playground for the rich and famous, and the automobile became the first choice for travel.

Road construction began in 1936 from Homestead to Key West. Cross ties were removed and replaced with concrete. Ultimately, it became the Overseas Highway and was finished in 1942.

After completion, along the highway north and south, it had been common for cars to pull off to the side of the road for sightseeing, picnicking, swimming, or plain old partying. There were four lanes. Two were paved, and two were limestone ruts on each side of the road.

Forcing her thoughts back to the present, she noticed that the Volkswagen had just passed over the first bridge leaving Upper Matecumbe Key going south. During the day, if one looked to the left one would see Indian Key, but on a moonless night, it was impossible to see.

Just past the third bridge CJ slowed, checked his rearview mirror, and made a U-turn. He pulled over and parked his VW Thing in the limestone ruts at Mile Marker 78. Twenty feet from where they sat was a deep channel alongside the road. Indian Key Anchorage lay just beyond the channel. Two hundred yards from shore was Indian Key.

Heat lightning flashed periodically to the southeast and occasionally left a faint outline of the tiny island they were to visit.

As CJ looked out toward the empty darkness, he felt a shiver run up his back, making the hairs on his arms stand up. He was extremely uncomfortable with the uncertainty they would soon face, but there was no way he would say that to Skye. *She'll think I'm a wimp, and that's the last thing I want her to think of me.*

Skye reached over and handed CJ a spray can containing mosquito repellant. "Here take this," she offered. "I know we'll need it."

"Thanks," he whispered.

"Why are you whispering? There's nobody around."

"I don't know," CJ whispered again. "It just seems right to whisper," he laughed softly. His laugh sounded a little shaky to him. He hoped that Skye couldn't hear the fear in his voice.

They had agreed before leaving home that evening that they would wear regular clothing with long-sleeved shirts instead of swimsuits. The channel was only about sixty feet wide, so swim fins, masks, and snorkels would be of no use. Sneakers were the order of the day. Once they were past the deep channel, the water was shallow enough for them to wade to Indian Key.

CJ got out of the car first, and Skye followed. He walked to the front of the car, opened the trunk, and removed a dive sack. It contained a hunting knife, two waterproof flashlights, and a liter bottle of water. He walked around to where Skye stood and began spraying her with the mosquito repellent.

"This stinks," Skye complained.

"You ought to be happy we have it." CJ smiled at her in the darkness.

Taking the can from CJ, Skye gave him his blast of repellant. Wrinkling his nose, he decided, *She's right. It does stink. Phew.*

Skye put the can in the bag, pulled the drawstring, and slung it over her shoulder.

"Let's go," she said and began walking toward the channel. "Be careful, there's a sharp drop-off ahead," she warned.

They passed a mangrove tree leaning out over the water. Mosquitoes began buzzing around their heads. *The repellant seems to be working,* CJ thought with relief. He remembered not too long ago when he and Skye had been out in his boat, the mosquitoes had been eating him alive until she had taken pity and sprayed him with insect repellent.

Skye took out her flashlight and examined the water's edge. Two feet out was a ledge, and then beyond the water it dropped off thirty feet. A mild current flowed along the ledge. She cautiously stepped out into the water with both feet, turned off her flashlight, stood there for a bit, and then bent her knees and fell forward. Hitting the surface, she managed to keep her head above water.

177

CJ wasn't as graceful. He stepped forward off the ledge and dropped straight down. A moment later he surfaced, spewing saltwater.

Eighty-seven degrees is comfortable, CJ decided. He had checked online that afternoon on NOAA's website for local water temperatures. He knew the water was unusually warm for this time of year and was thankful for that because he and Skye would be wet for quite a while. Trying not to think about what might lie ahead, he concentrated on his strokes.

Skye found it awkward swimming with clothes and sneakers. It took a lot more effort to stay afloat than it did in bathing suits. Wet sneakers were heavy, creating a lot more resistance, and with each breaststroke she took, her forward progress was just inches. It would take longer to cross the channel than she had anticipated.

CJ followed closely beside Skye. As he swam, tiny sea animals created a fluorescent light that sparkled all around them. The blackness surrounding them amplified the beautiful green color.

"You okay?" CJ asked, looking over at Skye. He could barely see her, and she wasn't more than three feet away.

"Yeah, I'm good. I just didn't think it would be this hard."

"Me either."

Swimming for several more minutes, Skye finally touched the bottom. After several more strokes, she stopped. She felt seaweed in her hands. *About three feet to go*, she thought. She put her feet down into the muck and stood.

CJ stumbled slightly after getting a foothold and then stood. They were in luck. The tide was going out, and the depth of the water would be much shallower, making wading easier.

While Skye stood in two and a half feet of water, she felt her feet slowly sinking deeper and deeper into the slimy mud. She was standing in rotting seaweed and algae. Taking steps became almost impossible. Each time she raised her foot, suction gripped it. She had to lean forward, and with significant effort she jerked her foot out of the hole and stumbled frontward, almost losing her balance. For a moment, she wondered if she would gradually disappear into the yucky mess. Shivering, she made herself move.

CJ realized what was happening right away. He reached over and took Skye's hand. Together, they used each other's hands to balance themselves. The secret, they soon discovered, was not to stay in one spot too long; otherwise, they would sink deeper.

Slowly, they made their way toward the island. Had there been an observer on the road, he would have seen two kids stumbling, walking like robots, hand in hand, clinging to each other for balance, and occasionally falling facedown into the water.

Twenty minutes passed, and their progress had been about fifty yards. Both of them were out of breath from exertion, and fatigue was taking over.

"Let's rest for a minute," Skye suggested, and CJ nodded his head. She sat down in the water, stretched out in a prone position on her back, and tried to relax. The mud felt soft and yucky on her body as she sunk down a few inches. Again, she felt a shiver of fear. Not so much about the muck they were trying to walk in, but what they might have to face when they made it to the island. She kept thinking about what Squeaky and Flapper had told her. *Could I have put both CJ and me in danger by asking him to come with me to this island?*

Pushing aside the thoughts of peril, she heard CJ say, "This is a great idea," as he lay down in the water next to her.

Thank goodness the water is warm, CJ thought. *Trying to walk in the muck is no fun, but it could be worse.* Even with the warm water temperature, he involuntarily shivered. He tried to clear his mind, but it didn't work. *I'm a little scared,* he admitted to himself. *Okay, okay, I'm a lot scared.*

Again, he tried to force himself to remain calm. He began to relax, and thoughts of the beautiful girl beside him filled his mind. *Will I ever have the courage to tell her how I feel? No, probably not. Most likely she will laugh at me.* He figured she wasn't interested in being anything but friends with him. That thought bothered him.

He wondered again if her parents were going to allow her to date

179

when she started the new school year. *I sure hope not. She is almost sixteen, and her parents told her she could date when she turned sixteen.* He felt sure she would want to go out with guys in her class. His heart ached to think that she might even have a boyfriend by next summer if she didn't already have one. *Heck, she might not even come back to Poppy's next year, especially if she is involved with another guy,* he thought sadly.

Trying not the think about what might happen between him and Skye, he again wondered what they might find on Indian Key. Rumors had circulated for years that ghosts of Indians and those they had killed inhabited the island. Neither he nor any of his friends had ever had the guts to find out. Heck, the only reason he was here now was for Skye. *She has enough guts for both of us.* Of course, he had no idea that Skye was afraid too.

As they lay in the warm salty water, they watched an occasional car move up and down the highway. *It's Saturday night. I wonder if any of those people are driving drunk*, thought Skye. Drinking and driving was a big problem in the Keys. God help the locals if there is an accident on a bridge. Traffic could be tied up for hours.

Once, it was backed up for over thirty hours when a semi-truck collided with a camper. Turned out the driver of the camper had a blood alcohol of 2.8. Thank goodness no one had been killed, but it sure made a mess on the highway.

Skye was so glad that CJ didn't drink. Some of his friends from high school thought it was cool to get loaded on the weekends, but CJ never went out with them. *When CJ isn't earning money on a fishing charter, he spends almost all of his summer with me,* Skye suddenly realizes. She was always dragging him from one adventure to another. He never had time to spend with anyone else.

Briefly, she wondered if he would date someone when she went back up to Connecticut. After all, he would be seventeen this year. *I wonder if he has dated anyone in school yet. He hasn't mentioned another girl.* The thought of CJ with another girl gave her a funny feeling, and she felt sadness deep in the pit of her stomach.

When she came back to Poppy's next summer, she wondered if

he would even want to spend time with her? She didn't want to think about that. She would be like Scarlett O'Hara in that old movie, *Gone with the Wind*. She wouldn't think about that today; she would think about that tomorrow… maybe.

Chapter 39

CJ was the first to get up out of the water. Eight minutes had passed since they had stopped to rest. Standing, he turned to the east but saw nothing, and then a flash of heat lightning revealed the outline of the island. He made a mental note, referencing lights on the road, as to the direction they had to take. He noticed the longer he stood, the deeper his feet were sinking into the muck. *How in the world did I ever get talked into this?*

Enjoying the warmth of the water, Skye hesitated before standing. A shiver ran through her as her body temperature adjusted to the cooling night air. *This is going to be a long night. We're going to have to wear wet clothes until tomorrow.* Shaking off the chill, she looked up at CJ.

"Ready?" CJ questioned.

"I suppose," she reluctantly answered. "My sneakers are full of yucky junk!" The thought of her feet in muddy shoes for several hours wasn't exactly appealing.

"Yeah, mine too." CJ thought once again, *Why in the world did I ever let Skye convince me to do this?* Answering his own question, he finally decided, *It's simple, I guess. I would do anything for her, even wade in this slimy mess to find God knows what when we get there.* Shivering, he wondered why they hadn't thought to bring dry clothes in a plastic bag to wear when they got on the island. Starting again, they held hands, mostly in the up position, trying to keep their balance as they struggled to lift their feet from the suction of the muck. It was a slow process.

After struggling for several more minutes, CJ noticed the water was becoming shallower, making wading a little easier. Eventually, they waded out of the water at the edge of a narrow beach. Exhausted again, they stood there for a couple of minutes, trying to catch their breath, wondering which direction they should take and what they should do next.

Below the ground, the temperature was cool and comfortable. Unlike the eighty-five-degree temperature eight feet above them, the tunnel stayed around sixty-eight degrees all the time. Unfortunately, humidity was a problem. Everything had become soaking wet. Alexei Kovalchik and Anatoli Krasnoff had not anticipated this particular problem when they had conceived the idea for the project. Now they had five dehumidifiers constantly running just to keep up with the moisture. Too much moisture could ruin their electronic equipment. Even if the equipment was knockoff electronics, they still intended to get rich with it.

Anatoli lay in a knotty makeshift bunk trying to get a little shut-eye before the next boat from the Bahamas arrived.

Alexei monitored the radio and the other surveillance equipment that had been installed around the perimeter of the island. So far, only birds and an occasional raccoon had set off any of their monitors.

The beeping noise from the monitor startled Alexei, who was nodding off in his chair when all hell broke loose. He straightened in his seat and quickly began surveying his equipment. The infrared instruments showed two large objects at the eastern side of the island. The images definitely were not raccoons or birds.

Also awakened by the noise, Anatoli rose up from his stupor. "Alexei, what's going on?" he asked with fear in his voice.

Even with the cool temperature, Alexei began to sweat. All they needed now was to be discovered. Their hopes of a quick fortune would vanish. He had to scare the intruders away from their hideout.

"There's somebody on the island!" he answered with panic in his voice.

"Use your acoustics," Anatoli urged.

Alexei pressed a button.

———————

Skye was moving her flashlight from side to side as they walked down the narrow beach when they heard a blood-curdling scream not more than twenty feet away. Skye dropped her flashlight as CJ pulled her to the sand, covering most of her body with his. Skye's heart raced with fear. *Oh my gosh, what was that?* Flashing through her mind were visions of scary ghosts, horrible monsters, and wild animals with sharp teeth. *Flapper and Squeaky both told me there were ghosts and bad things on the island. Maybe they were right. Why didn't I listen to them? What have I gotten us into?*

Tucked into CJ's protective arms, her eyes tightly closed, she wondered why she had talked CJ into this crazy idea. She wondered if they would just disappear and never be heard from again. She could feel the wetness of tears at the corners of her eyes.

On his side, with his arms around Skye and not moving a finger, CJ waiting uneasily for what was coming next. His face and clothing were covered in sand. Finally, he got the courage to move his arm to his lips to wipe the sand from his mouth.

Frozen in fear, Skye refused to move or even open her eyes.

———————

Alexei studied his instruments. A faint display of infrared

184

remained on the screen but not as clear as it was before. To his relief, whatever it was it had not moved, and he relaxed a little, but he knew something was there. Minutes passed. He just couldn't help worrying. To prove to Anatoli that he wasn't afraid, he said, "It must have been a deer or something. Everything's okay now."

Anatoli wasn't as sure as Alexei. He paced back and forth in front of the monitors. *What if we can't scare them away?* he thought. Unlike Alexei, he was certain it wasn't animals. There were people snooping around.

At first glance, when the alarm went off Anatoli got up and looked at the screen, and he could see two images. *Could it be the cops? Would they be able to find the tunnel in the dark?* He couldn't let Alexi know he was worried.

Of the two, Alexei was the one who always worried, even though he tried not to show it. "What if it's the cops? What will we do?" he asked.

Anatoli was quickly becoming annoyed with Alexei. "Just stay calm, okay? Our research indicates these measures will work. Whoever or whatever it is will be scared away by the noise."

————————

"What do you think it is?" CJ softly whispered in Skye's ear. He noticed she was shivering and pulled her closer.

"I don't know," she whispered as her teeth chattered from fear and the wet clothing in the cooling night air.

"I thought you could use a little more body heat."

"Thanks, that's better."

Not sensing any immediate threat, and thinking more clearly, CJ said, "You know what I think? Whoever is here is just trying to scare us off the island."

Skye moved her head and looked at CJ. "You could be right, but why?"

"I don't know. Maybe it's smugglers. The island is deserted, and this would be a good place to hide drugs or stolen goods."

Loosening CJ's hold on her, Skye slowly turned to face him. "This reminds me of that movie, *Dr. No*. You know, CJ, the James Bond movie?"

"This isn't a movie, Skye. This is real. Whoever it is doesn't want us here. They're trying to hide something, and we're in the way. Why else would they have that screeching, noisy alarm, or whatever it is?"

"What should we do next?" asked Skye.

Deep in thought, CJ didn't respond right away.

"I know one thing we need to do, and that's to get moving, or we'll freeze to death in these wet clothes," Skye urged. "The temperature has started to drop a little."

CJ stared down at his dive watch. It was 1:33 a.m. *What do we do now?* he wondered and finally said, "If there are smugglers here, what are we going to do when we find them? Hold them at gunpoint with guns we don't have? What if they capture us? Who's going to come to our rescue? Nobody even knows we're here," CJ whispered.

With no other loud noises, Skye's fear was abating and her adventurous streak was returning. She thought for a moment about what CJ had just said. "Well, we've already made it this far, so we might as well find out what's happening here."

CJ frowned at her remark. "If we had any sense, we'd get the heck out of here and let the authorities handle it, assuming there is anything to handle."

"For heaven's sake CJ, we've been lying here for over half an hour. If there's anybody here, don't you think they'd already have shown up?"

He didn't like the way the conversation was going. He had known Skye had a stubborn streak, but never realized it was this bad. He needed to discourage her, but he had no idea where to start. Sighing, he remembered that Skye always won their arguments.

Skye was saying, "If they're smugglers, they probably have their stuff stored somewhere. Maybe it's camouflaged, and they only come out here to the island when they need something. Surely, they wouldn't have somebody camped out here all the time, would they?"

Relenting, CJ thought, *That makes sense.* "Okay," he acknowledged, "let me get into the water and get this darn sand off of me."

CJ moved away from Skye and crawled toward the water. He squatted and walked like an alligator out into a foot and a half depth and started rolling around, rinsing off the sand.

Skye followed him into the water and did the same.

Chapter 40

CJ and Skye finished cleaning off the sand while welcoming the warmth of the ocean. Skye had finally stopped shivering and lay in the water, not wanting to get up. Off in the distance, she heard a splash. She reached over and touched CJ's arm to get his attention. A moment later came another splash, but this time it was a little closer. Skye froze, still a little scared from their experience earlier in the evening. Suddenly she asked, "Squeaky, is that you?"

"Yep, it's me."

"How did you know I was here?"

"It's a small world in this big pond," Squeaky said. "You know your Poppy is going to kill you when he finds out you're over here! Besides, I was worried about you."

"Well, let's just hope he doesn't find out." Skye looked pointedly at Squeaky.

"What? Me? How could I tell him? You're the only one who can talk with me. Besides, I wouldn't do that to you. You're my friend. Just be careful, okay?"

Squeaky had trouble negotiating the shallow water. He worked his way over to Skye and put his head in her lap in a loving gesture.

CJ reached over and patted the dolphin on the head. "Did you find anything?" Squeaky asked.

"Not yet, but something is going on here. We just heard a horrible screaming noise. CJ thinks it could be smugglers trying to scare us off. We're going back to the island to find out what's going on here. Would you mind keeping a lookout just in case we need your help? The screaming noise could be ghosts."

That thought made him worry for Skye and CJ.

"What can I do?" Squeaky asked, wondering how he was supposed to help.

"If something happens and we need help, you can get Poppy or CJ's dad. Make a ruckus so they will follow you. Will you do that?"

"Oh, okay. I can do that." He was happy that Skye had asked him to help. He couldn't wait to tell his friends. None of them had ever communicated with a human. His friends all envied him and Skye that ability.

Listening to Skye, CJ knew she and Squeaky had been having a conversation, and he knew that eventually Skye would let him know everything they had been discussing. He could only hear Skye's part of the conversation.

"CJ, are you ready?" Skye asked.

"Sure, why not," CJ grumbled and thought, *Yeah, I'm ready all right, ready to get into trouble.*

———

Alexei looked at his watch for the fiftieth time. It was two thirty-eight a.m., and there was no boat. He and Anatoli had finally been able to relax. The infrared images had disappeared, and the emergency seemed to be over. He decided it was probably a couple of Key deer. Still, Anatoli wasn't completely comfortable with the situation. He didn't want any intruders around while the boat was offloading supplies.

———

CJ could be more perceptive than Skye at times. He always analyzed situations before he acted, and most of the time Skye just approached them like a bull in a china shop. He surmised that as long as they stayed in the water, there was no danger. It seemed that the detectors only worked a few feet in from the shore. The cloud coverage had passed, and the starlight had helped improve their visibility. They could see the shoreline and mangrove trees at a distance of about thirty feet, much clearer than they had been able to earlier in the evening.

It was a good deal easier wading in the muck closer to shore, but as CJ and Skye worked their way around to the north end of the island, they still had to hold hands to keep their balance. Suddenly, Skye's right foot tripped over a solid object. Her momentum propelled her forward as she threw out her right hand to counteract her motion. She let out an "Oops" as she fell forward. *I'm such a klutz.* She was embarrassed at her clumsiness.

CJ quickly twisted around, grabbed her left hand, and pulled her up. He held back his laughter. Lucky for him, Skye couldn't see the tickled look on his face.

"Thanks," she said and continued wading, acting like it was no big deal.

CJ guided Skye closer to the water's edge. Once on the beach, he strained his eyes to see what appeared to be a path leading to the island. He stopped Skye abruptly, placing one finger over his lips as if to say "quiet." He saw the questioning look on Skye's face as she looked up at him.

He leaned down next to her ear and whispered. "Let's walk down this path and see if there's anything of interest."

Skye nodded her head and took a step forward.

———

Flashing lights shocked Anatoli from his much-needed slumber. He jumped from his chair and ran over to the infrared video monitor.

To his surprise, he saw two ghostly figures slowly moving down the path toward the cistern. The figures seemed to be having difficulty, occasionally stopping to get their bearings. Now and then the screen would flare bright red. He figured it was probably caused by a flashlight.

Alexei stood by Anatoli's side. "What are we going to do?" he said, fear shaking his voice.

Anatoli reached over and pressed a button on the tape recorder.

Skye and CJ both stopped abruptly in terror. Neither could believe what was in front of them. They stood looking up, petrified. A giant dragon stood over them, spitting fire from its gnawing mouth. Bellows of smoke and flame shot from its nostrils. A sound like ten thousand banshee's screaming held them mesmerized. It was as if they were suspended in time; neither could move.

Ten seconds later, the giant monster disappeared, leaving Skye and CJ standing in the dark in shock, hearts pounding like overworked drums. It was only a moment later, but it seemed like hours before either could move or speak.

Skye finally reacted. "What in heaven's name was that?" she whispered, her heart still racing. She took in a long, deep breath. She hadn't realized that she had been holding her breath for what seemed like forever.

Taking a breath, and seeming to recover from the shock, CJ finally came to his senses. "Is that what it looked like? No way. It can't be. Dragons don't exist."

Her racing heart finally under control, Skye answered, "Of course, they don't exist, CJ. That wasn't a dragon. It must be a projection or something."

"A what? You mean a holographic image?"

"Yeah, something like that," she said, emphatically. "Whoever did it is trying to scare us off, but it's not going to work with me," she said, stubbornly.

Fearless was the only word he could come up with for Skye. *She has to be the most fearless person I know.* "Well, it sure is working for me," CJ said, his voice a little unsteady. "Let's get the heck off this island right now. Can't you understand? It's dangerous here, Skye. We could be hurt or even worse. These people mean business." He turned to leave. "Are you coming?"

Skye grabbed CJ's arm. "Come on, CJ. If these people were serious, they'd already be doing something a lot worse than just scaring us. They'd be out here with guns and stuff."

———————

Anatoli didn't believe what he was seeing. The two images continued moving up the path.

"They're not buying into our tactics," Alexei whined. "Maybe we should make a run for it. It's probably the cops."

"No way!" Anatoli commanded. "We're staying right here. Besides, they'll never find us in this tunnel. Just shut up about leaving. We're not going anywhere!"

"Yeah, and what will we do if they do find us?"

"Then we'll just have to deal with it if that happens," he said, benignly. He had never killed anybody, but he knew if they were discovered by the intruders, he would have no problem eliminating them and hiding their bodies. Of course, he didn't know the intruders were two curious teenagers, and that a pelican and a dolphin had told them there was someone on the island.

———————

Skye flipped her flashlight on, shining it up ahead as they walked along the narrow path. Giant aloe plants lined their way. They

192

passed an occasional, scrawny scrub oak that was scattered about the island. Broken bottles and litter were strewn about the area. *Who in the world had been over here on the island and made such a mess?* Skye wondered. *This is supposed to be a deserted island.*

CJ reached over and took over the flashlight and the lead from Skye. What appeared to be a clearing loomed ahead in the darkness. CJ's stride, which was much longer than Skye's, left her six or eight feet behind him.

Skye heard a crackling in the leaves and trees rustling as CJ unexpectedly disappeared in front of her. Her flashlight lay on the ground. She ran over to pick it up and heard CJ swearing above her, and he never swore. She shone her light on him. He was swinging upside down in a net-like material about five feet above her head. Tangled in the net, CJ was unable to move.

"Run Skye! Run for help!"

———————

Anatoli still couldn't believe his eyes. Milliseconds after he had flipped the switch, his monitor showed a blue-green image being scooped up into his camouflaged snare. To his horror though, the second image hesitated for a moment, turned, and then began running down the path toward the ocean.

"We have to get them!" he screamed at Alexei.

Both men were out of their chairs at the same instant, heading for the tunnel entrance. On their way out, each snatched up a pair of infrared goggles, stumbling as they struggled to put them on their faces.

Anatoli was the first to reach the entrance. He waited for Alexei to catch up. He needed help moving the heavy door. Alexei's weight was a detriment, but he was strong. Puffing from exertion and anxiety, Alexei finally managed to help push the door open.

Their goggles were of little help. The ambient light was almost non-existent. Fortunately, the moon was beginning to rise from the east, which gave them a hint of visibility. They reached the five-foot wall of the cistern.

Anatoli was up and over in one powerful jump, while Alexei struggled to no avail. Anatoli left him behind as he ran down the path. He passed a struggling CJ hanging in the air. He had to catch the one who was running toward the beach. That person was probably going to call the cops. *Maybe that is a cop,* he thought. *That's all we need. There's no way I'm going to let that happen.*

Chapter 41

Skye ran as fast as she could on the uneven terrain. Occasionally stumbling, and overwhelmed with fear, she made her way toward the beach. Her flashlight beam was shining everywhere but on the narrow path. It was impossible to keep a steady hand as she haphazardly ran down the trail.

Suddenly, her left foot hit an unseen root, causing her to stumble headfirst to the ground. The flashlight fell from her hand as her palms hit the dirt, trying unsuccessfully to break her fall. Her face hit the uneven landscape, and she felt pain as her skin tore in several places. Her lungs ached for breath as they convulsed, trying to fill the need. She lay there unable to move. She knew she had to get up, but her body would not respond. *I can't stay here,* she told herself. Her mind screamed for her to get up and go. She had no idea how far behind her assailants were, but every second she lay there she knew that both their lives were in mortal danger.

The thought of saving CJ brought her back to her senses. At last, she was able to gulp a breath of fresh air. Slowly, her right hand moved to her mouth. Sand and leaves seemed embedded in her cheeks. Her sandy fingers brushed it aside as she tasted blood. *It's broken glass*, she decided. Her hand moved up to her forehead, and she discovered a knot the size of a goose egg. Her right eye felt swollen. Blood dripped down the side of her face. "Move, Skye. Get up or you'll die," she mumbled, forcing herself to roll onto her side. Her body ached from the sudden and hard impact of the fall. Dizzy, but with her lungs filled, she slowly mustered up enough strength to lift her body to a standing position. One foot moved forward, and then the other. She had no idea how she was doing it, but the process continued until she was in a full run. She didn't remember picking up the flashlight, but it was in her hand. "Guardian angel, please help me," she prayed as she continued on the uneven path.

I have to make it to the beach. Her mind raced. *What will I do when I get there? Squeaky, yes, Squeaky will help,* she remembered with relief. *I have to find Squeaky.*

Suddenly, as if her guardian angel had heard her, the moon cast a beam of illumination, lighting the rest of her way to the beach. As her feet touched the water, she stopped, gasping for air from the run as her heart pounded.

About ten feet in front of her, she saw a splash and knew it was Squeaky. "Thank God," she said as she dropped to her knees. Feeling them burn from the salt water, she knew that they had also been cut by the broken glass. Blood continued to drip down her face.

"Squeaky, I need your help," she said weakly.

"I'm here," Squeaky responded. "What's wrong? What happened to your face? Why are you bleeding?"

"Don't worry about me. They have CJ. We have to get help right away!"

"Who has CJ? The bad people who talk funny? Skye, you'll have to come out here. The water's too shallow for me where you are."

Skye's emotions filled her throat. "Please God, don't let anything happen to CJ," she murmured. It was all she could do to mutter those words. Still dizzy, she picked herself up from the shallow water, stood, and began wading out to the deeper water where Squeaky waited.

When Skye was knee-deep in the water, Squeaky swam up beside her. "Grab my dorsal fin, and I'll take you to the car."

Skye lay down in the shallow water, took hold of Squeaky's dorsal fin with both hands and held onto her friend.

Squeaky began towing Skye out into deeper water where it would be easier for him to swim.

"Is CJ hurt too?" Squeaky asked.

"I don't think so. I'm not really sure, but he's in a lot of danger. We have to get the police out here. There are booby traps everywhere."

"Really? Oh, my goodness, then we'd better hurry. Uh, Skye, what's a booby trap?"

"I'll tell you later. Just hurry, Squeaky!"

When they reached Indian Key Channel, Squeaky picked up speed. Skye held on tight, hardly noticing the saltwater burning her face, hands, and knees.

Resting as Squeaky pulled her swiftly through the dark water, Skye thought about what her next move should be. *Should I go directly to the police? Should I call Poppy and Mr. Jansen first? How am I going to explain our dilemma to Poppy, much less Mr. Jansen?* She knew she and CJ probably would be on restriction until they were grown, but first in her mind was how to rescue CJ.

Clearing her mind, she concluded that she would go to the police. *Yes, the police,* she thought. *They have all the resources to deal with these people.*

As Anatoli finally reached the beach, out of breath and with minor scratches from running into several aloe plants, he found that the intruder was gone. He navigated his way to the west side of the island. *Nothing.* He backtracked and walked in the opposite direction, searching the bushes close to the path. *Still nothing,* he thought, wondering where they had gone. He looked down at his watch and touched the light on it so he could see the time. It showed 5:56 a.m. *It will be light shortly. I had better get back and help*

Alexei deal with the captured intruder.

The longer Skye remained in the water, the burning in her face, legs, and hands began to subside a little. As they reached the bridge, Squeaky made a left turn and entered a narrow channel running alongside the highway.

He had begun to tire from the weight and drag of towing Skye through the water, even though she wasn't that heavy. "How much further?" Squeaky groaned.

"I think it's the next bridge down."

Seven and a half minutes later, Skye spotted the Volkswagen parked exactly as they had left it. She couldn't remember if CJ had taken the keys with him or left them in the car. *It doesn't matter. He hides an extra key under the front fender.* Thinking about him and the trouble she had gotten him into made her determined to do whatever it took to get him off that island safely.

Squeaky eased Skye up to the edge of the bank.

"Thank you so much Squeaky. I owe you one."

"It's okay. I was glad to help. Skye, what does owe me one mean?" he asked.

"Don't worry about it now. I'll explain it later," Skye said softly, patting his head.

"Will you do me another big favor and keep an eye out for CJ?"

"Yeah, I'll stay around. You just be careful."

Chapter 42

CJ's eyes felt like they were bulging out of his head. He figured he had been in an upside-down position for nearly ten minutes; at least that's how long it felt. Blood had rushed to his head, giving him a major headache. The net was like a tight sack, gripping his entire body and robbing him of any movement.

Continually struggling, he was finally able to free one arm, which was now sticking out through the camouflage trap. He grabbed the net and pulled it away from his face, feeling a little relief. He heard someone stumbling and grunting down the path, coming in from the beach.

CJ began to panic. He was helpless and at the mercy of his adversaries. His mind raced. *What can I do to free myself?* He was unable to reach his pocket knife in his right pants pocket. *Maybe if I stay still the guy won't see me hanging here.* He wondered where Skye was now and if she had managed to escape. *Am I going to die on this island and never be found?*

A beam of light began flashing in the trees as if searching for something, or someone. CJ froze, holding his breath, hoping the beam wouldn't hit him. Several seconds later the beam blinded his eyes. *What will they do with me?* he wondered, terrified.

"Oh, there you are," Anatoli Krasnoff sneered, shining the light all around the net, checking to make sure his intruder was secure. "Where is your little friend?"

CJ wondered about the guy's accent. *Russian, maybe?* "Please, would you get me down from here? I'm about to pass out," CJ begged. He was weak, but he knew if he got the chance he would run like heck for the beach. Alexei Kovalchik finally came running up. He stopped, bent over, hands on his knees, gasping for air.

"You okay?" Anatoli asked, shining his light on his friend.

CJ looked at the short, heavyset man who looked like he was about to have a heart attack. *The weak link, CJ thought.*

Several minutes passed before Alexei finally stood. "So, this is our problem?" he said, looking up at CJ. "What should we do with him?" he asked, looking over at Anatoli.

"Whatever it is, we need to do it fast, before any other visitors arrive," Anatoli answered flatly. "It looks like his friend escaped, and that means the cops will be here in a couple of hours, maybe a little longer with the coming storm if we're lucky."

CJ wondered what "do it fast" meant. *Who are these people? Are they going to kill me?* He wondered what in the world had he and Skye stumbled upon. Because of his cautious nature, he should have been firm with her about leaving after they saw the holographic dragon, but as always, he pretty much did as she asked. Listening to her this time might get them both killed.

He knew he had to find a way to get out of this trap and find Skye. He wondered if she had made it back to the beach and if Squeaky had helped her get to the car. He was scared, but he was more afraid for Skye. He had to get away from these guys, so he could find her. That was all that mattered to him. Taking a deep breath, his courage grew, and he knew he would do whatever it took to get away from these guys and ensure Skye's safety. He also knew in that instant that he would always protect her, with his life, if necessary.

Skye found CJ's keys to the Volkswagen under the front fender weld. Her hands were shaking so badly from her wet clothes and from fear that she could barely open the car door. She jumped into the front seat, slammed the car door shut, and then managed to get the engine running. *He's going to kill me for getting his seat wet.*

"Why the heck am I worried about a wet seat?" she said aloud. "I need to find help for CJ...and fast." She wondered if the bad men had found him in the net. She prayed that he was okay.

She didn't bother to check the traffic as she lurched out onto US 1. The transmission gears ground into second and then into third as the car jerked forward. "Phooey!" she said. CJ had taught her to drive his VW Thing, but she wasn't nearly as good at it as he was. *About ten miles to the Sheriff's office.* Skye pressed the accelerator to the floor.

As she entered Upper Matecumbe Key, the Volkswagen's speed had maxed out at sixty-eight miles an hour. *Three miles to the next bridge*, she thought. She had just passed Mile Marker 83, when on the right side of the highway she saw a Supper Hess Station, brightly lit and already open for business. It was a blur as the Volkswagen passed by.

Simultaneously, Skye saw what she thought was a Monroe County Sheriff's patrol car at the station. She stomped on the brakes as hard as she could. The little car lowered its nose as all four tires began smoking and squealing, leaving black skid marks on the road. With both hands gripping the wheel, her body was thrown forward. It was all she could do to control the direction of the car. A hundred thirty-eight feet later, the car skidded to a stop.

———————

At the same time, Detective Sergeant Callahan stood by his cruiser pumping fuel into its gas tank. He glanced down at his watch. *6:15 a.m.* Daylight began casting a gray shroud over the Keys. *I'd better hurry, or I'll be late for breakfast.* He had an early breakfast meeting with his dive team. Meetings were held every Saturday morning, and it wouldn't look good if he were late.

Callahan heard the whine of the Volkswagen's engine as it sped up the road. At first, he paid no attention until he heard the squealing of tires. As he looked up, he saw black smoke boiling up from the melting of the tires. That's when he recognized the car. *CJ Jansen. Why is he driving like that? Something must be wrong.*

———————————

As the Volkswagen stopped, Skye fell backward in her seat. She looked back over her shoulder and sighed with relief when she saw the patrol car was still there. She threw the gearshift into reverse, gunned the engine, and expertly turned the car around in the direction of the gas station.

Still pumping his gas, Callahan stood there, staring at the car. He watched it spin around and head toward the entrance to the station. Skye pressed the gas pedal down as she made a sharp turn into the drive and headed for the cruiser. As she came alongside Callahan's car, she slammed on the brakes, jumped out of the car, and ran for the detective.

Callahan couldn't believe his eyes. Seeing that it was Skye Somers and not CJ, he noticed that the beautiful young girl was wearing wet clothing; her hair was dripping wet, and she had some pretty bad scrapes and lacerations on her face, hands, and knees.

Without saying a word, Skye ran into the detective's arms. "Please Detective, you've got to help me," she sobbed.

Callahan felt odd just standing there not knowing what was going on, or what she wanted him to do for her. He felt Skye's wet clothing soaking his uniform. He looked down at her, and with his left hand, he lifted her chin and looked at her. Gently, he pushed her back a little and said, "It's okay now. What's going on, Skye?"

Callahan had never seen her like this. She had always seemed so confident. He knew he had to find out what had happened to upset her so badly. *Had someone hurt her? Where was CJ?*

Chapter 43

"Now slow down, little lady," Callahan said. He tried to make his voice sound as calm as possible. Words not making any sense were pouring out of her mouth non-stop.

Skye's knees were weak from all the adrenalin she'd been pumping for the past couple of hours. She held on to Callahan's hand for balance as she sat down on the curb next to the gas pump.

Callahan sat down next to her, putting his right arm around her shoulder and pulling her close. *This kid is a mess. What has happened to upset her so badly?*

Sighing in relief at finding Detective Callahan at the gas station, Skye put her elbows on her knees, placed her face in her hands, and began crying, quietly at first and then louder, finally becoming hysterical. She slowly began to realize that she was safe and had nothing else to fear except CJ's safety. *Did the bad guys find him in the net? What have they done with him?* Just thinking about CJ made her cry harder.

Callahan quietly comforted her, not saying anything yet, hoping that just his presence was enough. He let her cry until she was "cried out." He knew she needed the release.

Skye finally began to regain her composure. She looked up at the detective and began rattling off what had happened in the past few hours. Callahan would have to stop her now and then to clarify what she was saying. "We have to get somebody over there, right away!" she pleaded. "If we don't, they're going to kill him," she cried with certainty, the tears starting to flow again.

Callahan raised himself up by reaching for the car handle and lifting his trim one-hundred eighty-two-pound frame to a standing position. His long legs had cramped from sitting on the low curb. He reached inside the car, grabbed the mike from the radio, and made his call.

Skye was weak with exhaustion. She leaned back against a gas pump, closed her eyes, and began to pray. *Lord, please, please, keep CJ safe.* She drifted off into a light sleep, still leaning against the gas pump.

Skye was awakened by Callahan gently shaking her shoulder. "I think we should transport you to the hospital and get you checked out," he said. "I don't like the looks of that knot on your head, and you're going to need some stitches. The EMT's will be here in a couple of minutes."

Slowly rubbing her eyes, Skye tried to familiarize herself with where she was and what was happening. Suddenly, she was completely awake and remembered something. "Detective, I have to call Mr. Jansen and Poppy," she said, trying to stand up from where she sat.

"You just stay where you are. I've already made arrangements for a squad car to go by their houses."

"What about CJ? We have to do something," Skye pleaded to Callahan once again.

"Don't you worry about a thing, little lady. It's already been taken care of, okay? We'll have a helicopter in the air shortly, and my boat is on the way to pick me up. If CJ is there, we'll find him, I promise."

A green truck with flashing lights pulled up next to the pumps, EMT lettered on its side.

"I can't go to the hospital," Skye announced. "I have to go with you on the boat," she said, looking up at Callahan. "I have to find CJ. Don't you understand? Those bad men will kill him. When he told me to run, he was upside down in a large net."

"Oh, no, you won't!" he admonished. "You're going straight to the hospital and get checked out, and that's final. Besides, we just received a weather report that a small tropical front has just popped up, and a squall line is heading this way. It'll be here in a couple of hours, and I don't want you anywhere near it."

A small crowd had gathered in the parking lot at the Hess station. Curiosity seekers were breaking their usual monotony on an early Saturday morning, wondering what all the fuss was about.

————————

Tropical Storm Diane was gaining strength over the Tongue of the Ocean, due east of Andros Island in the Bahamas. It was heading straight for the Keys.

Chapter 44

Detective Sergeant Sean Callahan met the boat at Bud & Mary's Marina at the lower end of Upper Matecumbe Key.

Officer Courtney Morgan had picked up the boat at the Coast Guard Station and brought it to the marina to meet up with Callahan. Morgan had been assigned to assist Callahan with the search.

Heavy overcast skies shrouded the lower half of the Keys, with prevailing winds coming out of the east at fifteen to twenty knots. NOAA's forecast was not good. Tropical Storm Diane was scheduled to arrive at Islamorada around 12:45 p.m., just four hours away. Winds were forecast with gusts up to seventy miles an hour, which was almost hurricane strength. Sustained winds would be around fifty miles an hour and would bring heavy rains and probably do some damage. It was dangerous to be out in a boat when an impending storm was near.

Callahan looked to the east moments before stepping aboard the boat. Although the county owned it, he still thought of the craft as his. He had spent a good share of his time in the boat, cruising the Keys. "How 'ya doing Morgan?" Callahan asked as he took the wheel.

"All right, I guess. Looks like we're in for a big blow." Officer Morgan was not a typical-looking police officer. He looked more like a chef who ate a lot of his own food rather than a policeman. At five feet five inches in height, with a belly almost as round as he was tall, his uniform certainly didn't fit the image of a Monroe County

Deputy Sheriff.

With all of Morgan's shortcomings, Callahan was fond of the man. He had a good sense of humor and was pleasant to be around. In addition, he was a particularly good policeman. When they were together, their friends said they looked like Mutt and Jeff. A small smile creased the corners of his mouth as he thought about it.

"What do you think, Morgan?" Callahan asked, looking him straight in the eyes. Callahan had always respected the man's opinion.

"I think we're going to be in for one heck of a ride," he answered.

"Well, hold on then," Callahan ordered. "Let's go find the boy."

Michael and Maria were the first to reach Fisherman's Hospital. Maria was halfway out of the car door as Michael slammed the gear into park. He finally caught up with her as she reached the emergency room entrance. He grabbed the handle, and Maria rushed inside. Michael knew his wife too well. When Maria got something in her head, or when she was on a mission, he had better step aside. He had learned that a long time ago. He also noticed that Skye was a lot like that too. The thought crossed Michael's mind that CJ had his hands full.

Maria dashed up to the counter and immediately asked to see Skye.

"May I help you?" the nurse said from behind the counter.

"Skye Somers. We're here to see Skye Somers," Maria said, a little breathless. "She's supposed to be here in the ER," Maria said, now sounding a little agitated.

"Oh, yes, she's with the doctor. Just have a seat. He'll be finished in a few minutes."

CJ's life is at stake and she wants me to have a seat? That's not going to happen, Maria thought. Her first son Jeffery flashed through her mind. *His death almost destroyed Michael and me. I will not lose another son.* Ignoring the nurse, she started walking down the hall, looking left to right and then right to left, eyeing each cubicle as she passed.

Other than CJ's birth, she had only been in a hospital twice. The first time was when her first son Jeffrey had been born. The second time was in the emergency room where she and Jeffrey had been taken on the day he had died.

The nurse jumped up from her chair and hurriedly followed Maria and Michael down the hall.

"Miss, you can't go down there," the nurse half shouted, racing forward.

Maria stopped at a cubicle with the drape drawn closed. She listened briefly, heard a man say something, and then reached over to pull the drape open. Skye was lying on a gurney with an IV stuck in her arm.

Maria hesitated, trying to collect her thoughts. Her mind clear, she boldly walked into the cubicle as if she owned the place. Michael followed.

A man dressed in green hospital scrubs turned to see what the interruption was about.

Maria rushed over to Skye and grabbed her hand. "Oh, honey, are you all right?" she asked with tears in her eyes.

Groggy from a concussion, Skye turned her head to the side, recognized Maria, and began to cry. "Oh God, they have CJ, Mrs. Jansen, they have CJ," she sobbed.

――――――――

"Sheriff's *Avenger*, this is *Trauma Star*. Over."

"Go ahead *Trauma Star*," Callahan answered above the whine of his outboard engine.

"We are approaching Indian Key from the south and will be in the area in about five minutes."

"Roger," Callahan said. "Hey, do me a favor. Fly over the island

and let me know if there's anything unusual. Over."

"Roger that."

Callahan left shelter on the lee side of Upper Matecumbe Key, turned left into Indian Key Channel, and then motored under the second bridge. As he lined up the boat for the channel, three-foot waves began crashing into the bow of his boat. Forty-five-knot winds blew his jowls and eyelids backward, and the wind was increasing.

Officer Morgan held to the railing with his left hand, and his right hand held onto the windshield. The tropical force winds shrieked around the small boat. The noise was terrible, as if a pack of screaming monkeys were after them. He lowered his head to keep the stinging salt spray from entering his eyes. He wondered how it must be in the ocean if it was this bad in only ten feet of water.

"*Avenger*, this is *Trauma* Star. Over."

"Go ahead," Callahan shouted over the mike.

"We've located a small skiff tucked up under some mangroves on the north side of the island. There's a small outboard motor attached. Other than that, the place looks deserted. Over."

"Is there any place for you to sit down?"

"Negative, *Avenger*. Nothing here but scrub oaks and mangroves; over."

"Crap!" Callahan complained.

"What do you recommend, Skipper?" Morgan asked.

"We'll keep on going until this weather forces us to turn back," Callahan shouted over to Morgan. *We have to find CJ before the worst of the weather comes. It could mean the difference between life and death for him.* He brushed the thought from his mind. *I can't let myself think that way. We will find him.*

Chapter 45

CJ slowly lifted his head for what seemed like the hundredth time. Sleep made his mind foggy. Fatigue hung over his body like a black shroud. *It must be at least twenty-four hours or more since I've slept. I wonder how long I've been here.* His wrists, arms, and shoulders ached from having his hands tied behind the back of the chair.

He looked around the tunnel in the almost nonexistent light and realized that the Russians had gone, or at least he thought they had gone. *Where did they go? Do they have Skye?*

He listened intently for any sounds that would betray their presence. *Nothing,* he thought to himself. *I suppose that's a good thing. At least if they've abandoned me, I won't have to worry about being killed. But that,* he thought, *is unlikely. Why not let me go if they're not going to kill me?* His immediate problem, however, was how to get loose from the chair that was holding him captive.

"What the heck!" CJ shouted aloud as he looked down at his feet. Chilly water was beginning to cover his sneakers. With a confused expression on his face, he couldn't believe what he was seeing.

Where in the world is all this water coming from?

Alexei Kovalchik and Anatoli Krasnoff huddled against the lee side wall of the previously dry cistern as a helicopter passed overhead. Prop wash from the huge chopper competed with the increasing speed of the wind coming in directly from the east.

The two men knelt in two feet of accumulated water against the wall that kept them from being blown across the man-made hole that had been excavated over a hundred fifty-five years earlier. They had panicked at the sight of water flowing in from the cistern.

Wading through water, Alexei had hurriedly followed Anatoli to the entrance to investigate the anomaly. In all their planning, it never occurred to them that there was always a strong possibility of flooding, particularly during hurricane season.

"They are looking for the boy!" Alexei shouted above the roar of the wind. "If we stay here, we will drown with the kid!"

"We must get to the shore now!" Anatoli yelled as his slender body shivered in the wind and downpour.

Torrents of rain began sweeping across the tiny island. Band after band of rain blasted in from the ocean as the wind increased gusts to over seventy miles an hour. Alexi and Anatoli again heard the whooping of the giant blades of the helicopter approaching this time from a different direction.

"Do not move!" Anatoli shouted at Alexei. "In this dim light, maybe they will not see us."

The helicopter passed within fifty yards of where the two men squatted. In the torrential rainstorm, it was impossible for the flight crew to see the island, much less the two Russians clinging to the wall.

"We must get to the boat right away!" Anatoli yelled and pointed in the direction of the concealed skiff.

"What about the kid? He will drown."

"We're going to drown if we don't get out of here right now. Forget about the kid!" Anatoli shouted. "Let's get out of this hole and get to the boat!"

———————

Callahan fought the controls of the twenty-foot Angler boat. By the time he and Officer Morgan reached the end of Indian Key Channel and got ready to make a right turn for the Island, the small boat almost capsized from a seven-foot wave rolling in from the ocean. Visibility was down to less than three hundred feet, and from this distance Indian Key was invisible.

"*Avenger*, this is *Trauma Star*. Over."

"Go ahead *Trauma Star*," Callahan shouted.

"We're going to stop for the day. Winds and visibility are below minimums. We'll be on standby for you when this storm passes. Over."

"Roger, *Trauma Star*. We're going to have to abort too."

Callahan carefully turned his boat into the rolling seas, reduced his speed, and began surfing the seven-foot waves back into Indian Key Channel.

———————

Skye opened her eyes and saw a stark white ceiling and bright lights shining from behind her bed. She moved her head from side to side. The room was empty of all its previous occupants. She lay there trying to remember the events of the past hour. She remembered asking the doctor if she could go home.

"No, sweetheart," he had said, "I think it's best that you stay here for at least one night. Maybe in the morning we'll talk about it."

No way. I have to find CJ, her foggy mind thought. She knew she was his only chance.

She looked over and saw an IV in her left arm. "I've got to get out of here," she groaned.

Suddenly, her body froze. She heard the howling and screaming of the wind around her hospital room window. Occasionally, the window pane would shake as waves of rain shrieked at the glass, looking for a place to weep.

The same thought kept going through her mind. Even knowing what she would be facing, she was determined. *I've got to get out of here.* Images of CJ flashed in her head. *God only knows what those guys are planning to do to him or have already done to him. Where is he? Is he still in the net in this storm?* Tears welled up and slid down her cheeks, as she thought about what he might be going through right now.

She lay back and tried to relax. "I've got to get my mind straight," she whispered to herself. Almost methodically, she thought, *I've got to help CJ. I've got to find him. I need to get out of here. What can I do?* she wondered, still trying to clear her mind.

Flapper came to her mind. *Where are Flapper and Squeaky?* She looked at the big clock on the wall that showed 12:52 a.m.

Skye raised herself to a sitting position at the edge of the bed. Her head spun momentarily as her equilibrium adjusted to the sudden movement. She looked down at the IV and shuttered at the thought of having to remove the thing. She hated needles more than she hated spiders, and she really despised spiders.

Skye suddenly realized that her clothes were gone. "Oh, no, what am I going to do?" she said, looking around the room for any signs of clothing. "The closet," she murmured.

She reluctantly reached down and started pulling at the tape surrounding the needle. She grimaced as she began to remove it. CJ kept popping into her mind, and that gave her the courage to continue.

With the tape finally removed, she took the end of the needle, closed her eyes, held her breath, and pulled it out. She felt no pain as she looked down and saw a small amount of blood oozing from the tiny hole. Glancing at the needle in her right hand, she briefly wondered why needles had to be so long.

Tossing it in the trash can, Skye grabbed some Kleenex from her nightstand and applied pressure to her arm. She bent her elbow against the wad of tissue and then slowly slid from the bed to the floor, where she immediately steadied herself and headed for the closet.

"Thank you, God," she quietly said as she found a dry set of clothing Poppy had left for her. She quickly got into her clothes and then into her sneakers. "Now all I have to do," she said, "is to escape from this darn prison!"

Chapter 46

Alexei Kovalchik and Anatoli Krasnoff finally reached the skiff, but not without great difficulty. Alexei had scrapes and bruises on his arms and hands as he had clawed his way through the dense underbrush. Occasionally, he would run into a large cactus or aloe plant, causing him to scream out in pain. His eyes were red from the strong wind that caused the saltwater to blow against his face, blinding his sense of direction.

On a cloudless day, they could have made it to the skiff in less than five minutes, but today he had stumbled around like a mad man, going in every direction except toward the skiff.

Anatoli Krasnoff had fared much better than his partner. Anatoli had followed directly behind Alexei as he had pushed through the underbrush, paving the way for him. Unfortunately, also like Alexei, he had burning red eyes from the saltwater spray.

As they reached the skiff, to their dismay they discovered that it was almost full of water. The tidal surge had pushed the tiny boat fifteen feet inland from the shore, breaking its bow line and wedging it deep in the underbrush.

The two men were gasping for air, suffering from exhaustion, and cold from the blowing rain that had soaked their clothing. Trying to catch their breath and regain their senses, they dropped down into two feet of water, unable to move. The brunt of the storm seemed to be passing much too slowly, but the urge to leave the island was overwhelming. They knew they had to get away before the law came to the island, found the kid, and arrested them. After a couple minutes of rest, Anatoli was the first to stir.

"Come on Alexei, we have to get moving. When this storm is over, the police will be all over this island like ants at a picnic looking for us. I don't think the other kid who got away can identify us. But if they find the boy drowned in the tunnel, and I'm sure he will be after all this rain, we need to be miles away in Miami. If we can get up there, we will call our Russian Mafia friends, and they will protect us.

Alexei began to move, opening his eyes and trying to focus on the task at hand. "What about our big shipment in the tunnel from the Bahamas? That amounts to a lot of money, and we're just walking off and leaving it."

"Forget about the electronics, you idiot! It's all ruined from the water. We'll get more iPhones and Xboxes from the guys in the Bahamas later, and we'll find a better place to hide them. Let's just get the heck out of here before the cops come," Anatoli said sharply.

Anatoli turned to Alexei and said, "I don't know if I told you or not, but I don't know how to swim." His face reddened in embarrassment.

Still sitting, Alexei lowered his head. "I don't either," he confessed.

Anatoli looked down into the boat, searching for life vests. Alarmed when he didn't see them, he shouted above the wind, "Where are the life vests?" Looking around the area where the boat had finally settled, he exclaimed in a panicky voice, his face pale, "Oh, no, the storm has washed them away! Now what are we going to do?" Realizing they would never find them, he groaned, "We will just have to take our chances. Come on, let's get the water out of the boat."

Alexei rose unsteadily to his feet. He went to the bow, and Anatoli moved to the stern. Grunting together, they managed to lift the heavy, water-filled skiff several inches off the ground, and tilting it to the side just a little, they were only able to empty out a small amount.

Giving up, Alexei dropped his end of the skiff to the ground and collapsed where he stood. *Anatoli is nuts*, he thought. *We will never be able to empty it out all by ourselves.*

"Come on!" Anatoli shouted to his friend. "We cannot stay here! Get your butt up and move!" he commanded.

Alexei stirred for a moment, tried to get up, and then collapsed back on the ground. "I can't! It's too heavy."

Anatoli looked over at his obese friend in disgust. He moved toward Alexei. Once beside him, he reached down, grabbed his friend by the shirt, and pulled him to his feet.

"You tub of lard, I said move, or I'll kill you right here!"

Alexei opened his eyes and stared at his antagonist. He got the message. He reached down and took hold of the edge of the boat at the stern.

Anatoli moved back to the bow, looked again at Alexei, and with a nod of his head heaved as if it were life or death. Alexei also reached deep inside for strength and once again gave a last heave. The boat tittered for a moment as water poured from inside the skiff. With a final effort, both men pushed, and the skiff fell upside down.

Exhausted, Alexei collapsed against the flat-bottomed boat. Anatoli dropped to his knees in two feet of water, leaning over the bottom of the overturned boat.

Five minutes passed, and with renewed resolve Anatoli stood up. "Let's go," he commanded.

The pneumatic door quietly closed as Skye left the hospital through a rear exit. She found herself in a back alley next to several green garbage containers. Within seconds, she was drenched with rain. Her wet hair clung to her swollen, bruised, and scratched face. Shivers ran up her spine as chilly rain and wind blew against her fragile body. It seemed to her that the storm might be slowly abating. *It doesn't make any difference. Even if it's not slowing, I have to find CJ.*

Where is Flapper? I need you, Flapper. I need *you to find Squeaky. He's the only one that can help me. Hurry Flapper!*

Skye made her way to the edge of the building and looked around the corner. *How I am going to get transportation to the bridge? she wondered. CJ's car is still at the gas station. If I can find a way to get to his car, then maybe with Squeaky's help, I can make it to the island.*

She momentarily stood there, deep in thought, and immobilized from the hard rain that felt like cold needles against her skin. The light blouse and shorts Poppy had left her was of no help against the elements. She wrapped her hands around her shoulders, seeking warmth.

As Skye peeked around the corner, she realized that she was looking at the emergency room door. An overhang for passenger drop-off stood out about ten feet from the entrance. She watched as a red Chevy Nova pulled up to the entrance access. A young teenager, whom she recognized as one of CJ's classmates, was dropping off his girlfriend.

Taking a deep breath, she thought, *I'm ready. It's now or never.*

The driver's girlfriend leaned over and gave her boyfriend a quick kiss on the cheek, jumped out of the car, and ran for safety through the ER doors. Skye could tell from her uniform that she was a volunteer candy striper. Candy stripers assisted the patients by refilling water containers, passing out magazines, and sometimes even helping the nurses by taking patients' vital signs. The thought flashed through Skye's mind that she might enjoy doing that on weekends at one of the hospitals close by when she got back up to Connecticut.

Ready to make a run for it, Skye noticed that the boy took a moment to adjust his windshield wipers before pulling out from underneath the canopy. It was just the amount of time she needed to make her move. She sprang from the corner of the building and sprinted straight for the car.

Before the kid realized what was happening, Skye yanked the passenger door open and jumped inside. "Hi Travis," Skye said in greeting. She had met Travis at a cookout on the beach when she had been with CJ.

Travis was startled by this wet stranger jumping in his car. He sat there, mouth open, staring at Skye. "What the...?" he stammered.

"Travis, it's me, Skye, CJ's friend," Skye said as she shivered. "We met at a cookout last summer."

Travis continued to stare for several more seconds before his face relaxed as he recognized Skye's familiar face. Realizing that she was no threat, he seemed to be more concerned about his wet front seat than he was about Skye, or why she had jumped into this car.

Chapter 47

In the tunnel, CJ was in panic mode. He had been sitting in the dark for hours, and with no sleep he was beginning to hallucinate about trolls, the creature from the black lagoon, giant crabs, and large hairy spiders.

Icy water had reached his waist and was continuing to rise. The temperature in the tunnel was very cool, and with the rainwater rising, he was freezing. If he didn't hurry up and get out of the tunnel, and quick, he would surely drown. His chances of escape were dwindling as the water rose. His wrists were raw from fighting at the tape and stinging from the swirling saltwater. "God, please don't let me die this way," he prayed.

Skye was talking so fast that Travis had a tough time keeping up with what she was saying. Finally, realizing that his buddy was in danger, he reluctantly agreed to her request. "Okay, I'll take you to CJ's car," he said, shifting the four-speed transmission into first gear and spinning the 1979 Chevy Nova out of the parking lot. "You ought to let me call the police," he urged. Skye did not respond.

She huddled in the corner of the front seat, trying to get warm. Rain was still falling at a rapid pace, but the wind had slowed a little. Travis had his wipers flapping back and forth as fast as they would go. Still, it was hard to see the road.

Fourteen minutes later, they pulled into the Hess Station. Skye saw CJ's car parked where she had left it and pointed in its direction.

Realizing Skye was shivering, Travis reached over the front seat and retrieving a black windbreaker, he handed it to her. "Here you go," he said. "Maybe this will help."

"Thanks," Skye whispered.

The Nova came to a stop next to the Volkswagen, and Skye got out of the car. Travis waited for her to get in the VW before he peeled away. He was going straight to the police. He knew Skye needed help, and quick. Plus, he didn't want anything to happen to her or CJ. *She must sure like CJ a lot to be searching for him in this weather. Lucky guy,* he thought.

Sky got into CJ's VW, seated herself, slammed the door shut, and then reached for the seatbelt. She took a deep breath as she folded her arms and leaned against the steering wheel. Her mind was fuzzy and felt like it was full of cobwebs as she tried to concentrate on her next move. *I'm sure the police are looking for me by now.* She figured the hospital had told them she had disappeared. *Driving the VW around is probably not a good idea, but I'll just have to take the risk.*

She reached down to start the car as her eyes caught sight of Flapper sitting on the trunk of the VW, which was in the front. A wind gust shook the car as he turned away from it. Skye sat back in her seat and folded her arms for warmth.

"Flapper! I've been looking all over for you."

"Sorry Skye, but this is not a good time to be flying."

"Please, I need your help," Skye begged. "Some bad people have CJ out on Indian Key, and I've got to find a way to get out there. I was hoping you could find Squeaky for me. He can give me a lift to the island."

"I don't think that's a good idea," Flapper said. "I had trouble getting here as it is, and now you want me to go looking for that dolphin?" Squeaky wasn't exactly Flapper's choice of friends.

"I know," pleaded Skye, "but there's no other hope of saving CJ. I don't even know where they're holding him, but if Squeaky can get me to the island, I can search for him. He's in terrible danger, Flapper. Please don't say no."

Through the windshield, Flapper looked into Skye's serious blue eyes. He saw the terror for CJ in them. He could see that she was injured, desperate, and pleading for his help. He knew he had to help her and CJ. She was his friend; the only human who had ever spoken to him. He would find Squeaky for her and give him her message.

"Okay," Flapper replied. " I'll see what I can do."

Skye's spirits perked up for a moment. "If you can find Squeaky, tell him to meet me where he dropped me off before at the bridge."

Flapper spread his wings and let the wind pick him up. In a flash, he was gone.

Detective Sergeant Callahan waited in his boat for the storm to pass. He and Officer Morgan had returned to the Coast Guard station to wait until sea conditions improved. They had tied up to the dock thirty-six minutes earlier and were sipping cups of the hot coffee that Morgan had retrieved from the mess hall.

Both men were dressed in yellow foul weather jackets and pants. Callahan wondered why they had even bothered to wear the suits. They leaked like a sieve and barely worked as wind breakers. The back of his shirt and pants were soaked, and he would have liked nothing better than to change into a set of dry clothing. The storm was slowly passing, but the wind was still gusting to about forty miles an hour on the water. He had decided that once the wind was down to thirty miles an hour, they'd try it again. The one thing he was sure of was that the longer it took to find the kid, the worse things could be for him.

"*Avenger*, this is Coast Guard Station. Over."

Callahan was shaken from his thoughts. "Go ahead Coast Guard," he answered over his mike.

"*Avenger*, we just got a call from the Sheriff's office. Skye Somers, that little girl that you took to the hospital this morning is missing. Security at the hospital thinks that maybe she just walked out. Oh, and another call just came in a couple minutes ago from a kid named Travis Jackson, a friend of the boy who is missing. He said Skye Somers jumped in his car at the hospital and asked him to drive her to some Hess Station so she could get the missing boy's car. He said she kept saying, "I've got to find CJ.""

"Roger Coast Guard. Thanks for the info. Out."

Callahan was stunned at what he had just heard. *Surely, she's not going back over to the island. Crap! More problems.* Now he would have to look for two teenagers.

Morgan looked over at Callahan. "What are you thinking Skipper?"

"I don't know," Callahan groaned. "I guess we'd better try it again," he said, looking up at the sky that was still dropping heavy rain. It did look a little better, but not much.

———————

Alexei Kovalchik and Anatoli Krasnoff finally reached the shore, dragging the skiff behind them. They had to pull the little boat fifteen feet out of the underbrush down to what used to be the beach. They stood in two feet of water on the sandy shore as the four-foot waves broke. Each time a wave came in, the men would have to brace themselves against it to keep from being knocked back into the water.

Alexei managed to climb into the back of the boat as Anatoli held the bow line, allowing the skiff to rise up and down in the rolling waves.

Alexei pulled the starter rope on the ten-horsepower Johnson. After several more pulls, the engine started purring like a little kitten. He shifted the gear lever forward, and the boat began to move. Anatoli moved to the mid-section and heaved himself over the side and into the boat.

Alexei gunned the engine, turned the boat, and almost flipped it as a wave slammed against the side of the skiff. He lined the bow up with the road and went to full power. The boat began surfing in the four-foot waves. Alexei and Anatoli started to relax as they headed toward the highway.

Suddenly, the skiff began going down the crest of a wave faster than Alexei had realized. The bow dug deep into the water in front of them. As it dug deeper and deeper, a gust of wind picked up the stern, flipped it into the air and spun it like an out of control kite. The black ghost of death had moved out of the tunnel and was hovering over the boat.

Chapter 48

Skye moved slowly and carefully down Highway US 1. Salt spray had settled on the windshield of the Volkswagen while it had been sitting in the parking lot at the Hess Station. Even with the windshield washers going at full blast, a stubborn film obscured her vision. She leaned forward against the steering wheel thinking that maybe the closer she got to the windshield, the better her vision would be. Lucky for her, with all the rain and wind, traffic on the road was almost nonexistent.

Between poor visibility and wind gusts of almost forty miles an hour, it was almost impossible for her to keep the little VW on the road. She constantly weaved across the road's center line like a snake slithering its way down a pig trail. She shivered every now and then as she thought about having to get back into the water in the pouring rain. She felt like she was driving at a snail's pace.

Wondering if CJ was okay, she silently prayed that Squeaky would be at the designated spot when she arrived.

———

The water seemed colder and was rising. It had just reached CJ's shoulders. Realizing that he might die set off a major panic attack that he had never experienced before. "Somebody, please help me!"

he shouted into the darkness.

He wrestled with the tape holding his wrists, not realizing that they were bleeding pretty badly from his constant tugging and twisting, trying to get them loose. The stinging from the saltwater was becoming almost unbearable. He let out an animal-like groan from frustration. "I'm in here!" he screamed, knowing that no one was there to hear him. He thought about Skye, and with a sense of foreboding wondered if she has made it across the water and back to the car. *Probably not, or she would have been back with help by now.*

Just thinking about her and what might have happened to her made him forget for a moment that he probably wouldn't make it out of the tunnel. His heart twisted in sorrow and loss at the thought that he might never see her beautiful face again. With a deep sadness, he also doubted that his parents and Skye's Poppy would ever know what had happened to him and Skye. Silence permeated the tunnel.

———————

Skye had just passed Mile Marker 78. After the third bridge, she slowed the Volkswagen to a crawl and prepared to make a U-turn on U.S. 1. She knew Indian Key was out there not more than two hundred yards.

She wondered how CJ was managing. *Is he injured? Where are his captors? Have they hurt him?* The thought that he might be hurt, or worse, flashed through her mind, but she wouldn't accept it.

Heading back to the island, she briefly wondered if she might be their next victim. *Where are the Sheriff and the Coast Guard?* Her mind was jumbled with questions as she maneuvered the car over to the south side of the road and pulled up next to the channel running alongside the highway.

As she opened her door, Skye noticed that the wind was still blowing, but it had lessened, and the rain was lighter. Still, she could barely make out the island in the distance. She hunched over as she walked toward the edge of the channel. "There you are," she heard Flapper say.

"Flapper, I'm so glad you're here. Where are you?" she asked, looking around.

"Up here in the mangrove tree."

Skye looked up and saw Flapper clinging to a limb high in a mangrove tree. He was holding on for dear life.

"Thank you so much, Flapper. When all this is over and done, I'm going to treat you to a bucket of the freshest fish money can buy."

"Thanks, Skye, it sound great, but it's not necessary. You're my friend, and friends help each other. Oh, I found Squeaky. He is waiting for you down in the water."

Skye carefully made her way down the side of the seven-foot bank, slipping and sliding in the loose limestone rock of the steep incline. When she reached the water's edge, she heard Squeaky making his boisterous noises. Suddenly, his head popped out of the water, no more than five feet in front of her.

"There you are," Skye said, her body sore and fatigued. Her emotions bubbled to the surface as tears flowed freely down her cheeks. She was so thankful that both Flapper and Squeaky had come through for her. Squeaky and Flapper had just been elevated from her good friends to her knights in shining armor. She would never understand the connection between the three of them, but she was thankful for it.

"You look terrible," Squeaky said, moving in closer to the bank. "You're white as a ghost. Flapper told me that CJ was still on the island with the bad men, and that you were coming back to help him. Where are the policemen? Aren't they going to help?"

"I found a policeman, but he called the rescue unit to take me to the hospital. I escaped about thirty minutes ago."

"Escaped? They don't know you're gone?"

"Don't worry about it now," Skye said with a wan smile. "Squeaky, I need you to take me back to the island. I have to find

CJ. He's in real trouble."

"Are you sure that's what you want to do?" Squeaky asked, with concern. "That's a bad place, and you'll be all alone."

"Yes, I'm sure," Skye answered. She was injured, exhausted, soaking wet, and already cold from being in the wind. She gasped as she lowered herself into the water.

"Well, if you insist. Come on, grab hold," Squeaky offered.

Skye reached out and grabbed Squeaky's dorsal fin as they began moving out into the channel. Had she looked to her right about fifty yards down the channel, she would have seen the overturned skiff that had washed ashore in the storm just minutes before her arrival.

————————

Detective Sergeant Callahan turned his boat into Indian Key Channel and headed out toward the island. The rain was slowing, but the wind was still about thirty knots. Clearer visibility and smaller waves made their ride much more comfortable than it had been earlier in the day. He was thankful for the reprieve. He wondered what was in store when they reached the island. He thought about the boy, CJ. He had grown to like him and Skye, and although he was not a particularly religious man, he prayed that they would find the teen and that he would be okay.

With binoculars, Morgan had been scanning the channel. Unbelieving, he reached over and tapped Callahan on the shoulder as he pointed toward the island. Callahan took the binoculars and focused in where his partner had been pointing and was shocked at what he saw.

The wave action was still high, and the distance was at least a half mile away. For a moment, he thought his eyes were playing tricks with him. At first, he wondered if it might be a submarine, but he knew the water was too shallow. Finally, he realized that it was a dolphin pulling something. "What the heck is that?" he shouted over at Morgan.

"It looks like the dolphin is pulling a girl!" Morgan shouted.

After studying the object for a few moments, "Yep, you're right, that's Skye," Callahan agreed. "I can't cut across because it's too shallow. We'll have to go around and come in on the southeast side. By that time, she'll already be there."

Callahan reached for the radio. "Islamorada Coast Guard, this is the *Avenger*. Over."

"Roger *Avenger*. Go ahead. Over."

"Better get *Trauma Star* in the air. I think we'll probably need her."

Chapter 49

Michael, Maria, and Poppy sat quietly in a booth at the Days Inn restaurant at Mile Marker 82 in Islamorada, each deep in thought. Poppy kept glancing at his watch. It was 2:47 p.m.

Maria was a nervous wreck. She had been crying off and on since early in the morning when the hospital had called Poppy to notify him that Skye had disappeared. Poppy had immediately called them. Maria's nose and eyes were red from constantly wiping them. Most of her makeup was gone. *Not only is CJ missing and in danger, but now Skye is missing too.* Her left hand held a crucifix that had been her constant companion all day.

Michael sat stoic, but occasionally his emotions would get the best of him, and a silent tear would roll down his cheek. Thinking of their first son, Jeffrey, he knew that neither he nor Maria could survive another loss. His outward appearance seemed cool, calm, and collected, but internally he was just as bad, if not worse, than Maria.

Poppy was as quiet as a church mouse. He hadn't had much to say all day. He had contemplated calling his daughter, Amanda, to tell her what was going on but had decided against it. All it would do was upset her. She was having some health issues since she and Skye's father, Alex, had returned from their trek in the Himalayas, so he decided to wait to contact her when he had more information.

Besides, he knew his granddaughter. He had learned not to jump the gun. Skye was very smart, and she always came out on top. That thought had kept him going all day.

Michael looked up from the table and watched a deputy sheriff walk through the restaurant's entrance and move toward them. He held his breath until the officer reached their table. Poppy and Maria looked up in surprise.

"Mr. and Mrs. Jansen, Mr. Hudson, my name's Officer Hernandez.. Detective Callahan asked me to let you know that we've located Skye, and she seems to be okay." Looking directly at Michael, he said, "We haven't located your son yet, but we are searching for him as we speak."

"What do you mean she seems to be okay?" Poppy interrupted with concern in his voice.

"She's been spotted at Indian Key with a dolphin."

"A dolphin? In this storm?" Maria asked, her face ashen as she fell back against the booth.

Michael stood. He knew he had to find CJ and Skye right away. He was certain that Skye had gone to the island looking for CJ. "Officer, I would like to go to the island."

"Sir, at the moment it's not possible. We have a rescue operation in progress as we speak. I suggest you folks stay put right here, and we'll get back with you as soon as we have more information."

———————

Squeaky had towed Skye to the southeast side of the island without incident, except for Skye swallowing an occasional mouth full of saltwater. He lay in the shallow water, exhausted from the exertion of pulling Skye across the rough waves, even though it was only a distance of a couple hundred yards, and she was light.

Skye let go of Squeaky's dorsal fin when they reached two feet of water. She lay there beside him gathering her strength and occasionally patting him on the head. "Thank you so much,

Squeaky," she kept repeating, as if once was not enough.

Slowly, Skye lifted herself out of the water. Chills from the wet clothing and the brisk wind caused her to shiver as she began wading ashore. A few feet away, she stopped and turned slowly toward Squeaky. "Mind waiting here for a while?" she asked. "I may need your help again."

Squeaky rolled to his side, waved his right flipper in affirmation, and said, "I want a bucket of fresh fish like you promised Flapper. I heard you tell him that. Of course, I would help you even if you didn't give me any fish, but with all this weather, pickings have been slim."

Skye managed a weak smile. "It's a deal, my friend; I promise." She turned toward the island, and not knowing what she faced, she reluctantly moved ashore.

Before entering the underbrush, she stood for a moment, gathering her bearings. She was trying to decide which direction to take to get back to where the camouflage net was located. Her decision made, she walked toward the center of the island. Not more than ten feet inside the mangroves, the mosquitoes began their relentless attack. Skye dared not make any noise. She didn't want CJ's captors to hear her. She quietly suffered the unending bites of the bugs. She closed her mind to the gnawing pain and moved forward.

As she waded to higher ground, she noticed that the water was receding. It gave her some reassurance that the island was not flooded too badly.

In the distance, she heard the sound of an outboard motor and wondered if it was the bad men moving CJ off the island. Her adrenalin began to flow, urging her forward. As she progressed faster, palmetto prongs and tree limbs slashed at her tender arms and legs. A dinner of blood was on the table for the insects, and they ate hungrily.

Please, help me find CJ, she prayed. Suddenly, something inside screamed for her to stop. She abruptly paused. Peering through the underbrush, she saw what appeared to be a huge hole in the ground.

She pushed aside the bushes and moved forward to inspect the crater. For a moment, she didn't recognize what it was.

Water covered the bottom of the hole. She realized that it was manmade. Brick and mortar made up the sides of the pit. *A cistern. It's a cistern to store water!* Poppy had told her and CJ about it.

Walking closer to the edge, she bent down to get a better look inside the hole. To her right, she saw a crack in the side of the wall. Going around the edge of the pit, she peered down to inspect the crack. In an instant, it occurred to her that it wasn't a crack at all but a makeshift door of some sort. Fear swept over her. *What if those bad guys are in there? Did they leave? Did they take CJ?* Regardless, she knew she had to find out.

Callahan and Morgan held tight to the railing as Callahan drove the boat up and onto the sandy beach. It lurched to a halt.

Officer Morgan's agility surprised Callahan as the heavy man jumped out of the boat, moved forward to the bow, and reached in and grabbed the anchor and line. He then walked forward about ten feet and planted the anchor in the sand. Callahan was impressed. Who would have known that a short, overweight guy like Morgan could be so agile and quick? Callahan's admiration for the officer grew exponentially.

Unlike Skye, Callahan had prepared for the bugs. He sprayed himself with a liberal dose and handed the can to Morgan.

"Thanks," he said, grateful for the gift.

"I think it's best if we stay close to each other," Callahan suggested. "This underbrush is pretty thick and it will be easy to get lost."

"I'm all for that," Morgan agreed.

"Let's not get out of sight of each other. Let's just keep a little distance apart, okay? There is no telling what we might find in there." Something told Callahan to head for the center of the island.

He couldn't explain it, but something kept nagging at him, so he just started moving in that direction.

Chapter 50

Skye looked down into the darkness of the hole in the ground.
There was no way of knowing how deep the water was. Debris left
by the storm floated on the surface. Like a green carpet, leaves,
branches, palmetto fronds, and coconuts were visible.

In the far corner, she spotted a large rat floating upside down.
She hated rats almost as much as she hated spiders, and she really
hated spiders.

Still peering over the side, she wondered what else could be in
the water. It was creepy looking. The thought of snakes and other
slimy reptiles sent chills running up her spine. *How am I going to
get down into this godforsaken hole? It's too far to jump, and I have
no idea what's on the bottom.* Regardless of what was down there,
she knew she had to find CJ, and through that nasty water was
probably the only way.

After deliberating a few moments, Skye bent down and sat on the
cement edge of the cistern. She dropped both feet over the side, put
her right hand down on the cement, and with a quick twist of her
body, she slapped her left hand onto the edge. She hung there
precariously, with her body leaning forward and her back facing the
pit. Slowly, she lowered herself, using her elbows as leverage until
she was hanging by the tips of her fingers, her feet swinging in the
water. She closed her eyes, and with one fluid motion, she pushed
her body away from the wall and landed in the water. Excruciating

pain followed her fall. Her ankle had twisted on some unknown object sticking up several inches above the floor. Not able to stand on her injured foot, she fell backwards into the water up to her neck. With effort, and gasping from the pain, she managed to stand and right herself on one foot.

As she bent down to assess her injury, her face touched the putrid water. Spitting and sputtering, she again placed her weight on her good side and noticed that the water was just below her breasts. Standing barefoot, she stood about five-one.

Wincing in pain and not thinking with her usual clarity, she estimated that the tunnel was flooded with about three and a half feet of water or maybe more. *Is the floor level? Does it go down to other rooms?* Numerous thoughts raced through her mind.

With her weight on her good side, Skye eased her bad foot down to test the bottom. The moment she touched solid ground, her foot involuntarily jerked back, her face grimacing in pain. *"Oh, no! It's probably broken. I've got to get to that door,"* she groaned. *Are the men who captured CJ in that room? Is CJ in there?* She pushed off with her uninjured foot, heading for the wooden structure ahead.

Dog paddling, she slowly made her way toward the opening while kicking with one leg and stroking with her free hands.

CJ fought the urge to scream. He suppressed the rising hysteria, managing to keep it under control. *Thank God I'm tall,* he thought; *otherwise, I'd have drowned by now.* The water had reached his shoulders and for some unknown reason appeared to have stopped.

Bending over, he tried to stand with the chair attached to his body, but he was unable to keep his balance in the water. *I'm a prisoner in this chair.* He sat back down, shivering in the dark chilly water and continued his never-ending prayer. "God, please keep Skye and me safe," he prayed. He wondered why she had not come back. He started freaking out, thinking that the guys with the

Russian accents may have caught her. *I have to get out of here. I have to find Skye.*

———————

Sean Callahan led the way through the underbrush. Within minutes, he and Officer Morgan were soaked to the bone from water droplets falling from bushes and trees. Callahan saw clouds through the thick underbrush. *A clearing*, he thought as he carefully made his way forward. Twenty paces more, he found himself standing in a clearing with a big hole in the ground not more than thirty feet away.

As Morgan came out from the bushes, Callahan motioned for him to stop and be quiet. Together, they eased forward, carefully making their way to the edge of the hole. As Callahan leaned over the side, he was stunned by what he saw. Skye stood there holding onto the frame of the door, half in and half out of the opening. She seemed to be having trouble standing.

"Skye," Callahan called out, "wait for us! You don't know what's in there!"

Skye appeared to be in shock as she turned her head to stare up at the two officers. Not immediately recognizing them, her expression conveyed fear. Finally recognizing the detective, she relaxed, but the pain from her broken ankle was evident on her face.

Callahan knew the teen was in trouble. He reached up to his shoulder mike to call the rescue helicopter. "*Trauma Star*, this is the *Avenger*. Over."

"Roger, *Avenger*. How can we assist you? Over."

"*Trauma Star*, we are at a clearing in the center of Indian Key. We need a medevac ASAP. Over."

"Roger, *Avenger*. Our ETA is approximately twenty minutes."

"Thanks," Callahan replied.

———————

Unexpectedly, the water quickly started to rise again. CJ's fear rose with it. *Is this the end? Is this how it feels to die?* Debris floated across his face, and foul-smelling water splattered his mouth. He couldn't scream. His heart was pounding. He lifted his face toward the ceiling, trying to breathe through his nose without taking water into it.

He thought again of Skye. If she had survived, why hadn't she contacted the police and come back to find him? He knew something had to be wrong. Copious thoughts rushed through his mind in what he thought were his last moments. The rushing water had reached the bottom of his nose. He closed his eyes, accepting his fate.

Suddenly, calmness came over him. Peace and serenity flowed through him. His body relaxed, and the pain in his wrists vanished. He was perplexed at what was happening to him.

In the darkness, a tiny, gold luminous glow the size of a baseball appeared in front of him. It moved about the tunnel and finally came to rest directly in front of his chair. He thought his eyes were playing tricks on him, or his imagination was overworked from the stress under which he had been. He wondered if maybe he was dead and didn't know it.

As he watched the gold ball, it began to grow slowly until it was about six feet around. A moment later, its color began to change from gold to white. It became brighter and brighter until the light hurt his eyes. Warmth flowed throughout his body as he smiled at the glow. *Is it an angel?* he wondered.

Slowly at first, almost imperceptibly, a figure began to appear inside the light, eventually forming into the shape of a human body.

CJ sat there taped to the chair, feeling weightless as if he were floating on air. Momentarily, the image of an Indian man took form. *An Indian?* CJ wasn't a particularly good judge of age, but he figured the Indian was about thirty-five.

A white bandana circled his forehead and held back shiny black hair that fell down past his shoulders. Warm brown eyes looked at CJ from a broad face with beautiful white teeth. A quiver holding arrows hug loosely from his naked shoulder. In his right hand was a bow. Sinewy muscles covered his chest, and a red arm band tightly circled his forearm. To CJ's surprise, there was no malice on his face, just peace and tranquility. As the Indian looked into CJ's eyes, a small smile crossed his face.

For a moment, CJ thought he was imagining it, but then he again felt the movement of water. To his amazement, the water moved faster and faster and dropped lower and lower around his body. Within less than a minute, it was rushing past him so fast that its force began to move his chair. Not understanding what was happening, CJ sat calmly as his chair moved in large circles around the tunnel.

He wondered what was causing the water to speed up so fast. It was as if someone had pulled the plug in a bathtub. *Where is the water going? Does the Indian man have something to do with it?* Rationally, he thought that the Indian was probably just a figment of his imagination. *Am I dead? If not, what power is causing the water to move with such force? Why am I unafraid?* He knew at that moment that he was alive and realized that something miraculous and supernatural was happening in the tunnel.

———

Callahan and Morgan stood on the edge of the cistern, not believing their eyes. Skye held fast to the door frame as thousands of gallons of water emptied from the tank, flowing past her at an alarmingly fast speed. Suddenly, the force swept her off her feet and into the rushing water. With panic on her face, she looked up at the two officers, her eyes begging them for help.

Callahan, seeing Skye's distress, stepped to the edge of the pit prepared to jump. Morgan's hand reached out and grabbed his belt.

For some strange reason, Callahan didn't resist. In less than sixty seconds, the reservoir was completely empty, leaving Skye lying on the ground completely dry.

Both men were having difficulty comprehending what had just happened. As they looked into the pit, each realized that all the debris had disappeared and that the bottom of the cistern was completely dry. "My God," Callahan whispered. "What just happened? Where did all the water go? It's completely dry down there, Morgan. Do you see that?"

Chapter 51

Together, the two police officers managed to lower themselves into the pit. As Callahan's feet hit the ground, his two-way radio went off, and Morgan rushed to Skye's aid.

"*Avenger*, this is *Trauma Star*. Over."

Callahan grabbed his mike. "Go ahead *Trauma Star*."

"We'll be with you in two minutes. Over."

"Roger that," Callahan answered. *That was a fast twenty minutes. He must have broken the sound barrier, thank goodness.*

When Callahan reached Skye, Morgan had her leg elevated and had put his foul weather jacket over her. Callahan immediately recognized that her ankle was badly broken. It hung to the right in an unnatural position. He looked into Skye's eyes and could see that she was in terrible pain. "How are you doing little lady?" he asked softly.

Still in shock, Skye opened her eyes and tried to control her shivering. "In there," she said, pointing a finger toward the tunnel.

Callahan stood, removed his Glock from its holster, and moved toward the opening. Standing at the entrance, he stared into the blackness. *I can't see a thing without a flashlight.* As he raised his Glock and stepped into the tunnel, he heard the sound of a helicopter hovering overhead. *Trauma Star* had arrived.

Five feet into the darkness, Callahan was suddenly showered in light. He raised his hand to his eyes and squinted to shield himself from the brightness. *What the heck is that bright light?* He stood paralyzed in fear for a moment, and then he heard a soothing voice inside his head say, *Don't be afraid.* He paused for a moment, thinking his mind was playing tricks on him. Finally, sensing no imminent threat, his body relaxed. He stood tall, removed his hand from his face, opened his eyes, and saw CJ sitting taped to a chair thirty feet from the opening. The bright light was gone. Callahan took a moment to look at his surroundings. His police training kicked in as his eyes constantly moved.

A cursory glance around the tunnel revealed boxes stacked atop one another all the way to the ceiling. A work bench filled with electronic equipment stood to his right. He glanced up at the ceiling and saw a line of electric lights strung along the roof. To his surprise, the bulbs were shattered. Callahan wondered from where the source of light had come a few moments ago. A diffused glow cast no shadows throughout the tunnel.

CJ stared at the officer. Recognition crossed his face, and an ear-to-ear smile appeared. "Thank God you're here," CJ said as he breathed a sigh of relief. "I thought I was going to drown, and then I saw an Indian and a really bright light."

What? An Indian? Callahan rushed over to CJ and began cutting the tape, first from his wrists, and then from his ankles. Puzzled, he noticed that CJ was completely dry, without a cut or scratch on his body. In fact, the entire tunnel was dry as if there had never been a flood.

"Come on, CJ," Callahan whispered. "Let's get out of here."

CJ stood, paused for a moment, and then looked around. "Where did all the water go? Where's the Indian?" he asked with a puzzled look on his face.

"There's no time for that now!" Callahan cautioned. "Let's just get out of here." He took CJ by his arm, and the two began to walk toward the entrance.

Strong gusts blew through the tunnel as Callahan and CJ made their way back to the cistern. Noise from the Sikorsky S-76A twin jet engines was so loud that it seemed as if the world was ending.

Unconsciously and instinctively, they bent forward in a protective position, not knowing what lie ahead of them.

CJ made it to the entrance first. He was surprised to see a U.S. Coast Guard rescue diver and a deputy sheriff lifting Skye into a rescue basket. A splint had been attached to her ankle. He ran to Skye, knelt on one knee, and looked into her glazed, pain-filled eyes. She didn't seem to recognize him. He said something into the wind as the basket left the ground with the diver dangling from the cable next to Skye.

CJ stood next to Callahan and Morgan as they watched Skye being pulled from the pit into the chopper. Moments later, the helicopter shifted to the side and began gaining altitude. Thirty seconds later, all three men stood in the dry reservoir surrounded by total silence.

Morgan finally looked down at his pants and realized that they were completely dry. Five minutes before, they had been soaking wet. Raised a Catholic, he had been taught to believe in miracles, but he had passed them off as something that had happened in the old days of the Bible. *Was this a miracle?* He knew with certainty that it was. Overwhelmed with emotion, he made the sign of the cross, lowered his heavy body to the ground, and began to sob quietly.

Callahan turned and leaned against the side of the cistern. He looked up into the clearing blue sky and began uttering a silent prayer of thanks.

CJ followed Callahan to the side of the cistern, sat down with both knees up, and leaned back against the wall of the pit. With both arms hugging his knees, he lowered his head to rest on them. Seeing everything dry, and the water completely gone, he knew the Indian had not been a figment of his imagination. "Thank you," he whispered to the spirit of the Indian that had spared their lives.

Chapter 52

When Detective Callahan got the call from a sheriff's cruiser saying that a Volkswagen Thing had been abandoned at Mile Marker 78, he immediately realized that it was CJ's.

Back in Islamorada, they had just finished tying up the *Avenger* at the Coast Guard Station when the call came in. CJ heard it on Callahan's radio.

"That's my car. Skye must have left it there when she came to find me."

"Yeah, I thought so. I'll drop you off so you can go to the hospital to see her."

"I need to call my parents first," CJ said. "They are probably worried to death about Skye and me, and Skye's Poppy is probably in a panic by now."

"That's all been taken care of for you. They're on their way to Fisherman's Hospital as we speak."

"Thank you so much, Detective," CJ replied. He reached over and shook Callahan's hand. "I owe you for helping save my life."

"It wasn't me," Callahan replied. "I think we both know what happened in that tunnel. Heck, we were trying to find your girlfriend. We weren't sure where you were. After being admitted, Skye walked out of the hospital, hijacked a ride with one of your buddies and crossed the channel hanging onto a determined dolphin. That's some girl you got there, CJ."

CJ just looked at Callahan and smiled. He had always known that Skye was "some girl."

―――――――

After the detective dropped CJ off at his car, he put the pedal to the metal and headed for Fisherman's Hospital in Marathon.

Rushing through the ER door, he saw his parents and Poppy sitting over in a corner, each nursing a cup of coffee.

When Maria saw CJ, she jumped up from her chair and ran into his arms. She hugged him so tightly that he couldn't breathe.

A moment later, Michael and Poppy joined the circle. Eventually, Maria pushed him away a little and began examining him from head to toe.

"Honey are you all right?" she asked with deep concern in her voice. "My God, we've been so worried about you."

"I'm fine, Mom," CJ reassured his mother.

"What in the world has been going on?" Michael asked. "What were you two doing on Indian Key? We thought you were at Skye's house until we spoke with Poppy. He had no idea where you were, but he knew you were together. Then we got a call from Detective Callahan."

Without answering his dad, CJ looked over at Poppy. "How is Skye doing? Is she going to be okay?" *Please, please say she will be okay,* he thought.

"She has a pretty badly broken ankle," Poppy answered. "She's in surgery now. Doc says she needs a pin and screws in her ankle, and a few stitches. She's cut, scratched up, dehydrated, and exhausted, but she'll be okay."

Feeling relieved, CJ asked as his emotions surfaced, "How long will she be in surgery? When can I see her?" He had difficulty holding back the tears.

Maria pulled him back into her arms. "It's okay, son. She's going to be all right."

Michael stood beside his son with his arm around CJ's shoulders. "When Callahan called me on my cell phone, he told me a little of what had happened. You guys are lucky to be alive."

CJ turned to face his father. "No, Dad, you're wrong. Luck had nothing to do with it. It's a miracle we're alive."

Michael looked at his son, puzzled. "What do you mean a miracle, CJ?"

"Dad, you guys won't believe what I'm about to tell you," CJ said, pulling his mother down onto the couch beside him.

At that moment, Sean Callahan walked through the emergency room entrance. He headed straight over to the group gathered in the corner. He shook hands with Michael and Poppy and then pulled up a chair in front of Maria and CJ.

"Well, son, it looks like you and Miss Skye have been having a busy summer. One of my deputies found a skiff beached close to the highway about a half mile down from where you guys swam over to the island. Not far from the skiff, he found two male bodies washed ashore by the storm. From all indications, they were Russian, and apparently, they recently had been using the island to smuggle in all types of electronic equipment manufactured in Third World countries. They had been flooding the market for several years with knockoff iPhones, iPads, TV's, and other cheaply-made electronics from China. They were in the Russian Mafia."

Callahan continued. " The Feds have been investigating and have been looking all over the place for the source. I guess you two hit the jackpot. There is a twenty-five-thousand-dollar reward out for any information leading to their arrest. Guess we can't arrest them if they're dead, though, can we?"

Michael, Maria, and Poppy sat in silence, not comprehending what Callahan was saying.

Maria was the first to speak. "You mean to tell us that these kids could have been killed while sneaking around that darn island?" she said in alarm as she rose from the couch and looked down at Callahan.

Callahan leaned back in his chair and stared up at her, trying to decide how to answer.

Michael took Maria's hand and pulled her back down to her seat.

"It's okay, sweetheart. They're safe now."

CJ stood, hoping to change the subject. Looking at each, he took a deep breath and said, "Mom, Dad, Poppy, while I was in that tunnel, I saw an Indian spirit. You can't imagine how peaceful I felt. I know he was the one that pulled back the water and saved my life."

"What do you mean pulled back the water and saved your life?" Michael asked looking puzzled. "What water? What tunnel?"

Everyone except Callahan just stared up at CJ, dumbfounded by his words. Callahan hadn't given them the details of CJ and Skye's adventure. He had only told them that both were safe and that Skye had been taken to the hospital.

A whoosh from a pneumatic door opening broke the silence. A middle-aged doctor dressed in a green scrub, with a white mask hanging from his neck, walked through the door. Seeing the couple, he figured they were probably the girl's parents.

Walking up to them, he said, "Mr. and Mrs. Somers?"

Poppy rose from his chair. "I'm Skye's grandfather," he said. "These fine folks are friends of mine."

"Oh, I'm sorry. I didn't realize your granddaughter's parents weren't here."

Interrupting the doctor, CJ asked, "How is she doing?" He had to be certain that Skye was okay.

"Well, she came through the surgery fine, but I must say that her ankle was pretty badly broken. We had to put a pin and screws in it, but it's just for temporary support. After the bone has healed, we can take it out. She'll have to use crutches for a while. We couldn't cast her ankle because of the risk of infection from the surgery, but we wrapped it with several layers of ace bandages. She won't be able to put any pressure on it until it has completely healed, probably in about three months. Her main issue now is exhaustion and dehydration. We've got her on fluids and antibiotics as a precautionary measure. She should be fine in a few days. In the meantime, she needs all the rest she can get."

"When can we see her?" CJ questioned.

The doctor smiled. "She's still in recovery, but when she gets to her room, I'll let you know." He turned to leave. "Oh, I have a message for CJ. Is that you?"

CJ nodded.

"She wasn't very lucid when they brought her in, but she kept asking about you. She was very worried from what the emergency room doctor told me." Then the doctor continued, "She kept saying, I've got to help CJ."

Tears welled up in CJ's eyes. "If you don't mind, would you please let her know that I'm fine?"

"I sure will," the doctor answered. He turned and walked back through the door from which he had come.

———————

About twenty minutes later, the phone rang at the reception desk. A pretty candy striper took the call, listened for a moment, and then hung up. She stood, straightened her pink and white striped uniform, and walked out from behind her desk. With a trained smile, she headed toward the family sitting in the corner.

"Is this the Somers family?" she asked as she approached the group.

Poppy stood. "I am," he said, "and these are my friends."

"Miss Somers is out of recovery and is in room 129 at the end of the hall," she said with a smile on her face. "She's still groggy from the anesthesia, but you can see her if you'd like."

The candy striper glanced down at CJ, who was about her age. *Boy, he sure is cute. I wonder if Miss Somers is his sister or his girlfriend.* Seeing the look on the young man's face, she immediately knew the answer. *Just my luck,* she thought, disappointed. She turned to go back to the volunteer desk.

CJ jumped up from the couch and was the first to lead the way. Moments later, he stood staring at the heavy gray door of Room 129, wondering what lay beyond. He eased the door open and found Skye sleeping. Her left foot was elevated on several pillows. Five

248

pink-polished toes stuck out from several thicknesses of ace bandages, which ran a third of the way up her calf. The rest of her body was covered with a white sheet and a hospital blanket. Two bags of fluid hung from a pole, each connected to a small tube going into the needle on top of her hand. Several chairs had been placed against the far wall for visitors. With the exception of the bed and seating, the rest of the room was sparsely decorated.

CJ tiptoed to the edge of the bed, reached down, took Skye's hand, and held it as gently as he could.

The rest of the clan followed him into the room. Poppy walked around to the other side of the bed and rested his hands on the bedside railing. Tears filled his eyes. Maria and Michael took positions at the foot of the bed. The four stood there in silence, wondering who was going to be the first to speak.

Chapter 53

Flapper sat on a piling at the end of Poppy's dock, resting in the late afternoon breeze. He was patiently waiting for his bucket of fresh fish that Skye had promised him on that stormy day she had asked him to help her.

As he waited, he watched guest after guest arriving for the grand party. He had heard from "that dolphin" that the governor and a bunch of other important people were coming today. What he couldn't figure out was what all the fuss was about, and the dolphin, as usual, only told him what he wanted to tell him. *I don't even know why Skye is friends with that showoff. Of course, he does always come through when Skye needs him, so I guess that counts for something.*

In the meantime, Squeaky was swirling around in the lagoon, occasionally putting on a show for any guests that accidentally wandered down to the dock. He, too, waited for the fresh fish that Skye had promised when he had towed her to Indian Key. He knew a lot of people were coming, but he couldn't figure out what all the fuss was about either.

From his perspective in the water, he saw a large white tent that had been erected earlier in the day. Since then, there had been a flurry of activity about the house, all orchestrated by Poppy, of course. People dressed in black slacks and white shirts moved around like busy ants. Funny, he hadn't seen them eat anything yet, which made him curious. *I wonder if they are having fish.* Thinking of fish made his mouth water.

Still sitting on a piling, Flapper looked to the west, and judging from the sun's position he knew it was early evening. When he glanced back at the house, he saw CJ and Skye standing next to the tent, each holding a soft drink. Something was wrapped around Skye's left ankle, and her arms were around some long wooden sticks that looked like they were holding her up. Her walk was awkward as she held her left foot up off the ground. Flapper knew there was something wrong with her foot since she was using those long sticks, but she seemed happy and bouncy. CJ, on the other hand, was acting shy, as usual.

Skye happened to look toward the lagoon and saw Flapper sitting on the piling all alone. She motioned to CJ to follow her.

"Hey, Flapper, how's my buddy?" Skye said as they approached the pelican.

"I'm waiting for my fish," he said flatly, disappointed that she hadn't noticed him earlier.

"Be patient, my friend," Skye soothed. "I'll have them for you a little later. Don't worry."

"Why are you walking with those long sticks?" Flapper asked.

"Oh, I had a little accident on the island and hurt my foot. These sticks are called crutches, and they help me to walk until my foot heals," Skye said and smiled at her feathered friend.

"What's going on here?" Flapper asked. "What is all the fuss about?" Skye told CJ what Flapper had asked.

CJ reached over and rubbed the back of Flapper's head.

"My summer vacation is over, my friend. I'm flying back home to Connecticut tomorrow, and Poppy is having a little farewell party for me. I'm going to miss you so much," Skye smiled, a little teary-eyed. "I'll come and say goodbye before I leave, I promise."

The news saddened Flapper. *Home?* He and Skye had talked about her living in another place, but having no concept of time, he didn't realize it was time for her to go. "How long will you be gone? Will you come back to see me?" he asked.

Every year, some of the birds from Connecticut flew down to the Keys during the winter, so he knew it was far away from Islamorada. He also knew it would be a long time before he would be able to communicate with her again. Just thinking about it made his feathers droop.

"I'll see you again next summer, Flapper. I have to go back to school. When the weather here starts getting really warm again, I'll be back down here. But CJ will be here, and I'd like for you to stop by to see him once in a while, okay? He can let me know how you're doing. Thank you again for your friendship and for all the help you gave me."

As Skye turned to leave, she heard Squeaky splashing about in the water below them.

"Hey, Squeaky, I'm so glad you could come to my party."

Squeaky shot out of the water, did a summersault in the air, and without a splash re-entered the water. As his head hit the surface, he began to back paddle, squeaking all the while. He had to admit he was showing off a little more than usual today.

"What are all those people doing here?" he asked. "Do you have my bucket of fish? I'm hungry."

Skye translated her conversation with Squeaky to CJ.

"I'm leaving here tomorrow to go back home to Connecticut. I won't be back until next summer."

Addressing Skye, he said, "Next summer? When is next summer? Does that mean I won't get to talk to you anymore?" He couldn't believe his friend wouldn't be here any longer.

Skye translated to CJ again. He nodded in understanding.

"I live pretty far away with my parents. We're a family, like you and your pod. Don't worry, Squeaky, I'll come back down here next summer. We'll see each other again; I promise. Oh, by the way, hang in there, and I'll get someone to bring your fish down here in a little while, okay?"

With that said, Squeaky jumped in the air and flipped over, making sure that Skye was watching him as he hit the water.

"You are one big showoff, Squeaky," Skye laughed as she and

CJ turned toward the house.

———————

Poppy, Maria, and Michael were all excited about the upcoming event. Poppy had gone to great lengths to keep everything a secret from both Skye and CJ. The celebration was supposed to be a going away party for Skye, but there was more to the secret than what had been revealed.

Poppy had hired a small "wannabe" Jimmy Buffet band that had set up their equipment in the far corner of the large tent. Margaritaville played softly in the background.

Twenty tables, each capable of seating eight people comfortably, were covered with white linen tablecloths. Each place setting consisted of Royal Doulton fine china and crystal stemware, along with high-quality stainless flatware. The walls of the tent were transparent plastic, rolled up to provide fresh ventilation, but in case of rain they could easily be lowered to protect the guests.

Poppy was hoping that the small podium and microphone wouldn't be too obvious. Neither Skye nor CJ had been inside the tent, and Poppy didn't want Skye to know what he actually had planned for the evening.

Caterers had set up a large barbeque grill next to the steps leading into the kitchen. The aroma of lobster, shrimp, beef tenderloin and chicken filled the air, all teasing Poppy's guests' taste buds.

Michael had sneaked a bite of tenderloin, "It is to die for," he said, running his tongue over his lips for the final taste.

As each guest arrived, they were greeted with a glass of champagne and hors d'oeuvres and then escorted to a table.

Finally going inside the tent, CJ and Skye moved about the tables. Skye was hugging and kissing their friends. She even hugged the occasional stranger that she figured was a friend of Poppy's.

CJ was much more reserved than Skye, as always. Big crowds weren't his thing. *Oh, well, just for tonight and only for Skye*, he thought.

Seeing many more strangers arriving and milling about, Skye finally became curious. She had never met most of the guests. Some were CJ's high school buddies and their girlfriends, but the rest left her wondering who they were. Poppy had insisted on compiling the list. He had told her that a lot of his old friends would be there as well as some recent ones.

Looking up, Skye saw Detective Callahan walk into the tent. She barely recognized him in his tailored suit. Michael and Maria greeted him as he entered. CJ rushed over to say hello. He thought the detective was a cool guy, and he liked him a lot.

As CJ walked over to welcome Callahan, Skye took the opportunity to browse before greeting the detective. Looking around, she saw Cap Anderson standing next to an open bar nursing a beer. There was something about the cranky old seaman that she loved. *It's probably his blunt honesty*, she thought. A smile crossed her face as she walked over to say hello. Touching his elbow, she smiled. "Hi, Cap."

Cap turned to see who had his elbow. "My goodness, don't you look radiant," Cap teased, looking down into Skye's deep blue eyes. "What's wrong with your foot?" he questioned.

"Just being clumsy," Skye giggled and then gave him a big hug. "I'm so happy to see you, Cap. I wanted to say goodbye before I leave tomorrow and to thank you for all you did for CJ and me, and especially for believing in us. Thank you so much for coming."

"I wouldn't have missed this party for anything," Cap smiled.

It was a subtle noise at first, but then it grew louder and louder. A second later, a red Robinson two-seater helicopter broke out over the mangroves, hovered over the end of Poppy's wide dock, and then slowly settled onto the wide, aging planks.

Guests scurried out from under the tent and began moving down to the dock to see about all the commotion.

Out of nowhere, a tall, very muscular young man dressed in a white uniform began pushing a wheelchair down the dock toward the helicopter.

Skye met up with CJ and waited to see who the mystery guest would be.

Slowly the rotors came to a stop, and the attendant moved the wheelchair next to the passenger door. As the attendant locked the wheels on the chair, the door popped open, and two long legs swung out. The young man reached inside the chopper and lifted the large man from the passenger seat, carefully placing him in the wheelchair. His head was covered with a baseball cap. A loose-fitting, long-sleeved white shirt covered his chest, and what appeared to be a pair of baggy, blue hospital pants hung down to his ankles. His feet were bare, and most of his skin was bright pink. Skye noticed a large bandage around his right hand.

The attendant made some minor adjustments to the chair, making sure his patient was secure. All the guests, including Skye and CJ, were wondering who in the world was making such a grand entrance.

The pilot eased out of his seat, walked around the chopper, and inspected the dock. At his nod, the wheelchair slowly began rolling toward the crowd.

Curiosity finally overcame Skye. She tugged on CJ's shirt, urging him to follow as she walked down to meet the stranger. For a moment, she didn't recognize him, but suddenly visions of the rescue that day on the water flashed before her eyes. She began hurrying down the dock as fast as her crutches would take her, tears filling her eyes. She stopped just short of the wheelchair as if not certain what to do next.

"Mr. Duncan," Skye whispered, a little breathless, "What a wonderful surprise to see you."

John Duncan raised his left hand, motioning Skye closer. She walked around to the side without the bandage, knelt down, and took his hand. He slowly moved it to her face and looked into her eyes. Tears were rolling down his cheeks.

"Thank you so much, young lady," he said, looking deep into Skye's wet blue eyes. "Without you and that young man over there, I'd be dead. Detective Callahan told me about all the risks both of you took to save me."

CJ moved closer and stood behind Skye. John Duncan moved his hand from Skye's face and raised his arm to shake CJ's outstretched hand. CJ took the man's hand with both of his and stood there, not knowing what to say. He was not particularly good at that sort of thing.

Skye finally broke the silence. "I'm Skye and this is CJ. You sure gave us a scare, Mr. Duncan." She smiled as she looked up at CJ.

CJ finally found his voice. "Sir, if it hadn't been for Squeaky," he said, pointing down at the dolphin in the water "you wouldn't be here today. We owe it all to him."

With CJ pointing in his direction, Squeaky sensed they were talking about him, so he took the liberty of putting on a small show for the important guest.

The three of them watched Squeaky as he went about his aerobatic antics. John sat stiffly in his wheelchair, smiling at the dolphin. "That's quite a friend you two have there. How did you get to know each other?"

"Oh, it was the day of the explosion. Squeaky was holding you on the surface of the water when we arrived at the scene. That was the first time we'd ever seen him."

CJ broke into the conversation. "We'd better get on up to the tent. It looks like Poppy's ready to serve dinner. He's motioning for us to come."

"Good idea," their guest replied. "I haven't had any good food since the day before I got on the boat."

The attendant began steering the wheelchair up the dock as CJ and Skye casually followed.

Guests were filing into the tent, looking for their seats. John Duncan, Skye, and CJ were the last to enter. As the three made their entrance, Poppy stood before the microphone.

"Ladies and Gentlemen, our guests of honor have arrived." All who were not already standing rose to their feet, and everyone began clapping loudly.

Skye and CJ stood next to Mr. Duncan. They looked around the tent completely surprised and confused. *What in the world is going on?* Her hand flew to her mouth, not knowing what to do or say.

That is a first for Skye, Poppy thought and smiled. *My little granddaughter is always so curious, but this time she had no idea.* CJ stood with his mouth gaping open, looking for the first opportunity to run.

Moments later, they were joined by Poppy, Michael, and Maria. Hugs and handshakes were exchanged as the guests began taking their seats. Michael led the group to their table and graciously offered John Duncan a seat. After getting him situated, the attendant quietly disappeared.

CJ sat across the table opposite Duncan. Skye sat on his right, and Maria sat to his left. Michael, Poppy, and Cap took up all but one of the remaining seats. As soon as everyone was seated, appetizers of escargot and large shrimp were served to the guests. The band played quietly in the background.

Skye and CJ were unaware of the events that were to follow. Everyone made small talk as Caesar salad was served, followed by a choice of filet mignon, lobster, chicken, or barbeque ribs.

Servers continually kept the drinks flowing as dinner progressed.

As a choice of several desserts was being placed in front of each guest, Poppy left the table, made his way to the podium, flipped on the mike, and began to speak.

"Ladies and Gentlemen, I would like to thank everyone for coming tonight. There are a few people here I'd especially like to recognize for participating in this special event. Please welcome our fine Governor of the State of Florida, Rico Browning." Applause filled the tent as the Governor made his way through the crowd to the podium.

Governor Browning was tall and slim. A loose-fitting suit in need of pressing draped his slender body. He was not an especially good-looking man, but his smile always captivated an audience. Long hands and fingers cradled a sheet of white paper that he gently laid on the podium. He took a moment, studying his notes before he began to speak.

"Thank you, Mr. Hudson, for inviting me to this festive occasion. It's not often that I have the opportunity and the honor to bestow Florida's highest civilian award, The Florida Citizen's Award, on two such young and brave people; Mr. CJ Jansen and Miss Skye Somers." The crowd rose to their feet and again gave a rousing, prolonged round of applause.

The Governor reached into his breast pocket and withdrew two pieces of paper. "On behalf of the State of Florida, I would like to present each of you with a check for ten thousand dollars, along with our enduring gratitude."

Skye and CJ stood, red-faced and embarrassed-looking. They locked their hands as they began moving toward the podium. The Governor removed two small boxes from his coat while he waited for the teenagers to arrive.

Maria was overcome with emotion and began to cry. Michael held his arm around her shoulders, grinning from ear to ear with pride at the two teenagers.

Poppy's blood pressure rose with excitement to the point that he had to sit down. He was so proud and overwhelmed with joy at his granddaughter and CJ. His only disappointment was that Skye's parents had not been able to attend.

The Governor reached out, shook CJ's hand, and then Skye's. "Congratulations," he said, with a big smile. From one of the boxes, he removed a gold medallion with a red, white, and blue ribbon attached. Turning, he placed the ribbon around Skye's neck and the medallion fell to her chest.

Tears began flowing down Skye's cheeks. Speechless for once in her life, all Skye could do was to stare down at the medallion and at then up at the statesman.

Governor Browning reached into the second box, turned and placed a duplicate ribbon and medallion over CJ's head. CJ's face reddened in embarrassment. The governor then reached out and gave the two recipients a big hug. In a farewell gesture, he stepped between the two, reached down, took one of each of their hands, and then raised them high into the air. The audience went crazy with applause.

"Thank you so much for your service," the governor said as he stepped away from the podium. The guests began clapping again, and then finally took their seats.

Before the governor could completely move away from the podium, Detective Sergeant Sean Callahan was at Skye's side. He took her arm and motioned for her and CJ to remain where they stood. He waited for the governor to take his seat and then moved to stand behind the podium. He introduced himself and continued.

"I'd like to start by saying that the people of Monroe County are deeply indebted to Skye Somers and CJ Jansen. Through their brave and courageous efforts, a murder, an attempted murder, and a smuggling operation have all been solved. With the unanimous vote of the Monroe County Commissioners, they have hereby decreed to make Skye Somers and CJ Jansen permanent Junior Deputies in and for the Monroe County Sheriff's Department.

Again, the guests gave them a standing ovation.

Callahan reached into his pocket and pulled out two gold shields. He turned and pinned one onto the pocket of CJ's shirt and placed the other one on the strap of Skye's halter dress. With a big smile, he shook CJ's hand and gave Skye a big hug.

With tears in her eyes, Skye looked over to her right and saw the attendant pushing Mr. Duncan toward them.

"Ladies and Gentlemen," Callahan said, pointing toward John Duncan. "I would like to introduce Mr. John Duncan, who is the CEO of Duncan Oil Company."

The guests applauded. They had been wondering all evening who the mystery guest could be. Now, they finally knew. Most were aware of his company and had read about the explosion, but none knew him personally.

Callahan remained standing beside the teens as the attendant handed John Duncan the microphone.

Turning his wheelchair to face Skye and CJ, he motioned them closer as his eyes moistened.

"Ladies and Gentlemen, if it hadn't been for Skye and CJ, I wouldn't be alive today. Oh, and that crazy dolphin outside in the water, too. I am so happy to be here to thank them publicly. In some ways, they remind me of myself when I was their ages, reckless and fearless." Everyone laughed.

"In appreciation," he continued, "and from the depth of my heart, I can't express the gratitude that I have for these two young adults."

Mr. Duncan reached down to the edge of the wheelchair seat and withdrew a large manila envelope. Tiring, his shaking hands took their time opening the packet. Tears welled in his eyes again.

CJ and Skye both wondered what was inside the envelope. Skye's heart was still pounding from all the surprises of this special evening. CJ stood immobile and almost in shock, and a little uncomfortable at all the attention.

"You kids are going to be graduating from high school in another year or two, and then it's off to college. I want to help make that transition a little easier for you." He withdrew several official looking documents.

"I had my attorneys contact the University of Florida. Arrangements have been made and finalized for your full tuition, which will be paid from a scholarship fund that has been set up in your names. If you wish to further your studies for a higher degree, those funds will also be available."

Open-mouthed and bug-eyed, Skye dropped her crutches and jumped into CJ's arms on one leg. She then turned to face John Duncan. Tears of joy were rolling down her cheeks. She knelt down and began hugging him. He wrapped his good arm, the one that wasn't too severely burned, around her shoulders and continued crying with her.

CJ walked around to the other side of Duncan's chair, knelt, and he, too, began hugging Duncan. Tears were streaming from all three faces.

The entire tent shook from the applause and the extended standing ovation the three of them received. Michael, Maria, and Poppy gathered around the small group and began giving everyone a hug.

To Cap, it looked like a love-fest from the sixties. Red-faced, he seemed to be ill at ease from all the commotion, but he got up and joined the group too.

Outside, Flapper sat on his piling, wondering what in the world was all the noise going on in the tent. He'd never heard such a racket. "Where's my fish?"

Squeaky bobbed in the water. "Hey, what's going on up there?" he shouted over at Flapper.

Flapper just ignored him. He had had enough of this noisy showoff for one day. *Worse than seagulls,* he thought.

Epilogue

The last time Poppy saw Skye that summer was when she and CJ drove out of the parking lot at the Green Turtle Inn. The two of them had enjoyed a delicious breakfast, although no one else seemed interested in eating. It was the last meal they would enjoy together until Skye came back to Islamorada next summer.

As CJ started his Volkswagen Thing, Poppy noticed that CJ's muffler had still not been repaired, and Skye seemed a little embarrassed as they rounded the corner in a roar. They were heading for Miami International Airport where Skye was scheduled to catch a flight to Boston. Her parents were going to meet her there for the two-hour drive home to New London, Connecticut.

Poppy stood alone in the parking lot with his arms folded against his chest. He felt as if a small death had just occurred with the departure of his only beloved granddaughter. He would surely miss her. His one comfort was in his knowing that she would be back next summer, God willing. *She sure puts spice in my life.* Thinking about his beautiful little granddaughter made tears well up in his eyes.

As he turned to walk back into the restaurant, a light southerly breeze began to dry the tears on his cheeks. He had been able to hold them back until Skye had left. He stopped at the entrance to the restaurant turned and nonchalantly wiped away what was left of the dampness. Maria, Michael, and Cap sat finishing their light breakfast as Poppy joined them at the round table for six. Before Skye and CJ's departure, none of them had much of an appetite. Now, the meal was more of a ritual than anything else. Mostly, they were just killing time, especially Poppy. CJ would return to Michael and Maria, but it would be nine months before Skye would return to Poppy, and the group realized that he needed the extra support from his friends.

"I'll tell you people one thing," Cap was saying. "Those two kids are something else. Smart as whips, they are, and braver than most adults I know. I sure couldn't have done what they did."

Sighing, Poppy ordered fresh coffee and a bagel. Though he didn't feel like it, he knew he had to eat something.

"I'm really going to miss her," Poppy said, his face showing his sadness.

At that moment, Detective Callahan entered the restaurant, looked around, saw the group having breakfast, and walked toward their table. "I'm glad I found y'all," he said as he approached them.

Michael motioned him to a chair. "To what do we owe the honor?" he asked. Callahan was a good cop, and Michael had grown to like and respect him. He still missed his NSA friend, Sonny Mitchell, but he enjoyed the casual friendship that had developed between his family and Callahan.

The detective pulled out a chair, sat down, and put his elbows on the table. "I thought you might like to know that I got a call from the prosecutor's office in Miami. Mrs. Duncan just made a plea bargain deal with the state attorney's office."

"Really?" Maria said, surprised. "They must have scared her to death. Either that or she has a very smart attorney."

"Probably both," Callahan smiled. "The state dropped the conspiracy to commit murder charge and agreed to two lesser charges. Anyway, the deal is involuntary manslaughter on one count and attempted manslaughter on the other for two consecutive five-year terms."

Enraged, Cap slammed his fist on the table. "That may be a bargain for her, but it's certainly not for the two victims. One guy's dead, and her husband is badly scarred for the rest of his life. Not a particularly good deal for them."

"Unfortunately, there wasn't much forensic evidence left on the boat, and the only tie-in we had was from the phone calls she made to Roscoe Bertolli. The State Attorney's office is happy with what they got. She'll serve eighty-five percent of the ten years. That's one less felon my office has to worry about," he said with relief.

Poppy sat in silence pondering what Callahan had said. Those kids could have died from that woman's greed. *At least she'll be in prison for several years and good riddance.*

Looking over at Poppy, Callahan continued, "I sure was hoping to see Skye before she left. She's quite a young lady. Both of the kids are amazing."

Michael looked over at Maria. "Yeah, they sure are. Those two had quite a summer. Skye saved Flapper from the fisherman's line and communicated with the pelican and a dolphin."

"After seeing the explosion, they saved John Duncan's life, salvaged the wreck, discovered a smuggling operation, and on top of everything else, they helped solve a murder case without being killed. Yeah, I'd say they had one heck of a summer. I don't know if Maria and I are looking forward to next summer or not," he laughed.

Poppy looked over at Callahan, and with a twinkle in his eyes, he said, "I can't wait for next summer."

The End

Books by J Thomas Stovall

Marquesas Gold

Chapter One

Renaldo Rodriguez, an attractive, hard-working man, stood in his neat garage packing up his fishing gear for a weekend getaway from his nagging wife. He couldn't wait to get away from her. *The sooner, the better,* he thought. He picked up his gear and headed to his truck, not bothering to say goodbye. Once trim, beautiful, and vivacious, his wife had gotten fat, unkempt, and mean.

Fishing was his escape from his unhappy marriage, and he managed to get away nearly every other weekend. Strangely, she never nagged him about his fishing trips. *I think she's as glad to be rid of me for a couple of days as I am her. How did I ever get myself into this farce of a marriage?* Unfortunately, both were devout Catholics, so there was no chance of a divorce.

Renaldo, in beige cargo shorts and no shirt, and wiping beads of sweat from his face, stood at the stern of his eighteen-foot Sea Breeze boat. He had a larger boat, but he favored the smaller Sea Breeze when he fished alone. He was fishing with a donut-shaped yoyo. It was what poor fishermen used in Cuba, his birthplace. Renaldo had a job selling high-end luxury boats, and he and his wife lived very comfortably. He could afford expensive Daiwa spinning rods, but he preferred his favorite yoyo because it reminded him of his roots. Tired and sleepy from his second long night of fishing, his deep brown eyes kept slowly closing. His boat was anchored south of Sand Key, about two hundred yards from a lighted tower that winked at him every eight seconds. Finally, wiping the moisture from his face, he glanced down at his waterproof luminescent watch. 12:33 a.m. *It's about time for me pack up and head home,* he thought, part with relief that he would get to sleep in his own bed, and part with regret that he had to face his fat, annoying, wife again.

A warm, humid breeze blew in from the west at six miles an hour caressing the glassy surface. Renaldo did not need a light. His boat was well lit by the full moon overhead.

Fully contented from a fruitful catch, he did not realize that within forty-three seconds he would no longer have to worry about his nagging wife. Renaldo Rodriquez would be dead.

———————

Two eyes the size of large dinner plates quietly rose to the surface and lingered for a moment. The predator, analyzing its prey, moved within thirty feet of the boat. Hunger had driven the beast to the surface. Prey large enough to satisfy the predator's appetite was hard to find in these parts, especially in the warm shallow waters of the Keys. The need for food was overpowering, and the predator's instinct was to do what he had to do to survive.

Exhausted, but instantly alert, Renaldo turned when he heard the splash slam hard against the side of his boat, rocking it back and forth on the dark, glassy water. *What was that?* His heart skipped a beat. Focusing his tired eyes, he saw the predator, and he couldn't believe what he was seeing. Now fully awake, his eyes opened wide in terror. Fear instantly covered his handsome face, and his heart began racing wildly. *It can't be, not in this warm water! What the....!*

Before he could complete his thought, two lightning rod tentacles broke the surface, shot through the air, and entangled him. He saw them coming, but he was in shock and couldn't move. The rapid tightening grip of the massive creature forced Renaldo's eyes to

2

bulge from their sockets. Struggling was useless. Blood ran down his cheeks like red rainwater. His heart felt like a freight train trying to escape his chest. Bright red blood squirted from his open mouth as he bit into the meat of his tongue. A hysterical scream welled up in his throat, but it was quickly silenced as he as viciously jerked into the sea.

www.ingramcontent.com/pod-product-compliance
Lightning Source LLC
Chambersburg PA
CBHW020441270626
47155CB00022B/790